Bolan swiveled the barrel ninety degrees to his left.

He fixed the crosshairs on a crouching Colombian shooter who was still chopping away in Gaultieri's direction with an M-16.

One pull of the Accuracy International trigger and the man fell silent, weighted down with a 7.62 mm round in his chest.

Bolan was on the second box magazine, and from the counts he'd made, Carvaggio had done the same.

There were still a good number of targets to choose from.

Instead of making a break for it after the first several rounds of sniper fire as the Executioner expected, both groups dug in right away. Only then did they realize there was nowhere to go.

Bolan and Carvaggio had all the angles covered.

MACK BOLAN ®
The Executioner

DON PENDLETON'S
THE EXECUTIONER®
JUDAS KILL

A GOLD EAGLE BOOK FROM
WORLDWIDE.

TORONTO • NEW YORK • LONDON
AMSTERDAM • PARIS • SYDNEY • HAMBURG
STOCKHOLM • ATHENS • TOKYO • MILAN
MADRID • WARSAW • BUDAPEST • AUCKLAND

First edition April 1999
ISBN 0-373-64244-X

Special thanks and acknowledgment to
Rich Rainey for his contribution to this work.

JUDAS KILL

Histories are more full of examples of the fidelity of dogs than of friends.

—Alexander Pope

If you have loyalty you don't need to watch your back.

—Mack Bolan

To the ceaseless efforts of the
Organized Crime Task Force

1

A curtain of driving sleet and rain swept across Madison Avenue, intensifying the frantic pace of rush-hour commuters heading for either Penn Station or the Port Authority to catch their trains and buses out of the city.

The Executioner didn't mind the icy downpour.

It was the perfect weather for stalking a man.

Mack Bolan stayed a half block behind his target—the man in the Burberry trench coat. He could have given him an even longer leash if he had wanted to. Rupert Sawyer stood out in a crowd, even a wet, cold and agitated midtown Manhattan crowd.

Streetlights and illuminated storefront shops cast dull glows on the street while meandering headlights from a fleet of taxis punched holes through the early December darkness.

It was a vale of icy tears no one wanted to linger in. The street echoed with the cadence of rapidly moving feet smacking onto the slush-filled sidewalks, leaving their footprints behind in a field of ice-crusted craters. The fast-moving crowd provided Bolan with plenty of cover. Not that he needed it. The Executioner's mark hadn't looked back once.

Sawyer was so intent on his impending undercover rendezvous that he'd neglected the basics of street survival—know where you are and know who's there with you.

The silver-haired producer of *Case Closed,* one of the highest-rated true-crime television shows in syndication, continued trekking as covertly as possible up Madison. For the former network newsman, that meant hastening along with the collar of his trench coat turned up to protect himself from the cold. It also meant tipping the brim of his hat to shadow his eyes as he furtively glanced left and right—but never behind him—like a man on secretive business who wanted everyone to know he was important enough to be on secretive business.

At least he had the right technique for the job, Bolan thought.

In the side pocket of Sawyer's trench coat was a collapsible miniature camcorder. In his front shirt pocket was a state-of-the-art voice-activated minicassette recorder.

Less than a half hour earlier Bolan had sat three tables away from Sawyer in a walk-down bistro on 29th Street, watching the man check the batteries of his spookatronic gear over and over while savoring his upcoming covert rendezvous. The producer had also repeatedly fingered his gold tiepin, which might have been a 35 mm fly's-eye camera or perhaps just a good-luck piece.

Newshounds were just as superstitious as soldiers when it came to carrying good-luck charms with them.

But this day those kinds of charms wouldn't be enough for Sawyer.

The top-rated host was being closely watched by a critical and unseen audience whose members often voiced their disapproval with a quick slash of a stiletto, a soft pop of a silenced .22-caliber round to the back of the head, or if they really wanted to make a point, a heavy-metal drive-by that left the victim shredded on the street with autofire.

So far Bolan had seen a couple of vehicles that could have been casing the producer—a black van with bubble windows; a Lincoln with tinted windows.

Within a minute of each other both vehicles had slowed as they came up behind Sawyer, then cruised parallel to the curb. They could have been looking for a parking spot, or they could have been tailing the producer. It was impossible to tell. The Executioner had watched them with a casual eye, making certain that he stayed behind them until both the Lincoln and the van flowed back into the sea of traffic and went on their way.

But Mob hitters were out there somewhere. Bolan could sense the strike team even if he couldn't see it. It was the same feeling he got whenever he went into battle. The enemy was on the move, and it was only a matter of time before he encountered them.

One thing he was certain of. The hitters wouldn't strike now. Rupert Sawyer would be safe—at least until he met his underworld source. The source was the real reason both the Executioner and the strike team were interested in the movements of the producer.

Sawyer was the conduit to a man who could bring down the Mafia machine that had been quietly carving an invisible empire for itself in Manhattan and other Mob towns across the country. The man's name was Nicholas Carvaggio, and lately an alarming number of people who got too close to him ended up dead.

Carvaggio had proved to be just as deadly as the Mob rifle team hunting him, mainly because he used to be one of them. But when he'd refused a contract on a female witness in a Mafia trial—someone he considered an innocent civilian and therefore untouchable—Carvaggio himself was targeted for elimination.

His code of honor made him a pariah among the so-called honorable men in the Mafia hierarchy.

Among the dead were some well-known underworld hit men that Victor Sienna had sent after Carvaggio, along with a federal agent who'd been negotiating with Carvaggio to turn himself in.

The circumstances surrounding the agent's death were still unexplained, and a certain faction of the Justice Department was out for Carvaggio's head.

In a desperate attempt to clear his name, the Mob hit man contacted the producer of *Case Closed* to offer his side of the story—he was set up by his underworld enemies who wanted to pin the agent's murder on him. It seemed a logical enough move at first. Thanks to tips from members of the audience, Sawyer's program had broken several other exposés of the underworld. And it did have contacts with law agencies across the country.

But Rupert Sawyer wasn't a man who could keep a secret for long.

For that reason Sawyer had no idea of what he was walking into or of the clandestine parade he was leading.

As the Executioner kept an eye on the rotund figure of the producer, he matched the pace of the people around him. Some had umbrellas to shield them from the icy onslaught, but the sudden downpour had caught most of them by surprise. They were hurrying on their way with heads down and hands in pockets.

Bolan kept his head up in the cold slicing wind and rain so he wouldn't lose track of his man. He also kept his hands free in case something unexpected came up. In Manhattan that could be anytime or anywhere, and he had to be ready for it—with or without a Mob task force on the prowl. The last thing he needed was to be caught off guard by some street toughs strolling for dollars. Even professionals could get taken by surprise if they were too focused.

Besides, his hands were warm enough in the thermal half gloves that kept his fingertips free to handle the Beretta 93-R machine pistol. It was holstered in a breakaway underarm rig beneath his leather jacket, and the jacket was half unzipped in case he had to move quickly.

There was another pistol in the holster at the small of his back—a .45ACP that was easily concealed and easily fired. A few other odds and ends were stowed in the jacket, including a blue-steel triangulated knife pick about a half-foot long with a matte-black contoured fist grip. The thin but inflexible pick was embedded in the outer lining of the jacket.

Just about everything he needed for a walk in the park.

Bolan carried a lot more with him in case the city streets turned into a battleground. There were no boundaries in the war that he was fighting—except the one between life and death. And Bolan meant to stay on the right side of that border.

Like just about everyone else in the city, the Executioner had a small carryall slung over his shoulder. The briefcase-sized black canvas bag had several pockets and zippered pouches that carried the tools of his trade. Some of it was disguised, but there was nothing much he could do with incendiaries and spare magazines.

Bolan glanced around now and then, idly gazing at the cars that crept from streetlight to streetlight, traffic jam to traffic jam. That was one reason why there were so many people on the sidewalk. In New York it was often faster to walk than to ride.

The traffic was made up mostly of taxis that rode one another's taillights with only inches to spare, fighting tooth and nail for every square foot.

Bolan continued looking-without-looking for signs of any additional surveillance—either a foot patrol or some possible shadow cars that showed an interest in Sawyer.

There was a bottleneck up ahead at the next street corner where people were waiting for the lights to change. A few of them broke out of the herd and played chicken with the oncoming cars, but most of them waited impatiently in line.

Bolan stood near the back of the crowd, keeping one eye on the traffic and the other on Sawyer, who was about five rows ahead of him near the curb, shying away from the splashing of cars.

Just as the light changed, a woman who'd been standing behind Bolan pushed in front of him, stepping on his foot for a split second before he slid it out from under her. She glared at him as if it were his fault, then pushed on through the crowd.

Bolan smiled. He loved New York.

The Executioner continued on, drifting through the surging pedestrians until he was almost right behind Sawyer.

When the producer was halfway across the street, he finally decided to look around. But his eyes moved too quickly to register anything, let alone a man who was right behind him. The soldier adopted a dull gaze and looked past Sawyer until the producer turned and continued on his way.

Maybe they were getting close, Bolan thought, if Sawyer was getting spooked enough to look around for a tail. He wondered what the man would do if he discovered he really was being tailed. Unlike the recreations on his documentary show, reactions weren't controlled and scripted. Sawyer would probably jump right out of his wing tips and try to go to a commercial.

From the smug expression on his weathered face, it was obvious that Rupert Sawyer still didn't have a clue that he was a small-time player in a big-league game.

But at least the man was starting to show some caution.

Maybe now he regretted how his excitement at his exclusive interview with Carvaggio might have caused him to let bits and pieces of his secret slip to some of his associates on the show. And to his friends. And bartenders. And women he chatted to at parties. And law-enforcement contacts he tried to pump for background on Carvaggio.

Information was currency, and it had passed through several pairs of hands before it made its way to Hal Brognola.

The head Fed had a razor-wire fence to walk upon. His top people wanted to bury Carvaggio. Brognola wanted Carvaggio alive if it was possible—if Carvaggio was innocent of the agent's murder. But the Justice man was realistic enough to know that given the choice between taking out Carvaggio or taking him in, some of his people wouldn't think twice before pulling the trigger.

Carvaggio was a potential Rosetta stone of Mob operations. He could help decipher the latest mosaic of cooperation between the U.S. and Italian Mafia and the Russian *mafiya*. If the Justice Department managed to turn Carvaggio, it would be like setting off a backpack nuke in the Mob's own backyard.

Bolan was the point man on the Carvaggio situation. He

had the ability to bring him in alive. Or dead if Carvaggio really was the one who had whacked the agent.

The big Fed had called in the Executioner to finesse the situation.

It was an unofficial operation, but if Bolan needed logistics support or intelligence, Brognola would make sure he had it. There would be liaison with the Justice Department action team, and the big Fed would run interference with any bureaucratic matters if Bolan needed him to pull some strings or bend some rules.

But the game plan was up to Bolan.

Right now that plan meant keeping Rupert Sawyer in sight.

The producer turned down 34th Street and headed past Macy's. The soldier fell in behind him and maintained a discreet distance until they got closer to Penn Station and Madison Square Garden, where the crowds grew thicker. Then he closed the gap.

A couple blocks later Sawyer headed north again, moving up a narrow alley lined with shops and storefront offices. The producer stopped at the next crosswalk and suddenly reached into his side pocket.

Bolan was amazed. The man was playing undercover.

Sawyer took out his spy-sized minicam and slowly turned in his best imitation of a G-man covertly filming all four corners of the intersection to get some color for his story.

When his mini-epic was finished, the producer dropped the camera into his pocket and turned back toward the three-story building on the corner across the street, the obvious site of his rendezvous.

Chipped gold lettering on the window said it was an office supply company, but it looked like it hadn't supplied anyone with anything for quite some time. There was a main entrance into the showroom and a smaller one on the side of the building, leading to walk-up office space.

As Sawyer walked slowly toward the building, the Executioner stepped inside a long, narrow diner directly across the street, as if that had been his destination all along.

It was a traditional diner with red vinyl stools at the counter, booths running to the back along one wall and a couple of tables up front by the window. The tables were cordoned off.

Bolan tugged at his jacket to shake off the rapidly melting sleet, then stood by the cordoned area and glanced across the street where Rupert Sawyer was ringing the buzzer and waiting in the icy rain.

A waitress in a canary yellow uniform with a slightly smudged white apron drifted toward Bolan, murmuring softly to herself while she calculated totals on her order pad. She nodded distractedly at the soldier, then gestured to the back.

"Table up front," Bolan said.

"Sorry," the woman replied. "That section's not open yet. And you need a party of four."

Bolan flipped open his billfold and passed her a twenty. "Table up front," he repeated firmly.

The twenty vanished and a smile appeared on the waitress's face. "Up front it is," she said, unhooking the cordon.

She dropped a menu in front of him as Bolan took the seat with the best view of Sawyer's building.

"Just coffee," Bolan said.

"Sorry, hon, these tables are supposed to be for dinner items only—"

"Large coffee," Bolan said, dropping another twenty on the table.

That twenty vanished as quickly as the first. "Large coffee," she said.

Bolan pulled one of the nearby chairs closer to him and set his carryall on it, then watched Rupert Sawyer do a slow tap dance, annoyed that no one was buzzing him in.

Finally Sawyer tried the door. It was open.

Pushing the door inward, he stepped inside, hesitating a few moments before closing the door behind him.

The Executioner unzipped his jacket a bit more, careful not to reveal the holstered Beretta, then sipped from a ceramic mug of steaming black coffee while he waited to see who else was interested in Sawyer's destination.

RUPERT SAWYER STOOD in the darkened hallway on the second landing and rapped on the glass door. No lights were on inside the office. Just like the stairwell. He'd tried the light switch at the bottom of the stairs, but it wasn't working.

He rapped on the door again and pulled hard on the knob, shaking it loud enough for someone inside to hear it.

But it was locked, and no one came to open the door.

There was no sign of Nick Carvaggio.

At least a *live* Carvaggio.

Sawyer envisioned him lying on the floor somewhere in the office, dead from a shotgun blast, hanging from the ceiling, or maybe tied to a chair, bleeding to death from a hundred cuts.

He stood close to the door and shouted through the cracks. "Nick! Are you in there?"

Still no response.

"Mr. Carvaggio?"

With his voice echoing in the darkness, Sawyer stepped away from the door and backed against the opposite wall where a small window looked down on the street below. That was the only source of light in the hall. It wasn't much, but without it the hallway would be pitch black.

Sawyer called out one more time, not at all happy with the wavering timbre of his voice.

This felt wrong. Maybe he screwed up the time, Sawyer thought. Or the place. Maybe it wasn't Carvaggio who'd called him at all. It was only a voice on the phone. It could have been anybody. And the show had been scammed before with some of Sawyer's so-called informants turning out to be hoaxers or head cases.

Of course there was a more frightening possibility. Maybe the caller was someone who wanted to lure him to his death and figured the right bait would be to toss Carvaggio's name around.

Case Closed had brought down a good number of fugitives in the two years it had been on the air. That added up to a lot of enemies who might want to settle a score.

"Okay," Sawyer said, trying to calm down. "That's it! I'm out of here!" He turned back toward the stairs and was only two steps down when the door on the first floor opened and slammed against the wall. It banged loudly, then the shadowed figure of a man stepped inside, swiftly closing the door behind him.

The unyielding shadow stood in the doorway, looking up at him.

Sawyer couldn't see the man's face, just his silhouette, but he had the feeling he was being inspected. He also had the feeling that if he didn't pass the inspection he'd become a dead man.

"Nick? That you?"

The reply—when it came after a frightening pause—was soft spoken but certain. A man who carefully measured what he said and what he did. "It is."

"You're late."

"Yes." He started walking up the stairs.

"You were supposed to be here waiting for me," Sawyer said. "That's what you said when you called—"

"Correct," the man answered. "That's exactly what I said." Carvaggio gradually emerged into the dim light.

He had a dark blue coat on, with a white scarf wrapped around his neck, making him look like he just came from the opening of a Broadway show. Not at all the image that Sawyer had expected.

The man had a strong face and an imposing presence, but there was nothing intrinsically frightening about him. His short black hair was combed straight back, giving him an almost aristocratic look.

Nick Carvaggio wasn't at all the living mug shot that typified so many other underworld types Sawyer had met in his line of work. They were informers, con men. This man was different, a cut above. And there was little about him that seemed sinister.

Except maybe the eyes.

There was no greeting in them as he drew closer to the producer, just a cool and hard look, with a quick intuitive acknowledgment of Sawyer's strengths and weaknesses.

Carvaggio saw mostly weaknesses.

He stepped past Sawyer, keeping one hand in his coat pocket, and flicking the other near the side lock. The lock clicked open and the door swung inward.

Carvaggio stood in the open doorway, listening as he breathed slowly and calmly, as if he were trying to sense rather than see any presence within. When he was satisfied things were in order, he stepped inside and headed to a long table in the middle of the room.

Sawyer followed him, stepping carefully through the shadows past tables, counters, desks, shelving units. A dim glow lighted the interior of the office, coming from a computer screen.

Carvaggio picked up a slim remote control and clicked a few buttons, causing several other computer monitors to blink into existence. They were lined up in stacks and tiers on top of a long U-shaped work counter. It looked like the display wall of a television shop.

Without taking his eyes off the main screen, Carvaggio dropped into a wheeled office chair in front of the counter and ran his hand over the mouse and keyboard, adjusting the images in front of him. Lighted only by the green glow of the various monitors, he looked like the phantom of the opera playing a musical score as he manipulated the screens.

It looked almost like a production studio. Drawn like a moth to the green glowing television monitors, Sawyer said, "Who's your decorator? Nielsen?"

"Orwell," Carvaggio replied.

Sawyer grasped his meaning as he drew closer and saw that the green screens were night-vision monitors that covered every approach to the office building. Camera angles looked down from rooftops, street level and car level.

"Why all the gear?" Sawyer asked. "It's like you're expecting someone."

"I was," Carvaggio said without looking at him. "I am."

"Who?"

Carvaggio took another sweep of the outside approaches, then turned to face Sawyer. "I expected one of the teams to be here already, sharpening their knives and greasing their guns."

Sawyer exhaled theatrically, but it was a genuine physical reaction. He felt faint and cold. He also felt anger, but he didn't dare show it. Not to this man. "You thought there'd be trouble here…and you still let me go in first?"

"That was the game plan."

"Why?"

"I figured if someone was here, they'd drop the hammer loud and quick. That'd give me time to get away."

"You mean you were deliberately using me as a decoy?" Despite himself, Sawyer found his voice rising. "I could have been killed."

"Chances are," Carvaggio agreed. His voice still maintained an even and unhurried tone, as if he were explaining third-grade math to a slow student. "Don't be so surprised, Rupert. It only would have happened if you gave the address away to anybody. Did you?"

"No!" Sawyer snapped.

"And no one knows about me or that we had arranged this meeting?" Carvaggio asked. His voice hadn't risen, but his eyes had grown a lot more intense. "I mean not even a hint that I contacted you?"

This time the producer hesitated a bit too long before replying. "No. Well, I mean, not actually. Maybe people knew I was doing some preliminary research for an investigation, but, uh, no one knew what I was working on. I mean, no specifics were mentioned."

Carvaggio nodded, then he jabbed his finger toward one

of the security screens that showed a black van double-parked halfway down the block. "Then why do you suppose they're here?"

Sawyer looked at the van on the screen. Two men were in the front seat. Another man stood between a parked car and the passenger side of the van, talking to someone through the open window.

"You know them?" Carvaggio asked.

"No."

"Sure they're not one of your news team vans?"

"Of course not."

"Reason I ask," Carvaggio said, "is because the van was following you. It passed by when you were lingering at the front door, then it circled around the block. Take a closer look."

Carvaggio clicked the button on the mouse and zoomed in on the van, showing all three faces. The man outside the van was about six foot, lean and had nervous energy coursing through his lanky frame. Like an athlete warming up for a match, he was tapping his feet and clenching and unclenching his hands to deal with the adrenaline rush. He was ready to go.

The man in the passenger seat appeared to be a lot more passive. He had a huge blocky shape with heavy jowls and a gluttonous, feral look about him. He seemed calm, but there was an aura of menace about him, like an avalanche quietly building up momentum until it was time to bury the unwary target.

The driver was quiet and alert, watching the traffic and the building. He was totally focused on his part of the mission— get them in place, then get them out alive.

Sawyer had no doubt the three men were part of an underworld action team, and they weren't alone. At least two more shapes were moving around in the back of the van, but from that angle Sawyer couldn't get a clear look at them.

"So?" Carvaggio prompted. "What do you think? Know any of them?"

The producer shook his head. "Never saw them before. They're not with me. But you know who they are already."

"Yes, I do. I want you to get a good look at who you're dealing with so next time—in case there is a next time—you'll be a bit more careful."

"Well, who are they?" the producer demanded.

"That's one of Victor Sienna's mobile hit teams," Carvaggio said, pointing at the screen. "You know—the guy I used to work for. Good old Vic probably sent them to give me my severance pay."

"Got it," Sawyer said. "So let's get the hell out of here before they come after us."

"Relax," Carvaggio said. "They figure we're going nowhere. They'll take their time, call in some more soldiers to cover all the streets and exits." As he spoke, the ex-hit man zoomed in on another location. The green screen showed a backstreet delivery alley on the other side of the office building, where a second van had just come to a stop with its engine running and its lights out.

"And then," Carvaggio continued, "when they're all in position, they'll come in to take us out with overwhelming force. Something we all learned in the military. Of course, some of us learned a few other things."

It felt unreal to Sawyer. Outside were the type of people he wouldn't want to meet on their best days. This day they would kill him just as soon as look at him. They were out to give Carvaggio the traitor's death he deserved, and if Sawyer happened to be around when it happened, then he wouldn't be around much longer.

And Carvaggio didn't seem to worry about it at all. It was almost like he expected it to happen.

"Nick…" Sawyer stammered, with a dry mouth and shaky voice, "come on. We've got to run while we still can."

"No," the Mob fugitive said. "Not yet." He manipulated a few more screens, zooming in on alleys and streets. "All of their people aren't here yet. They're waiting."

"Well, I'm not," Sawyer said, as he headed for the door.

"No."

"What?"

"You're not leaving. You go out that door, it'll spook them into action. They'll take you down or in for questioning. Believe me, Rupert, you won't like that at all. What'll happen to you is the kind of stuff you can't show on television."

Sawyer backed away from the door. He knew the man was right. On his own he wasn't able to face the hit team. But at the same time, he had a growing suspicion that he'd just placed his life in the hands of a man with a death wish. "Okay," Sawyer said. "What do we do?"

Carvaggio leaned back in the chair, resting one arm over the back while scanning the screens. "We watch, Rupert, and wait for the inevitable to happen."

THE EXECUTIONER UNZIPPED his jacket as he crossed the street, making it easier to get at the Beretta 93-R when he needed it.

He'd walked halfway down the block away from the diner before crossing to the opposite side of the street where Carvaggio's building was. Without missing a beat, Bolan started walking back toward the corner where the ex-hit man and Rupert Sawyer were holed up.

That brought him a good forty yards behind one of the Mob spotters who'd been casing the street. Bolan picked up his pace slightly as he walked along the ice-slicked sidewalk, keeping his eyes down and using his peripheral vision to track the man.

Bolan didn't want to stare too hard or concentrate too much on the Mob soldier. It was an instinctive technique practiced by predators the world over. Whether man or animal, prey often had a sixth sense when they were being stalked.

The Executioner had been on both sides of the equation enough times to know that it was a real sensation. It was more developed in people with military backgrounds, or hunters and trackers who spent a lot of time in the woods, people who knew that death was often only a click away.

Though he was moving faster, Bolan made sure that he maintained a casual stride that shouldn't attract too much attention from the spotter.

So far he'd seen two of the Mob hit men sharing street patrol outside Carvaggio's building. Bolan had watched them from his vantage point in the diner across the street, getting their patterns down and trying to match their faces with the Justice Department files he'd scanned. With the naked eye it was difficult to tell for sure. He wasn't about to risk pulling out a handheld spyglass and watch them from the front table at the diner.

Bolan would find out soon enough when he went face-to-face with them, though he had little doubt that the spotters and the men in the van were part of the advance team.

The gunmen were alternating recons so both of them wouldn't be walking around at the same time. Two men covering the same ground over and over again would have been too obvious. At separate intervals each of them had stopped briefly in front of the walk-up entrance to try a furtive twist of the doorknob to make sure it was still unlocked.

Neither of them had been in a hurry to go inside. No one wanted to be a hero. Instead of waltzing in with guns blazing like it was an average hit, they were setting up their forward perimeters like streetwise rangers. Which meant that the hit team respected Nick Carvaggio's abilities. Which meant Bolan would do the same.

They wouldn't attack until the heavy reinforcements came in.

Bolan meant to be gone by then. A crew, yeah, he could take care of them. A clan, no.

He closed on the man in front of him, a stocky, overconfident gunner in a denim jacket who walked like he owned the street. Maybe on another day, Bolan thought. This day the street was his.

The spotter had about twenty more yards before he reached

the corner entrance, perhaps to try the door again. But this time he wasn't going to make it.

Bolan's footsteps slushed through the gathering muck on the sidewalk. It was just a normal sound for this kind of weather, but the man turned by habit. He didn't like to be followed anywhere by anyone.

The Executioner kept walking, hands apparently tugging on his unzipped jacket to keep it closed against the weather while the carryall thumped lightly against his shoulder with every step.

By the time Bolan was in striking distance, the man's sixth sense kicked in. His hand darted inside his denim coat and started to pull out his piece.

Bolan's weapon was there first. His hand had been inside the jacket all along, holding the butt of the 93-R. The 9 mm machine pistol swept free from the breakaway holster without a sound.

Like a man throwing his hand on the table, Bolan continued the move until the blunt sound suppressor pointed straight at the man who was a split second away from getting his weapon free.

Their eyes met, soldier to soldier, and there was no doubt in either man's mind that they were on opposite sides of the war. The only question that remained was who would fall.

Bolan answered the question with a single pull of the trigger.

A third eye erupted in the middle of the man's forehead, and a volcano of blood erupted across his shattered crown. The bullet continued out through the back of his skull, taking away his thoughts and his motor control all at once.

The half-raised gun fell from his dead fingers and clattered onto the sidewalk.

He was gone.

But he was still standing. Or half standing. Right after the shot, Bolan grabbed the collapsing man by his collar, twisted hard and propelled him toward the office building.

Bolan leaned the man against the glass while he twisted

the knob and pushed the door inward. The dead man's momentum carried him forward, causing a bit of blood to streak onto the glass before he hurtled inside like a zombie. Swinging the corpse all the way inside the hallway, Bolan held it up like a shield while he carefully studied the stairs. Then, as he backed toward the door, the soldier pushed the remains headlong into the stairs.

By the time the spotter hit the steps, the Executioner was back on the street again. The whole incident had taken less than half a minute and attracted little notice, not in a city where people made a point not to look around too much.

It went off just as he'd planned, the choreography of carnage that he'd rehearsed in his head several times before actually doing it.

Now it was time for act two of the performance.

With the Beretta back in the breakaway holster, Bolan rounded the corner and headed down the street toward the van, not even looking at it, not even thinking about it, except in the past tense. The crew in the van was as good as gone. That part of the operation had also been planned.

All the Executioner had to do was to act naturally when the time came and let his battle instincts take over.

NICK CARVAGGIO STARED at the monitors in a state of amazement. He'd seen the hit go down every step of the way. One of the outside cameras caught the approach of the man in black and the showdown.

The inside camera caught the dead man being thrown onto the stairs almost effortlessly, even though he was literally deadweight.

"Christ, did you see that?" Carvaggio asked.

"Yeah," the producer said, "I saw it." He was still seeing it in the shocked part of his mind that was replaying it over and over with grisly fascination. And Sawyer felt a chill— not a physical one, a spiritual one. He was now in another realm entirely.

"That man is stone cold," Carvaggio said, "and he's

good. Damn good. Didn't give himself away until the last
moment."

Sawyer didn't share Carvaggio's enthusiasm. If the man
was good, shouldn't that be bad news for himself and Carvaggio? Maybe he was some out of town hit man who didn't
want any witnesses, even people on his own team.

"Who the fuck is he?" Carvaggio said as he watched the
man in the leather jacket head for the van. "I mean, is he
one of yours?"

Sawyer shook his head.

"No, you're right," the ex-hit man said. "He's too good
to be a bodyguard or corporate security op for a studio. Any
studio. Show like yours couldn't hold a man like that. But
what's his game? What's he in it for?"

"I don't know," Sawyer mumbled. His knees felt weak,
like they were going to buckle and he was going to drop to
the floor. But then he wouldn't be able to get up in time to
get away. The bullets would start flying, and he'd never get
up again.

Carvaggio continued spinning out his conjectures on the
man in black and his black ops mannerisms.

"First I thought Justice Department," Carvaggio said. "It
only figures they'd be casing out Victor's crew. But, no, man.
No Justice guy ever just takes you out like that. Pop! None
that I know of."

"Me, neither," Sawyer said. And, as a sick feeling started
to spread through his stomach and a cold sweat broke out on
his skin, he realized that he never wanted to know a man
like that.

"If all of the Justice agents did that," Carvaggio said,
"there'd be nothing left of the Families anymore. Anywhere.
Justice Department I know about talks you to death. Not this.
Definitely not this."

Sawyer backed away from the screens.

And from the hit man.

He wasn't used to Carvaggio saying so much in such a
short a time. It was like the man had suddenly come alive,

as if he were finally engaged in something that really interested him.

Suddenly Rupert Sawyer understood. The man who so calmly watched another man get taken out was appreciating the artistry of death he'd just seen on-screen. Carvaggio was just one step away from breaking out in applause.

Both Carvaggio and the man in the leather jacket had a similar way of carrying themselves—military, menacing, no bullshit, no prisoners.

No wonder Carvaggio admired the sudden but certain kill. It was like seeing himself in action.

For a moment Sawyer wondered what in God's name he was doing there. It wasn't his world. Despite his endless shows about underworld rubouts, crime lords on the run, Mob-tinged political scandals and drugged-out bimbos on the rampage, Rupert Sawyer really hadn't known what it was like to live in that world.

Until now.

And very soon he might find out what it was like to die in that world. It was a shattering thought, and the only thing that kept him from running was the suspicion that he wouldn't make it ten steps outside the door.

At the same time another facet of his personality was coming to life. The fear that was slowly building inside him was tempered by something else, another quality that had an equally powerful effect. It wasn't quite courage, but it was close.

It was greed, and with greed came glory. And power.

It was an epiphany for Sawyer. This was what it was like for reporters on the edge—ultimate success or ultimate failure. He knew that if he toughed it out and somehow survived this night and managed to show this story to his audience, then not only would *Case Closed* stay on top, but it might get him a spot back on the networks again: Rupert Sawyer, a specialist on organized crime; Rupert Sawyer, a roving producer for the network with one or two specials a week.

Rupert Sawyer's *Eye on Crime.* He would be the subject of the story instead of someone just doing the story.

For a moment the producer almost felt glad that he'd walked into the middle of this. But then his eyes were drawn to the surveillance screen again, and he saw the man in black heading for the van. He walked with an easy gait, looking harmless and unconcerned, exactly the way he'd looked before he made his first kill.

Sawyer knew that the night was far from over and his survival somehow rested in the hands of the man in black, hands that were now digging into the pocket of his carryall.

He watched the screen with a hypnotic trance. It felt like a ten-second promo for the evening news—"Live at eleven, a shootout in midtown Manhattan."

And then the thought came to him unbidden, unwanted, but definitely a possibility. The ratings for his next show might shoot through the roof.

But not in the way he liked.

The objective part of his mind conjured up the ten-second teaser for that show. "Caught in the crossfire was Rupert Sawyer, investigative journalist for *Case Closed.*"

The subjective part of his mind told him to run for his life.

The fugitive hit man had to have picked up on his thoughts. He turned to Sawyer with an undertaker's gaze.

"Stay put and I'll get you out of this," Carvaggio said. "Move and you're dead."

2

The men who came to murder Nick Carvaggio waited silently inside the van. Light rain drummed sporadically on the metal rooftop like afterthoughts of the storm that had surprised midtown Manhattan.

Another time it would have been a soothing sound, but not this night.

The nerves of the five men were frayed. Hours of waiting and surveillance had put them on edge. They were tense and ready to explode. When the time came, they would roar into Carvaggio's safehouse, breaching whatever defenses awaited them.

There would be a brief foray into total madness with shooting, falling, screaming, smoke and blood in the air, the whole works. It would be quick and crazy, then it would be over.

But they had to wait, and that was often the hardest part—killing time until the rest of the crew got there.

Adding to their aggravation was the cigarette smoke that filled the van, permeating the carpets and the cushions, and adding another layer of streaky film to the windows.

But no one was about to tell the chain-smoker who sat in the front passenger seat to put out his cigarette.

The man with the cigarette was literally riding shotgun with a 12-round Armsel revolving shotgun perched across his knees. It fired tear gas rounds to flush out the prey and fléchette rounds to rip through and redistribute internal body parts. There were also lock-buster rounds and high-explosive slugs.

The entire magazine could be fired in a matter of seconds.

For most men the multitask Street Sweeper shotgun would seem like a large weapon with its thick tommy-gun-like revolving magazine. But in the large callused hands of the shotgunner it looked almost economy size.

So if he decided to smoke, the rest of them decided to breathe it in with no comment.

The only crew member not bothered by the smoke was the second spotter who was standing just outside the van, waiting for his next turn to patrol. All he had to contend with was the slight stream of smoke wafting through the half-open window while he pretended to be passing time with the occupants of the van. That and the condescending gaze of the shotgunner who regarded everyone else on the operation as deadweight.

It was a small price to pay, considering the bounty on Nick Carvaggio's head. No matter how many of them split it up, it was going to be a heavy piece of change.

For that reason each one of them wanted to move quick against Carvaggio, get the waiting over with, get in and out of the strike zone.

But they had orders that had to be followed, just like it was back in their days in the military. No one moved until all of the teams arrived and were in place.

Then they would erase Nick Carvaggio from the face of the earth with an overwhelming and unstoppable force.

Right now he was enemy number one of Vic Sienna's underworld clan, a cohort of genuine soldiers known as the Garrison.

Orders were orders, even if it was overkill.

MACK BOLAN SAUNTERED down the sidewalk like he had nothing on his mind but getting home. He made sure he didn't look too long or too hard at anything, but he took it all in just the same, like a man with nothing to hide.

It was a delicate balance.

If he looked away from people, that could attract their

attention because they might think he had something to hide.
If he looked too long at them, it might be considered a challenge and everyone would throw down at the same time.

Bolan played out his charade as best he could. He had some crucial ground to cover before he got to the kill zone. Once inside the boundary that he'd drawn in his mind, the hit team was as good as gone.

But to get there he had to mask his intentions.

It was a hard act to pull off, considering the amount of ordnance he was packing in the carryall. But he closed in on the van without any mishap. And now he was almost within striking distance. At this point, even if they made him, he would still have a fighting chance.

Through his peripheral vision Bolan saw the driver studying him. The man's senses were awakened. He was ready to roll, scanning the street and the sidewalk and the unconcerned eyes of the man in black. At the same time, he was talking on a car phone, maybe directing some other teams that were on the way, or perhaps waiting for the green light.

Steven? Bolan thought. No. The man's name filtered through his memory from the dossier of Sienna's associates. Stefan Gaultieri.

And the heavy guy in the passenger seat—the man with the scowling face who sat there immovable and unyielding? His name was drifting about somewhere in the Executioner's memory.

Laurenz Matteo?

Benny Arturo?

So many faces, so many felons. He couldn't remember the man's name, but he remembered the face that had looked out at him from one of Brognola's surveillance shots. He was one of Sienna's premium bulls. Before signing on with the Garrison, he'd done a stint with the Agency's Animal Farm, handling hard-core paramilitary ops. He was a spook who'd sold out to the highest bidder.

It was time for him to cash out.

Bolan was almost to the van, shielded by a row of parked

cars lined up along the curb, when the shotgunner pointedly stared at him. The man outside the van stared, and the driver stared.

It was the look Mob soldiers gave to people when something was going down that was none of their business, a look that told people to get out of the way or get hurt.

It also opened them up to attack.

From past experience terrorizing people on the side, they expected him to walk on by, and that gave the Executioner the few seconds he needed to surprise them.

Bolan sprinted between the parked cars straight for the spotter, moving like a halfback stiff-arming a tackle. His hand pushed hard on the back of the man's neck and propelled him face first toward the half-open window.

"Hey!" the man shouted. But it was the last thing he said. There was a crash of glass and a crack of bone as the impact broke the man's nose, giving him a concussion at the same time.

As the man bounced back off the window, Bolan grabbed the back of his collar and flung him away from the van, releasing him when he was almost horizontal.

With a loud thump the back of the man's head bashed into the parked car behind him, just above the wheel well. He made a slight teeth-clacking groan as he slumped to the ground.

He was out of it and registered no more threat.

It all happened within seconds, barely enough time for the occupants of the van to register what was going on.

But now the gunners were coming alive and scrambling for their weapons. A couple more seconds and they could open fire.

The shotgunner's gaze had changed from a tough-guy stare to wild-eyed rage. Not fear that he was being hit, but rage that he was going to be outclassed.

"Get him! Get him!" the shotgunner shouted when he saw what Bolan was carrying. He knew he didn't have enough time to bring his shotgun into target acquisition before the man in black made his move.

The Executioner pulled the pin on the Haley and Weller E-180 multiburst stun grenade he'd fished out of his carryall.

Bolan slammed the armed canister through the half-shattered window. It bounced off the heavy man's gut and clattered to his feet.

"What is it?" one of the men in the back shouted.

The shotgunner swore and reached down, his beefy hands scrambling for the canister when it went off in his face.

The flash-and-bang grenade concussed everyone in the tightly packed van, even the driver who was trying to scramble out the door.

Then it went off again.

And again.

The phased flash-bangs of the high-candlepower grenade went off in a sequence designed to catch even the best-trained commando off guard. A man could weather a single stun grenade if he knew it was coming, but the multiburst grenade overwhelmed the body's natural tensing and relaxing reflexes, temporarily blinding and disorienting anyone caught in the multiple shock waves.

Bolan raced to the back of the van just as the rear doors swung open, spilling two Mob soldiers onto the road. They'd started to bail as soon as the grenade landed inside the van.

But it wasn't soon enough.

The flash-bangs had enveloped them just as they managed to wrench open the door handle and push their way out. By the time they hit the ground they were in a state of shock, temporarily relieved of their wits by the sonic boom.

Still, they were pros, and they were armed.

The closer gunner had managed to hold on to his weapon, an automatic with an extralong stick magazine. He was flat on his back, pushing himself across the slippery road with his heels while aiming the pistol skyward. Even if the gunman couldn't see his assailant, he was still trying to sense him.

A wild shot could take out someone passing by, someone not even connected to this underworld war.

If the guy was lucky, it could even take out Bolan.

The Executioner took away his luck and his life with a 3-round burst from the Beretta. It was a reflex action. The nearest gunman was the greatest threat, so he was put down first.

The next burst took out the second gunman who had almost recovered from the stun grenade. Three 9 mm rounds caught him in the chest just as he was sitting up with his weapon, a silenced Ingram machine pistol that would stay silent this night—except for the dull splash it made when it skidded out of the gunner's fingers and came to rest in a puddle.

The Executioner took a split-second inventory of the opposition. There were two dead before him. The spotter with the cracked skull was still lying on the road between the van and the parked car, either out cold or out for keeps. Whatever his condition, he was no longer moving and no longer a threat.

That left two more to deal with—the driver, who was somewhere on the other side of the van where he'd scrambled out of the door, and the shotgunner who'd caught the full effects of the grenade.

As his scattered senses started to come back to him, the shotgunner thrashed inside the van like a wounded bull. The windshield was shattered and so were his eardrums, but he wasn't going out without striking back.

Bolan stepped back into the street as the passenger door hurled open and the shotgunner jumped onto the road. He was waving his automatic shotgun like a talisman.

When the barrel swung toward Bolan the 12-round wind-up rotary magazine looked twice its normal size.

The first burst of the Beretta cut a bloody red clothesline across the man's neck, while the second drilled into his massive chest, poking a few holes in his girth.

Six 9 mm rounds heavier, the big man dropped into the street, his bearlike head thudding wetly onto the road. His heavy paws smacked lifelessly into the water as if he were diving straight into hell.

The dropped Armsel shotgun came to rest almost at Bolan's feet like an offering. A trophy.

Bolan picked it up. He was already packing heavy, but the shotgun could come in handy. Who knew what else they had coming for him? Besides, the need for silence was over; the flash-bang had seen to that. The moment the sunlike nova went off inside the van, the covert operation had become high profile.

Now it was time to finish up and get off the street.

The Executioner jogged around to the driver's side of the van and saw that the door was open. The driver was staggering down the street toward a light blue Volvo that had stopped in the middle of the road, forcing traffic to go around it.

Reinforcements?

But then Bolan saw the stunned look on the man in suit, tie and overcoat who stepped out of the Volvo. He looked at Bolan as if he were seeing a ghost—or someone very capable of turning others into ghosts. The man looked at the driver of the van in a new light, realizing he was a part of whatever was going down and not someone in need of help. At least the kind of help he could offer.

He jumped back into the Volvo.

Definitely a civilian, Bolan thought, probably someone who'd been driving by when Stefan Gaultieri jumped out of his van. Maybe Gaultieri ran straight into the side of the car and got himself banged up.

Or maybe Gaultieri twisted an ankle when he jumped out of the van. It was hard to tell. Bolan just wanted to make sure the man wasn't a danger to himself or any of the civilians on the street.

But the concussed driver was running, hobbling down the street, no weapon in sight. Bolan could chase after him to finish him off, or he could pay more attention to the action on the street.

He'd been in a different world a few seconds back, the world of battle where time moved slow and background sounds faded to a whisper.

His senses had picked out the most crucial sounds to follow. Right now one of those was the acceleration of a Jeep Cherokee screeching from the road behind him, its tires alternately skidding on or gripping the slick road.

Bolan spun and found himself facing a pair of fast-moving headlights. The driver flicked on the high beams a moment later. Now it was Bolan who couldn't see.

It was either backup for the hit team or someone panicked by the gunfire in the street.

The Executioner got off the street and slid between two parked cars as the high-performance Jeep bore down on him.

There was no mistake now. He was their target, and once again the headlights were coming his way, trying to freeze him like a jacked deer.

Just before the bright lights hit him, Bolan saw a group of bunched-up silhouettes inside the vehicle. And then he saw the Heckler & Koch submachine gun poked out the front passenger window.

The barrel of the machine pistol was bearing down on him when Bolan let loose with the shotgun. He held the forward grip steady and triggered several rounds, shattering the headlights with a blast that shot clear through into the engine. The next round caved in the windshield, spraying fléchettes into the front seat of the kill car.

Bolan triggered a few more bursts from the Street Sweeper, appreciating the shot selection of the former owner—incendiaries, fléchettes, high explosives.

It was enough firepower to cause a lot of damage and confusion in the enemy and provide some time for Bolan to get away.

The Cherokee crashed into one of the cars next to the curb. There were probably some dead, some wounded, some worried.

Bolan made a split-second calculation. He could either stay

and try to finish them off or do what he came here to do—
hook up with Carvaggio.

That was his primary mission.

He double-timed it back to the corner building while scanning the street for any more of Sienna's reinforcements.

THE DEAD MAN WAITED for him on the stairs. He was sitting
there in a bloody heap like a true underworld sentinel, waiting for Bolan to give him the password.

The Executioner slammed the door behind him, then
looked beyond the shadowy corpse up at the dim staircase.

"Carvaggio!" Bolan shouted. "I'm coming up."

Dim light flicked on from the baseboard on the second-
floor landing, just enough to dispel the shadows. A voice
from above echoed electronically down the hallway, sounding slightly muffled through a hidden speaker embedded in
one of the walls. "Don't move until I say so. The hallway's
wired."

"I don't have a choice," Bolan said, leaning against the
wall to his right and looking through the door glass. The
shotgun was cached in the crook of his left arm and the
Beretta was in his right, loaded with a fresh magazine.
"There's some other people coming any second now—"

"I know," Carvaggio said, still through the speaker. "I
saw it. What I can't figure out is why."

"Let me up and I'll explain it to you," Bolan said. "I'm
working with the Justice Department—I came to hear your
side of what happened when you tried to come in."

"You don't look like any Fed I ever saw. Definitely not
Justice Department."

"Maybe just plain justice," Bolan said, tiring of talking
to the disembodied voice. "I'm working with the Feds on
this one, not for them. Never mind that for now. I'm coming
up before your Family comes visiting. Or NYPD shows up."

"Come halfway," the voice ordered. "No more. And
don't worry about them yet. They're regrouping. We've got

lots of time. Maybe even a minute. The cops'll be awhile longer.''

Bolan sidestepped past the dead man and continued up the stairs the same way, watching the stairs below and the shadowed landing above.

"This is your last chance, Carvaggio," Bolan said. "Either I come in now or I go away for good. All deals are off, and you can have Rupert there watching your back from now on."

"Hold on," Carvaggio said. "Look—maybe you are on my side. Or maybe this is just a slick way to get inside so you can take me out. How the hell am I supposed to know?"

Bolan nodded. It made sense, especially when you were dealing with a devious crew like Sienna's clan. "If I wanted you dead, I would have shot you when you followed Rupert inside. Or maybe I would have twisted your white scarf around your throat and broke your neck. I had opportunity."

"Yeah, you did," Carvaggio said. "Come on up. I'll hear you out."

Bolan heard a clicking sound from up above, then rounded the landing where he saw Rupert Sawyer holding a door open for him. The producer looked nervous but under the circumstances was doing his best to hold himself together.

Beyond the producer he saw the phosphorescent glow of a bank of surveillance screens, enough to furnish a sophisticated corporate security station or bankrupt a small business. Nick Carvaggio had obviously done well in his underworld enterprises. This was a one-time pad, a throwaway safehouse set up for just one clandestine meeting. The man had plenty of money to burn.

The Executioner brushed past the producer and took in the rest of the surroundings before focusing on the hit man.

Nick Carvaggio spun in his chair, totally at ease at the sight of the man with the shotgun and machine pistol, as if they were something every well-dressed guest would bring.

Carvaggio was also holding considerable firepower, gripping a 9 mm Steyr TMP with a compact 15-round clip about the length of the handle. The Tactical Machine Pistol was designed for up-close combat—crowded rooms, narrow alleys, subway cars. It gave a lot of control while still maintaining a solid speed of 900 rpm.

Bolan was more interested in the man than the weapon. He studied the eyes and saw a calmness there, a cold logic at work. Carvaggio wasn't about to risk a firefight. Just as Bolan tended to believe the ex-hit man's version of the incident that led to the death of a Justice Department agent, Carvaggio believed Bolan came here to bring him in if possible.

Carvaggio pointedly laid the weapon flat on the counter and nodded at Bolan. "You earned yourself a speech," he said. "Go ahead and make it."

The Executioner had also let his weapons drop. They were at rest, but available if the need arose.

"Actually," Bolan said, "I came here to listen instead of talk. If your story checks out, we can work out a deal satisfactory to all parties—"

"That's great," the producer interrupted, stepping forward and clapping his hands together. "We can—"

"You're not part of the deal," Bolan said. "Not yet. Right now you're just a complication."

The Executioner's gaze convinced Rupert Sawyer that complications could be easily removed.

"Say my story checks out to your satisfaction," Carvaggio said. "Do you have the ability to make a deal that sticks with the Feds? Even the ones who still want my head?"

"I've got a long reach," Bolan replied.

"Yeah, I saw that." Carvaggio gestured toward the monitors. "Actions speak louder than words. In your case, real loud. Which is why we're talking now. But what happens if you don't buy my story?"

"This is how it's going to work," the Executioner stated. "Whatever decision I make, the people who matter will back me up. If you're on the level, you've got nothing to worry about from me or them. If you're lying, then you're fair game."

Carvaggio nodded. "Good enough. I want my side known. I was going to tell it to him—" he pointed to Sawyer "—because of the reception I got from the Justice Department. A bit frosty."

The producer couldn't hold back any longer. "But we've got a deal! I won't allow this."

His words hung hollow in the air. He was in no position to allow or disallow anything. But Rupert Sawyer was a creature of habit who was used to getting his way. He was about to launch into more reasons why he had to be heard when Bolan silenced him with a sharp-handed gesture.

"We'll listen to you on the cutting-room floor," Bolan said. "On the killing floor you listen to us."

Sawyer nodded his head rapidly. "You're saying there will be a segment after all?"

"We'll figure something out for you later," the soldier said. "Something fair. Something that won't hurt any of us."

The producer smiled briefly. Amid all the carnage his mind was on the future, no matter how dim it looked at the moment.

Bolan glanced at the surveillance screens, which now showed a lot of activity on the streets near the intersection. About twenty yards past the building entrance a couple of cars had pulled up and double-parked. Doors opened, and some very intense men climbed out.

Another five-man group came around the corner, walking briskly with their hands sliding inside their jackets and working their guns free from their holsters.

"Unless you plan on fighting World War III here," Bolan said, "I suggest we start moving."

Carvaggio gestured for them to wait. "Not just yet. I've arranged a special welcome for this crew." He watched the surveillance screen as the first three men burst through the street-front door, weapons drawn.

Sienna's advance team saw the dead man on the stairs, took it as a personal affront and started up.

Carvaggio started pressing buttons on a small keypad remote control. The first radio signal triggered a blast halfway up the stairs, a shaped charge aimed at the gunmen's feet.

The stairway disintegrated in a blizzard of splintered wood, whipping into the hit men like toothpick-sized shrapnel.

Like human pincushions, all three men fell ten feet straight down into the dark well of the staircase.

The second round of plastic-explosive strips went off even before they hit the floor. This charge was heavier and cut through them like a fiery red guillotine.

"Jesus help us," the producer said as he saw the effects of the blast via the surveillance monitor.

"I doubt it," Carvaggio said. "Not this time around."

Carvaggio pressed another button. This one tripped a mine planted in the wire cage of the ceiling's light fixture just above the doorway.

Fire and metal rained on the heads of the two other hit men who'd stepped aside, so eager to be in on the Carvaggio kill that they died in his stead.

Both men fell back through the shattered glass door, leaving blood-filled shoes behind.

Carvaggio keyed in a couple more sequences, then gestured to Bolan and the producer.

"Now we can go," Carvaggio said, pushing himself away from the computer screens.

Sawyer fell in behind him and Bolan took up the rear-guard, now and then glancing back to cover their flank until they reached a wide and primitive-looking elevator.

As soon as the three men were inside, Carvaggio closed the folding metal gate, then aimed the remote control back at the high-tech monitoring station. With another press of the button he armed the remaining explosive charges planted throughout the office. "No one's going to make it through there alive. All we've got to worry about now is the rooftop."

"You think they're up there?" Sawyer asked.

Carvaggio shrugged. "No, not yet. But they're all around." He hit the up button and the elevator lurched into action, sounding decrepit and corroded as it shuddered its way toward the top floor.

They climbed a short flight of stairs to the rooftop garret and stepped into the darkness.

Bolan edged over to the protective stone cornice and scanned the neighboring roofs. There was no sign of the enemy, but there were plenty of shadows to provide a sniper's perch.

The Executioner took out the handheld thermal imager from his canvas satchel and looked through the green screen. No heat signatures were visible on the rooftop.

Bolan slowly crouched until he could see the streets and the alleys below, careful not to silhouette himself against the night.

He wasn't surprised to see Carvaggio doing the same type of recon, first looking through a night-vision scope at the other buildings, then using the naked eye to see what awaited them below.

There was a lot of activity on the street in front of the bombed-out entrance. Bystanders hurried by, some of them yelling for help. Mob soldiers gathered near the corner, waiting for the smoke and flames to clear before they launched their next attack. Their angry voices carried up to the rooftop.

The producer stood silently by the garret as if it were his anchor to safety, reluctantly looking at the two men scouting the horizon.

After they covered the entire perimeter, Carvaggio signaled Bolan from the far corner.

The Executioner eased away from the cornice and sprinted toward Carvaggio, keeping his head down until he was right beside him.

"It's still there," Carvaggio said.

"What is?" Bolan asked, carefully peering over the edge.

Carvaggio pointed at a narrow alley behind the office

buildings. The pothole-laden roadway ran between a maze of fire escapes, abbreviated loading docks and delivery entrances. Street debris, cardboard boxes and broken crates jutted from both sides, making it even more of an obstacle course.

The alley led to a side street just a short block away.

But there was a dilapidated black van blocking the alley about three buildings distant, exhaust fumes chugging away.

"I'm guessing that's your escape route," Bolan said.

"Yeah," Carvaggio agreed. "It was."

"And that van isn't here by coincidence?" Bolan asked.

"No. It's been here awhile. Noticed it on the cameras downstairs the minute it rolled up."

"You recognize it?"

"Oh, yeah," Carvaggio replied. "Matter of fact, I've ridden inside it a few times myself. Don't let the banged-up look fool you. That's a fast machine. High-performance engine, reinforced bumper. Use it as a portable arms cache or a taxi service. Rack of weapons hidden in the wall. Shotguns, pistols, grenades. The works."

"Friends of yours?"

"Not anymore."

"Good," Bolan said, "because they're definitely in our way. The longer we stay here, the less likely we'll all get out." He glanced over his shoulder at the producer.

Carvaggio nodded. "Time to move." He pointed toward the rubber-coated ladders leaning against the wall. There were two of them, both long enough to bridge the gap to the next building. The rubber coating was designed for quietly breaching walls.

SWAT team materials, the Executioner noted. Carvaggio used nothing but the best, even on a throwaway operation. Bolan helped him set the ladders across to the other rooftop.

Both men could have easily made it across the horizontal ladder rungs. Simple basic-training stuff. But Rupert Sawyer was looking wide-eyed and almost hysterical at the prospect, until he saw Carvaggio place a flat panel board across both ladders.

"Come on, Rupert," Carvaggio said. "Walk the gangplank."

"Can't do it," Sawyer replied. "I mean...it's...it's too high... The ladders...I can't make it..."

Carvaggio shrugged. "We won't make you do anything you don't want to. But I don't think you want to hang around and explain things to the boys when they get here. And get here they will—it's just a matter of time."

The pep talk had the appropriate effect, although Sawyer still looked unsure of his ability.

Bolan gripped the shotgun and the Beretta, balancing one in each hand as he crossed onto the other rooftop.

Behind him he heard Carvaggio urging the producer on. "You can do this, Rupert," the former mobster said, positioning him to step up onto the platform. "Forget can. You have to."

The producer stepped forward gingerly. Halfway across the makeshift bridge, Sawyer discovered that he really could do it. His steps went from timid to certain and then almost cocksure as he jumped down onto the opposite roof.

When the three men were safely across, they slid the ladders and boards from across the gap and carted them to the far edge of the building. The angle was a bit steeper there, but the ladders were long enough to provide safe passage. Carvaggio had planned his alternative escape route well, counting on the worst-case scenario to come true.

They carried out the same maneuvers across to the next building, bringing them to the rooftop just above the battered black van.

"I'll do the sweep," Carvaggio said, reaching out for the Armsel shotgun.

Bolan didn't argue and handed over the automatic Street Sweeper. This was Carvaggio's turf, his people, his conflict. He knew how they operated. Now it was a chance for Bolan to see the ex-hit man in action. If the two of them were going to be working together, the Executioner needed to know the man's capacity.

Carvaggio checked the rotary magazine, looking at the kind of firepower it contained. "This will work just fine," he concluded.

Then he opened his coat and revealed part of the arsenal he carried with him at all times. Holstered in a cloth sling in the lining was a small sawed-off shotgun and a canvas strip of shotgun shells. The pocket had a gap cut through it so Carvaggio could fire without having to withdraw the weapon.

Bolan had an image of Carvaggio walking the streets with his hands in his pockets, apparently unarmed and uncaring until someone made a move against him. And then it was lights out.

Carvaggio fished out a handful of shotgun shells, then reloaded and rewound the magazine of the larger shotgun. "This'll do," he said when he was satisfied with the arrangement.

With a practiced draw, he removed the lethal sawed-off piece from the holster and held it out for Bolan. "This one's designed more for shock tactics or a face-to-face encounter. Use it if you need it."

Bolan hefted the weapon and studied the cut-off barrel. The shotgun spray would flare in a wide pattern, which was good for close range, good for someone who wasn't the best aim in the world.

He handed it to the producer. Rupert Sawyer reluctantly accepted the shotgun and listened calmly as Bolan explained how to use it. And when to use it.

"We're climbing down the fire escape to that van," Bolan stated. "You wait on the top landing until we give you the all clear. Don't fire unless you have to. You might get us all killed. Understand?"

Sawyer nodded.

Bolan and Carvaggio inched over the side and slowly made their way down the fire escape, silently going from step to step until they were on the bottom landing almost on top of the van.

Carvaggio gripped the side railing, swung one foot onto it, then pushed himself up with the other. In one smooth motion he vaulted over the railing and sailed straight down toward the van, his coat fluttering like a cape in the air.

By the time his feet landed on the van, Carvaggio had a solid grip on the shotgun. He angled the barrel at the roof and let loose a two-second barrage.

Before the occupants could react to the thumping sound of Carvaggio's feet, a good portion of the roof disintegrated. Jagged metal strips coiled inward, singed by the high-explosive blast spitting from the Armsel.

Carvaggio pivoted to the back of the van and fired through the roof again, this time spraying the interior with an incendiary shell.

While death streamed into the van, two men managed to jump out the side door. As one of them aimed a revolver at Carvaggio, Bolan hit him with a triburst from the Beretta.

The Executioner fired another burst at the second gunman, who collapsed against the van. Carvaggio fired off the rest of the magazine, then speared the empty shotgun through the holes blown out of the roof.

Bolan and the ex-hit man spread out and covered both sides of the alley while the producer clattered down the fire escape.

Sawyer rode the extension ladder to the alley and jumped the last several feet to the ground. With Sawyer gasping like a fish out of water, the three men double-timed it through the alley to the side street where Carvaggio had a car waiting.

They scanned the road, looking for any of Sienna's crew before they headed for the car, an old Chevy with big fins and bigger dents, the kind of car no one would bother to steal.

Bolan climbed into the front seat. Sawyer flung open the back door and dived inside, slamming the door behind him now that he was in a cocoon of safety.

"Hell of a ride you got here," the Executioner said.

"Beats a hearse," Carvaggio replied, glancing back at the alley where flames had enveloped the van and turned it into a dull black coffin.

3

"This is where we part company," Bolan said, turning in the front passenger seat. "For now."

Rupert Sawyer nodded his agreement a bit too eagerly as he reached for the handle of the late-model black Mercury sedan parked in front of the Arris Hotel on Central Park East.

"Not so fast," Bolan said.

"What is it?"

"It's a matter of trust."

"I trust you guys," Sawyer stated.

Carvaggio laughed and shook his head as he drummed his fingers on the steering wheel. "That's not what the man's worried about, Rupert. Just pay attention. We all have to make the right moves from here on."

Sawyer shrugged and sat back in the seat, though he looked longingly at the brightly lighted alcove of the Arris Hotel, where a uniformed doorman awaited.

The Arris was his upscale refuge for the night, where he could escape the war the other two men had to see through to the end.

Now that the battle was over, Sawyer noticed Carvaggio was a bit on edge. Throughout the combat he'd maintained a casual, almost relaxed aura about him. He was totally in the zone then. But now that the shooting had stopped, Carvaggio was once again in limbo as far as his future was concerned.

The fugitive hit man had been driving them around Manhattan for nearly an hour now, after ditching the getaway junker for the Mercury that he had waiting for them in an underground parking garage. Since then they'd blended with the busy traffic and listened to the late-breaking news stories about the Big Apple Battle on the radio.

The reporters, almost ecstatic at the prospects of a blood-and-guts story, were breathlessly speculating that these were only the first rounds fired in an underworld war.

Every time a bulletin came on about the gangland slayings, Sawyer had bemoaned the fact that he'd been scooped on an incident he'd actually been involved in. The Executioner and Carvaggio had tuned him out, concentrating on the traffic flow around them and trusting their instincts to tell them if they were being followed by any reserves from Sienna's hit team.

Now it was time to explain the facts of life—and death—to the producer.

"Okay, Rupert," Bolan said. "Empty your left pocket."

"What?"

"The minicam."

"Oh," Sawyer said, as if he just remembered what he was carrying. He dug into his trench coat and took out the miniature video recorder that he'd used earlier to film the safehouse.

Bolan held out his hand until Sawyer dropped the minicam into the flat of his palm.

"I'll need that back," Sawyer said.

"After I look at the film."

"I just took a few shots," Sawyer insisted. "For background. If you think—"

"I'll tell you what I think after I look it over." Then Bolan pointed toward Sawyer's shirt pocket.

Sawyer sat back and managed to look like he was offended. "Now what?" he asked.

"Now you give me the voice-activated cassette."

"Oh. That."

"And the tiepin," Bolan said after Sawyer handed over the miniature recorder. "Let me see that."

Sawyer reached protectively for the tiepin. It was an ornately filigreed brass clip. "It's a family heirloom."

"Yeah," Bolan said, tugging on Sawyer's tie and studying the pin until he saw the lens and shooting mechanism of the pinhole camera. "Grandpa must have been a spy." He unclipped the tiepin and dropped it into his pocket.

"Man, you don't miss much," Sawyer said, unable to hide his admiration at Bolan's thoroughness. Though he'd already determined that Bolan was a formidable man, Sawyer suddenly realized just how closely Bolan had been following him and studying him. "You were there in the restaurant when I checked out my gear."

"Yeah," Bolan replied. "I was there. Ever since you left the studio I've been with you every step of the way."

"Okay, I'm sorry," Sawyer said, waving off his attempt at keeping the hidden camera a secret from Bolan. "Look, I'm in the business. It's habit. This is what I do."

"It's what you did," Bolan said. "Now you're in the business of staying alive, and that means you listen to us. You don't cross us, right?"

"Sure."

"You're saying that too easily. I want you to really think about things. About what you're promising here."

"I am!" Sawyer protested. "In fact I'm—"

Bolan held up his palm for silence. "Listen carefully to me, Rupert. Think about the people who paid us all a visit tonight. The ones who tried to take us out. You remember how you felt when they made their move?"

"Yes. Of course—"

"They were some of the meanest, soulless murderous bastards you could ever meet," Bolan said. "Right?"

"Right. I understand that."

"Understand this," Bolan said, pausing to let his words sink in. "They're dead. We're not."

Sawyer looked confused, as if Bolan were stating the obvious.

"So when it occurs to you during your more lucid mo-

ments to fear for your life because of people like them—
think of us. Think of what will happen to you if you betray
us.''

''I wouldn't do that,'' Sawyer said.

''Good. As long as you get it straight that the only exposé
will be the one we allow.''

Sawyer hesitated again, falling back on his old ways. As
a member of the press, he had assumed there was a right to
film anything his lens could capture.

''The pen may be mightier than the sword,'' Bolan said,
''and the video camera may be even mightier than that.'' He
raised the Beretta 93-R that had been sitting on the front seat.
''But there's no way a film clip is mightier than a 9 mm
clip.''

Sawyer's eyes focused on the barrel of the machine pistol
that he'd seen used with such telling effect.

''Putting our faces on-screen is the same thing as pointing
a gun at us,'' Bolan said, ''and that makes you an enemy.''

''But I need some film to put the story together,'' Sawyer
protested, nodding toward Carvaggio, who was scanning the
street to make sure no one was moving in on them. ''And I
need him to get the story!''

''You'll get the story, Rupert,'' Bolan said, ''but you'll
get it our way. Get in our way—that's the end of the story
for you.''

The producer raised his hands in surrender. ''No problem.
I want to work with you guys. Just tell me what to do and
I'll do it.''

''For starters,'' Bolan said, ''you can stay alive. That
means don't go back to your apartment for a couple of days.
Don't tell anyone about tonight. And get in touch with your
syndicate's security force to arrange for a bodyguard team
for the next few days.''

Sawyer's face paled. ''You think they'll come after me?''

''Maybe not this soon,'' the Executioner replied. ''But
they won't be too happy about tonight, and they'll want to
make someone pay.''

"Oh, God," Sawyer said. "How about you guys—"

"We're not in the baby-sitting business. We'll help you out as long as you do what we say."

"All right, all right," Sawyer promised. But even as he promised, he was still looking for a way to salvage his position and his profits. He leaned forward and looked straight at Carvaggio. "Where do you stand in all this? You and I had an arrangement all worked out. Now you're going to let him call all the shots for you?"

"I believe so," Carvaggio answered. "Once we talk things over."

The producer shook his head, then looked at Bolan as he slid across the back seat to the door. "Hell of a deal maker, man," he said.

"Everybody wins this way," Bolan said. "Nick gets to come in from the cold. I get the information I need. You get to stay alive."

"I'll do my part," Sawyer promised, "but how do I contact you?"

"We'll be in touch in a few days," the Executioner replied. "After we recon the opposition."

Sawyer nodded, then stepped out of the Mercury with dreams of Emmys swirling in his head.

As soon as the producer glided through the doors of the Arris, Carvaggio stepped on the gas pedal and swung into traffic. "You got a way with handling people," he said.

"Sawyer might be a big help."

"And me?" Carvaggio asked. "How you plan on handling my situation?"

"Let's have a sit-down," Bolan said.

"Deal," Carvaggio agreed. "And some food and a drink while we're at it. It's been awhile since I remembered to eat."

"You got any favorite places to go?"

"Sure."

"Make sure we don't go there," Bolan said. "They'll be scouting all your hangouts."

"No joke."

About twenty minutes later they were sitting at a corner booth in a quiet Upper East Side bar and grill about two blocks from the parking spot they found near 67th Street.

It was far enough away from the Brooklyn hangouts and the South Street Seaport haunts where Nick Carvaggio had been a fixture and his old teammates were looking for him.

Atmospherics was a two-story place with two separate bars and two different sets of clientele. Upstairs was a theme bar with electronic trance-and-dance music for the younger crowd who came there to meet one another while under the heady influence of drink or hormones. The sound system was extravagant but so was the soundproof baffle that separated it from the first-floor bar.

Downstairs was geared to a slightly older and a lot less edgier crowd. Some of the people sitting at the tables were couples who'd been together awhile and were comfortable just being out somewhere in the city. There were also a lot of singles who'd come to get away from people they'd met in other places, other bars.

It felt more like a tavern designed for serious drinking, thinking or talking. The music that played in the background was mostly old jazz and pop tunes rarely seen on jukebox playlists these days—Wes Montgomery blue notes, Bill Evans standards.

With the low music and quiet mumble of conversation, they could talk without being overheard, which was exactly what Bolan and his fugitive partner needed to plan their survival.

But just in case, they'd kept their coats with them. Carvaggio's long coat hung over the back of his chair, complete with the sawed-off shotgun in place.

Bolan kept his jacket on to cover the Beretta harness.

After a plate of pub fries, beef strips and a lager—which Carvaggio quickly dispatched—the ex-hit man was ready to deal.

Waiting until the waitress dropped off a fresh pot of coffee,

Bolan leaned forward, resting his elbows on the thick wooden table scarred with cigarette burns and beer-bottle rings. "All right," he said, "cards on the table. If we're going to work together, we got to know what the other's about."

"That's easy enough," Carvaggio said. "I'm about to get killed—unless I throw in with you. Provided, of course, you give me a clean bill of health with the Feds."

"Okay," Bolan said. "Let's start with the reason why they want you, which is the death of Justice Department Special Agent Hank Prescott."

Carvaggio nodded. "First let me tell you what led up to that. I know you've heard it plenty of times, but you haven't heard it from me."

"Go ahead," Bolan said.

Carvaggio launched into his version of events, starting with how he hooked back up with Victor Sienna. They were fast friends who came out of Brooklyn together and went into the service together—after the local parole board offered them a tour in the Army or a tour in jail.

They took to training well. Sienna stayed in the service for four years, Carvaggio for eight. After a stint with the Rangers, Carvaggio drifted into Special Forces operations, operating in Panama, Grenada and the Middle East.

When he came out of the service, he drifted back to New York and looked up Victor Sienna, who was in the middle of a war. Families were breaking up. Sienna's people were on the outs and being driven out of town or underground.

"He asked for my help," Carvaggio said. "I gave it. We went back a long way. Besides, this was hard-core crimies, man. No civilians, just soldiers. Everybody knew what they were in for."

Carvaggio paused, and his voice went a bit lower. "Tell you the truth, I found my calling. I stayed with Vic even after his war was over, and he hired out services to the other Families. There was always a war going on somewhere, and a lot of these people deserved what they got. You wouldn't believe what they're capable of."

"I've been a believer for years," Bolan said. "I've crossed paths with them more times than I can count."

Carvaggio studied him then, taking in his weathered, craggy face, his military bearing and his take-no-prisoners attitude from the moment he stepped into the building. A man on a mission.

A mission that had been going on for some time.

"Man..." Carvaggio said, exaggeratedly slapping his forehead. "It fits now. You're the guy..."

Bolan stayed impassive as recognition dawned in Carvaggio's eyes.

"The Execution—"

"Just call me Striker for now," Bolan said, cutting him off.

"Sure," Carvaggio said. "What the hell kind of name is that?"

"It's the kind of name you can drop in the right places if you need some help fast and I'm not around," Bolan said. "Provided I give you the right numbers to call."

"So give."

"You're not done yet. I want your story first. I want names, locations, everything you got. But first I want to know about Hank Prescott."

"Okay, Striker," Carvaggio said. "So you must know the kind of life I'm talking about here. The money was good. The cause was right. I was getting rid of people the world was better off without. And I thrived on it. I was trained for it. Things were moving along just how I wanted...and then Vic assigned me to hit a juror and her family."

Bolan was familiar with the juror situation. What Carvaggio told him in the next few minutes matched up with what the Justice Department had pieced together. Only they'd come to a different conclusion about the perpetrator.

Carvaggio's defection—or, in Sienna's eyes, his betrayal—began with the trial of a midlevel mobster who had a lot of favors to call in. One of those favors involved Victor Sienna, who offered his help.

Some of the jurors had already been reached and were going to bring in a not-guilty verdict. But one uncorruptible woman was determined to put the mobster away for good. A contract was put out on her and her family to make sure that couldn't happen.

"It started out the usual way," Carvaggio said. "Vic told me to gear up for a hit, a special one. I got my rig and was ready to start until he told me who the target was. It was a woman, an innocent one at that. That's when I broke with him."

Carvaggio paused, reliving the moment, almost savoring it. "I told him no, but Sienna said yes. Said it several times, said my life depended on it. He'd promised some heavy people that it would happen."

The hit man sipped his coffee and shrugged. "So I told him to make it unhappen."

"Something else was going on there," Bolan said. "He could have ordered other people to do the hit. He knew what you would and wouldn't do. But he came to you first. Why?"

"Maybe he saw me as a threat. I was getting a rep as the man behind his success—if that's what you want to call it. He didn't like it. Thought that eventually I would move against him."

"Would you?" Bolan asked.

"Never!" Carvaggio said. "As a matter of fact I was planning on moving out on him already. There were too many things going on that I didn't like. Sienna was changing, man. Heavy duty. This just moved up the timetable a bit. Like a matter of seconds."

From the files Hal Brognola had shown him, Bolan knew that Sienna didn't put up with any disloyalty. To question his decision was to ask for a death sentence.

"People don't tell Sienna what to do," Carvaggio continued. "Not if they want to live to a ripe old age. Anyway, after I walked out on Vic and took care of a couple of crew guys he sent after me, I dropped a coin to the cops. They put the juror on around-the-clock protection and Vic's man got put away. Seems he has a lot of making up to do with his compadres, and he has even more reason to put me away. He didn't like being made a fool of.''

Bolan listened attentively as Carvaggio filled him in on how he made the approach to the Feds.

Since Sienna had made Carvaggio number one on the hit list, there would be no rest for him. No sanctuary.

Unless he put Sienna away first.

Carvaggio made a call to some contacts in the Justice Department who put him in touch with the Organized Crime Task Force. In turn, that put him in contact with Hank Prescott who began negotiations to set up a meet.

But according to Carvaggio, Sienna's people heard about the meet somehow. They had one of their people call up Prescott to change the time and place. The Fed went to the rendezvous expecting to find Carvaggio but instead found himself looking down the barrel of a shotgun that took most of his head off.

"Now, here's why it wasn't me," Carvaggio said, leaning across the table and ticking off his fingers one by one.

"First, if I'm on the outs with Sienna, what am I doing attacking the one group that can help me take Sienna down? Second, there's the guy who made the call to Prescott pretending to be me—I'm assuming that's on tape. You can check the voiceprints and that'll prove it wasn't me. Third, I never heard of Hank Prescott before this. What reason I got to take him out? Fourth, say what you will about me, what I've done but I've never taken out anyone who didn't deserve it. Cops and Feds included. It's not how I operate, man. You know that?''

"Yeah, I do," Bolan replied. He'd seen the military jacket on Nicholas Carvaggio. He'd seen the other material that Hal Brognola had provided on Carvaggio and the soldiers working for Sienna. His military career was impeccable. And as far as his rep in the underworld, Carvaggio was a straight shooter. Literally. Anyone in the life was fair game, but civilians were off-limits.

"No one's going to canonize you for sainthood anytime soon," Bolan continued. "But from our point of view you were doing good. The better your aim, the less vipers on the street. No one was crying over the hits you made. Until Hank Prescott."

"That wasn't me."

"I know it wasn't," the Executioner said. "At least that's the way I'm leaning now. But I need something to take to the Feds looking to avenge Prescott. They want the people who set it up."

"So do I," Carvaggio said. "Sienna was behind it. It's his style. Look at it this way—he takes a Mob buster out of action and at the same time manages to frame me for the whack. So now with the Mob and the Feds after me, what chance do I have?"

"So that's why you turned to Rupert Sawyer," Bolan concluded.

Carvaggio laughed. "Yeah. Hey, I know he's one step removed from a carnival barker, but he delivers sometimes. He's got the audience, and he's got some good contacts. I figured I could tell my story and see what happened."

"What happened is that a lot of people heard about you."

"Yeah," Carvaggio said, "but it was worth a shot. I know for a fact other people have approached him and they haven't been blown yet. He keeps some confidences. He just didn't keep mine."

"Tell me about the others. And tell me about the crews you know are working for Sienna."

"Crews?"

"You're one of many," Bolan said. "Sienna had a lot more going on than just the New York Garrison. That's one of the reasons I was called in. He's putting together an underworld army."

"Hey, I know we were connected here and there. We got friends all over but nothing major like what you're suggesting. I mean, come on, he couldn't keep that quiet from me—"

"You're forgetting something, Nick," Bolan said. "You weren't Sienna's golden boy anymore. He saw you as a threat. That hardly puts you in the inner circle. Fact is, you're the last guy he'd tell about the empire he was building."

"Maybe," Carvaggio said. "I don't know about that."

"So keep talking about what you do know. And let's start figuring out ways we can land a few blows against the empire."

4

Victor Sienna sat in the warm glow of the hearth on his top-floor apartment on East 21st Street, listening to a parade of survivors explain why they were still alive and why half of the men who went out with them were dead.

He sat quietly in the darkened room which looked out on the New York skyline, a checkerboard of lighted windows highlighted against dark skyscrapers and apartment buildings that reached up into the night.

It was just one of several places he owned in the city where he could hold court or hide out, depending on the need.

Sienna was sitting on a leather sofa, leaning for support on the cane that had been with him for years now, stemming from an imaginary war injury. He'd come through the Army unscathed, and none of the underworld battles he fought had left him with any permanent damage.

But he used the cane just the same, perhaps to emphasize his power, his miter of authority, perhaps to have on hand as a weapon of last resort in case he was attacked in the heart of his own kingdom.

No one spoke of the cane. It was just part of the emperor's new clothes.

This night he leaned upon it more than usual. He clasped both hands upon the cane's carved ivory haft while leaning forward like an Old World baron passing judgment on the various reports his men made to him. They came in one by one and spoke in clipped military terms while Sienna listened to them in stonelike silence or asked probing questions in a deathly calm manner.

His angular face and narrow unblinking eyes held them in a feral gaze from start to finish, so they never knew what he was thinking. All they knew was that they had to tell him the truth, no matter how poorly it reflected upon them.

Sitting by his side was Andrew McNeil, the underworld quartermaster who had outfitted and recruited nearly every one of the soldiers who were now being measured for caskets or scraped off the ground. While Sienna was the hard-liner who called the shots, McNeil was the one who made them happen.

Unlike Sienna, who obsessively kept up with his conditioning, McNeil was a stout, friendly looking sort with a head of curly salt-and-pepper hair. He was always ready with a puckish grin and a pat on the back. He looked nothing like a killer until the very moment he stuck a gun in someone's face and pulled the trigger.

There was still considerable strength beneath his restaurant-padded physique, but these days he relied more on his experience and his deceptively mild looks to get the job done.

"Who's next?" Sienna asked after dismissing one of the soldiers who'd nearly gone up in the flames of Carvaggio's booby-trapped building. The soldier headed back down a long hallway that led to the sitting room where the others had gathered.

"Gaultieri," McNeil said.

"What's his condition?"

"Physically?" McNeil asked. "Not a scratch on him. He got shook up some by a stunner and got a little bit wet from running in the rain. Other than that, you'd think he was out for a night on the town."

"What about mentally?"

"Could be a problem. He's been shattered by whatever he saw happen in the street. Just like everyone else, until now he figured nothing could stand up to us and get away. Tonight he learned different."

"We all learned something tonight," Sienna said, "but we're all not quaking in our boots. What's your impression of him? Should we keep him or get rid of him?"

McNeil shrugged. "I vetted him myself. Seen him in action enough times to trust him. Maybe he broke just this one time or maybe he's broken for good. When he's at the top of his game, Gaultieri's a hell of man to have on your side. We'll find out soon enough."

"All right," Sienna said, "we'll give him another shot. If it doesn't work out, then we'll give him a final shot. Bring him in."

McNeil got up from his chair and walked down the corridor with a spring in his step. He returned a minute later with Stefan Gaultieri in tow, who looked sheepish and decidedly unhappy to be there.

Gaultieri stood in front of Sienna like a man at attention, except for the hands clasped nervously in front of him. His eyes looked down or to the side toward the flickering tongues of firelight. He didn't like looking directly into Sienna's eyes because in them he could see his own death reflected.

Maybe not this night, maybe not the following day.

But sometime soon.

He'd been around Sienna long enough to know his fate. He'd gone from being one of Sienna's invincibles to one of his disposables in one short night, unless he could redeem himself in action.

Sienna let him stand there and worry for a while before he spoke. "Stefan," he said, in a neutral tone, "tell me about your role this evening and what seems to be an almost miraculous escape. You're the only one from your team who survived."

The wheelman was about to explain himself when Sienna cut him off by reciting the names of the men in Gaultieri's unit who'd fallen in battle. After every name on the somber roll call, Sienna mentioned how and where each man died—right outside the van.

"That gives us four dead just a few feet from the van,"

Sienna said. "No one got away from that van except you. How'd that happen?"

"The man who was walking on the street," Gaultieri said. "The man in the leather jacket."

"This man," Sienna said. "I keep hearing about this man who came out of the darkness somehow. Who is he and how did this one man get away from so many of us?"

"I don't know."

Sienna's voice stayed calm, although his bone-white knuckles clenched the haft of the cane as he leaned forward. "We had a rifle team out there. We had patrols moving in the area. And you're telling me one man caught you all by surprise?"

Gaultieri shook his head. "We were going after Carvaggio. No one else. But then this man appeared. One minute he was walking on the sidewalk minding his own business—I looked him over like I looked over everyone on the street. Then all of a sudden he was by the window and a grenade thumped inside the van. We all tried to book out of there."

"Yet you're the only one who escaped," Sienna said. "The others tried to fight him. That we know. Somehow they recovered long enough to at least try and stop this enemy of mine."

Gaultieri looked at McNeil, but the man was impassive. No help there. He was on his own.

"I was out of it," Gaultieri explained. "The explosions, the flash. Everything was ringing in my ears. I couldn't see. I remember staggering in the streets, I thought I was dead, then I was on the ground. Something hit me."

"Hand-to-hand combat?" Sienna suggested.

Gaultieri studied him, knowing that the question was a trap. The other survivors had reported on the role he played in the engagement—or more than likely the role he failed to play. "No combat. I think a car sideswiped me when I jumped out of the van. I don't know for sure. All I remember is that farther down the street the same man attacked one of our other cars."

"The Jeep," Sienna said. "Half the men who were riding in it are dead. He blew it apart with a shotgun barrage. A shotgun taken from your team. Maybe because you didn't do your part."

"I tried," Gaultieri said.

"I'm not saying that you ran away. I'm just saying that there are some questions about your behavior."

Gaultieri fell silent until Sienna prodded him. "But you've been with me a long time," he said. "Almost from the time Carvaggio was here. I respect what you've done for me, and for that you will get another chance at this man who helped Nick evade our trap."

Gaultieri nodded, grateful that he was spared for now.

"One more question before you go, Stefan," Sienna said.

"Anything."

"It is the same question I must ask all of our people." Sienna pushed down on the cane and leaned back into the sofa, a world-weary statesman whose kingdom was under attack. "Were you glad to see Carvaggio get away?"

"What?" Gaultieri stepped back, stunned by the question and by the implication. Maybe he wasn't back in the good graces of Victor Sienna.

"Nick was a good man," Sienna said reasonably. "Everybody liked him when he worked for us."

"But you no longer trusted him, Mr. Sienna," Gaultieri said. "That was enough for me."

Sienna nodded at the correct response. "And one more question, Stefan. Do you know anyone among our group who wanted this to happen? Someone perhaps who warned Nick about the attack? Or maybe someone who actually joined his side and plotted against me?"

Gaultieri fell back into silence, aware that it was a dangerous question to answer or to avoid. He was also aware of the touch of paranoia glinting in Sienna's eyes.

The Garrison leader raised his right hand in an encouraging gesture, coaxing an answer from him. "Come, Stefan," he said. "Feel free to tell me whatever you're thinking."

"I'm thinking there's no way it could happen like that, Mr. Sienna," Gaultieri said. "You were against him—we were all against him."

Sienna studied his eyes long enough to make Gaultieri uncomfortable before finally nodding his dismissal.

As Gaultieri walked out of the room, he had the same look of concern on his face as the others who'd been questioned, wondering what they'd said about him. Did someone think he was an accomplice in Carvaggio's treachery?

Two MORE HOURS passed before Sienna had completed his questioning of the survivors, checking their answers against one another until he had a good idea of the firefight and the men who fought it.

It didn't bode well for the Garrison or their reputation. For the past couple of years Sienna had built up a solid operation that was respected and feared throughout the underworld.

That fear and respect could evaporate as quickly as the lives of the men he'd sent out to war that night.

It was a considerable detachment, and he'd taken considerable losses.

Fourteen dead.

Fourteen veteran soldiers had been chopped to pieces outside Carvaggio's building or trapped inside the inferno it had become.

And three men got away unscathed—three men who now occupied the top rank in Sienna's murderous thoughts.

The producer. It was a miracle that Rupert Sawyer hadn't died of fright, he thought. Sienna hadn't decided what to do about him yet. He still might be useful. Alive, he could provide a lead to Carvaggio. Dead, he could send a message to those who thought of going against the Garrison. He wasn't a real threat just yet, but he definitely had to be attended to.

Nicholas Carvaggio. A different matter entirely. That was blood. Family. Sienna thought back to the days in the old neighborhood and the usual adolescent troubles they'd gotten into, running across the rooftops and swinging down the fire escapes, boosting small stereos or TVs. Then came the more significant stuff, going out on jobs that could bring in some serious money or some serious time.

Back then Nick had stayed by him every step of the way. Sienna was glad to have him back at his side once again when he mustered out of the service. At least he was at first. But Nick hadn't learned what the others in the crew had.

Nick didn't fear him like they did. He knew Sienna too well and traded too much on their past friendship. He questioned Sienna whenever it pleased him. Carvaggio laughed at him and with him just like the old days, unaware that the old days were gone. These days people didn't question Sienna; they did what he wanted. They didn't betray him, and they didn't run from him.

Sienna had become a power to be reckoned with. Unless he took out Carvaggio in a splashy way, others might get the mistaken idea they, too, could move against Victor Sienna and escape with their lives.

Unfortunately, Sienna thought, it looked like he'd underestimated Carvaggio. Apparently the wayward hit man had a very powerful friend who stepped up when the time came.

That brought Sienna to the third man on his list.

The man in black.

None of his men got a good look at him, but those who did all said the same thing. The man could either stand his ground or take ground at will. He was skilled enough to materialize just long enough to wreak havoc before vanishing into the darkness, leaving men reeling from the onslaught.

"We need to bring in some new people," Sienna said. "A lot more than we lost. Enough to crush Carvaggio and the man foolish enough to help him."

Andrew McNeil nodded. He'd sat by silently while Sienna had been mulling over his options, waiting for him to talk, to lead.

That was why McNeil was his right-hand man. He knew when to listen, when to talk. And he always knew to follow orders.

"I'll start calling tonight," McNeil stated, "then I'll follow up with a few visits. But it's going to cost a fortune."

"Money we got plenty of," Sienna said. "Manpower we don't. Not enough to fight an extended war." The Garrison captain had enough men to still conduct his business affairs, but he didn't have the foot soldiers necessary to cover an extended front.

"I'll start with our auxiliaries," McNeil said, "people we've used before in one form or another. Then I'll scout some new talent if we need to."

Sienna nodded. They had people with the right kind of background in Chicago, Kansas City, Los Angeles, Miami, even up in Canada. These people weren't made yet and didn't strictly belong to any of the Families, although they'd done their share of work for them.

This was a chance for them to move up in the world. The underworld. Many of them would think twice before joining, but along with the recruitment bonus there would be another incentive. Anyone who took out Carvaggio would earn a field promotion and move up through the ranks.

Sienna and McNeil discussed the pros and cons of the candidates for recruitment before turning back to the identity of the man who'd helped Carvaggio.

"It doesn't make sense," Sienna said. "From here on in Nick might as well have a bull's-eye tattooed on his forehead. Who would throw in with a man who's got a death sentence?"

"The guy sounds military," McNeil said. "Someone Nick toured with? If so, he shouldn't be too hard to find. Or his family. We can get to him through them."

"What if it's not a pal from the service?"

McNeil looked doubtful. "Who else could it be? No one else has the kind of chops to do what he did."

"I'm thinking government," Sienna said. "Maybe spooks or special operations people worked Nick without him knowing it."

"And?"

"And now they come back to pull him into another special op they've cooked up," Sienna said. As he spoke, he sounded more and more convinced, as if his speculations could become fact just by the force of his will. He was so used to making things happen that it was difficult for him to accept it when someone made things happen to him. "They came to Nick because they needed someone with his talents. When they saw he was under fire, they... Hey, that's it!"

"What is?" McNeil prodded.

"There had to be more than just one man helping out Nick," Sienna said. "Our guys saw only one man at a time, so they assumed it was just a lone wolf. But there must have been an entire squad of Special Forces guys involved. No wonder they took us on."

McNeil let Sienna's enthusiasm die down before slowly shaking his head and answering. "No squad, Vic. I don't buy it."

"One guy, then?" Sienna said. "You're trying to tell me one guy did all this?" He turned his head slowly toward McNeil and gave him the stare he used on his underlings. But McNeil was immune. He'd seen it too many times, and he knew that Sienna needed him.

"If it was special ops or Special Forces," McNeil said, "then Nick went to them for help. Called in favors from people who owed him. They helped him set it up, and we walked into it." McNeil waited a few moments before venturing another scenario. "But that's no guarantee. We can't get locked into that, Vic. There's a chance it was just one guy."

"Who?" Sienna said. "Who could do it?"

"Same guy who did it to the Families awhile back. Fought a one-man war, made a lot of openings so guys like us could move up."

Sienna shook his head. "You kidding? You're thinking Executioner, right? Forget about him. He's history."

McNeil shrugged. "History has a way of repeating itself. There's been a lot of wars between the Families lately. Lot of disappearances. We chalk it up to rivalries, to the Russians, to the uptown crew. Maybe it is them...or maybe it's him.''

Sienna seemed to grow a bit pale, then felt the blood rush to his face, embarrassed by the fear that had momentarily taken over. The Executioner had died, supposedly years earlier. If it was the Executioner, then this problem might not go away as quickly as he hoped. Sienna might be the one going away.

''Look,'' Sienna said, ''we don't know anything for sure. But we're scaring ourselves like kids telling ghost stories around the fire. Somebody's helping Nick. Whoever it is, we take him out.'' He leaned forward on the cane and pushed himself up off the couch.

He walked slowly toward the window and looked out at the glittering lights of the city. His city. A cold wind shuddered against the panes of glass, and he could almost feel the tower sway, as if he were under attack by the elements themselves.

Sienna turned and glanced at the door just beyond the fireplace, a door that led to his private quarters. Out here was business. In there was pleasure.

It was no longer time for counsel. It was time for consolation, and he would find that in the arms of the dancer who'd been a regular at one of his clubs. Now she was a regular at his bedside. He headed for the suite where she waited.

''Vic,'' McNeil called after him, ''I think we have to talk about this some more. If it is the Executioner, then he can bide his time, hit us when we're not ready, then fade away and hit us again. Remember, this guy's not doing it for money or for power—he's doing it for a cause. That's what makes him so dangerous. It's what he lives for.''

''Yeah,'' Sienna said as he walked away. ''Just see it's what he dies for.''

5

The snowbank moved.

Inch by inch the white-blanketed shape edged closer to the rim of the snow-covered slope.

Mack Bolan was virtually invisible beneath the winter camouflage shroud—just one more amorphous and undetectable mass nestled in the rolling forests that looked down on the Hudson River.

The Executioner slowly exhaled, watching his breath billow away in a thin mist of frozen air, drifting up around the end of the sniper rifle that he'd trained on Danillo, one of the gunners in Sienna's crew.

The man had a long brown leather coat and a rakish beard, making him look like a Long Rider from a hundred years earlier. But this underworld cowboy lacked a horse and a hat, and in a few short minutes he would be lacking his life.

The enforcer was standing in a gully behind a shut-down Amtrak station along with a half dozen other soldiers from Sienna's Garrison, including Stefan Gaultieri. Bolan had recognized the wheelman who escaped him the first time. Perhaps growing skittish at being trapped inside a car, Gaultieri had accompanied the rest of the soldiers this time.

A few more gunners were hidden in the edge of the forest at the bottom of the slope, ready to cover their comrades from the heavily armed group of Colombians who'd also come to the isolated rendezvous.

Their headman, Jacob Patricio, was taller, heavier and a bit more wary than the cartel enforcers backing him up. They were cocksure types who somehow managed to look as if they were swaggering even when they stood still. In their minds this was business as usual, and there was no danger to face. After all, this was just like back home where the cartels owned the police and made their deals under their protection.

There were two carloads of gunmen, giving them the same number as the Mafia squad.

It was all part of the etiquette of the dope trade: equal numbers, equal precautions and equal value.

The Garrison would provide cash, the cartel would provide coke and then both parties would go their separate ways. The arrangement had been in effect for a couple of years now.

Sienna's crew had originally been hired as muscle for other Mob teams dealing with Patricio, but as Sienna's group increased in numbers and influence, they started cutting deals for themselves. Now they dealt directly with the Colombian who'd adopted New York City as his own.

Yet another party had come to the rendezvous.

Overseeing the transfer between the Garrison and the Colombians was a decorated Manhattan vice detective who was on the pad for both groups. He was a full-service skell who warned them of pending investigations into their activities, gave up names of informants, and now and then provided protection for their transfers.

The vice cop was the perfect referee. He'd sold out to both sides and had no particular allegiance to either of them. His loyalty was to money, plain and simple, and there was a lot to be had in the suitcases that were about to change hands.

Bolan swept the barrel of the Accuracy International PM sniper rifle slightly to the left, just enough to put the referee in the crosshairs. It was twilight, and the man's silhouette against the station house made him a good target even without the night vision scope.

The negotiators for each group stepped forward. Little more than a hundred yards away, Bolan swept the sniper rifle across the kill field, rehearsing his hits.

The thermal imager swept over the familiar faces from Justice Department dossiers. With Carvaggio's input on their hangouts and associates, Bolan had provided Brognola with enough leads for the Justice Department's Special Services Unit—SSU—to shadow Patricio and Gaultieri.

Carvaggio knew a deal was in the works and where it would happen. He just didn't known when.

The big Fed had tasked the Washington-based SSU intelligence team to Manhattan for the duration of Bolan's mission.

It was a strictly compartmentalized operation. The SSU reported the movements of their targets to Brognola, who in turn fed the intel to Bolan. When it was obvious the deal was going to happen soon, the big Fed called off the SSU. The team pulled back, no questions asked. They had a part to play, and they'd played it. Until they were called on again, they were out of it.

Bolan and Carvaggio had set up camp in the cold hills along the Hudson and waited for the games to begin.

With the magnification of the sniper scope, Bolan could easily study the expressions on the faces of the traffickers. Some put on stone-killer faces, but it was more acting than anything else—the usual masks worn by criminals at work and play. Others were almost smiling as they talked and joked among themselves, making comments about the opposing team while the deal went down.

Their casual schoolboy attitudes sickened the Executioner. They showed so little apprehension that it seemed like a night out to them. First they'd do a little business, then they'd celebrate back in the city. They'd used the train station enough times now that it seemed like they were showing up at the office.

The abandoned station was a short drive north of New York into Sleepy Hollow country with plenty of small hamlets separated by long expanses of wilderness. The access road was out of view of the railroad tracks. So were the cars they'd arrived in.

On the other side of the tracks, an overlook provided a scenic view of the Hudson River with its ice floes drifting toward Manhattan. The river looked dark and desolate with a touch of moonlight skidding across its broken surface.

The crews thought they were alone, and the deal would go off without a hitch—just like all the other times.

They'd conducted a cursory recon of the area, but they were confident no one—cops or competitors—would move against them. But they hadn't looked deep enough into the woods. Carvaggio had seen to that. He'd moved slowly around the perimeter to see if the Garrison had any free-roaming scouts.

Now he was back from his recon, about ten yards downhill from Bolan.

Carvaggio also was shrouded in winter whites and moved just as quietly and slowly as Bolan until he was at the Executioner's side.

"No one's out there," Carvaggio said in a hushed voice. "All we got are the crews down there."

"I counted twenty," the soldier said. "Maybe one or two more hiding out in the cars."

"Two clips' worth," Carvaggio replied, not too worried about the odds. It wasn't just bravado or overconfidence. Both he and the Executioner knew the damage that one well-trained sniper could inflict on the enemy. First take out the key men, throwing fear into the others, and then pick them off when they gave in to panic.

Bolan and the ex-Garrison gunman had already picked out their targets, deciding who had to die first and who should be kept alive, if possible.

They were both armed with modified Accuracy International rifles, each with a 10-round double-row box magazine of 7.62 mm subsonic rounds. The barrel, stock and ball-mounted detachable tripod were snow white. So were the spare magazines in case there was need to reload.

That was unlikely.

"How's the kill zone?" Carvaggio asked.

"About like we figured before. From this angle we can hit anybody in the Garrison. But the Colombians are a different matter."

The Colombians were keeping close to the side of the station house. Maybe it was a normal defensive position they took with the Garrison deals, or maybe they sensed something else was prowling in the woods. But from Bolan's position they were at a hard angle to hit.

"I'll move down and cover Patricio's team," Carvaggio said, inching back from the ridge, then moving slowly and silently toward the east where he'd picked out a sheltered stand earlier.

Bolan turned his attention to the gathering below and swept the sniper scope across the field. He stopped when the cowboy in the leather coat came onto the green screen.

The Executioner kept his right hand gripped firmly around the stock, thumb touching his cheek, the fat part of his finger above the second joint feathering the cold metal trigger.

He held the crosshairs on his target and swiveled minutely left and right, testing the amount of distance he'd have to move the barrel to hit targets two and three.

He waited until Carvaggio was in position.

STEFAN GAULTIERI HELD the Ingram M-10 in his hand, ready to pull the trigger at a moment's notice. He didn't expect any trouble, but this time if it came, he was going to get involved real fast.

A few other crewmen were carrying the Ingrams, thanks to a shipload that made its way up from the Caribbean where the machine pistols used to be the weapons of choice.

He glanced at the Colombians and saw only hard eyes and grim smiles looking back at him. Falling back on his military training, Gaultieri started making calculations of who he would take first if a battle erupted.

But the Garrison had this down to a science.

Two men stepped forward with the suitcases full of money.

Two enforcers accompanied them with nothing in their hands but gun metal.

Patricio's people did the same thing. Two carried the cocaine bricks in waterproof wrappers inside the gym bags. Two more Colombians followed closely behind, also with guns at their side in case anything went wrong.

There was little chance of treachery out here, Gaultieri thought. Not between these crews. They'd dealt with each other enough times before. They'd also done this enough times to know where to strike if they had to. If a battle broke out here, war would break out back in the city.

Then it would be impossible to conduct business, and that's what the Colombians and the Garrison were about. Making deals together, making money together.

Gaultieri forced himself to relax. From habit he scanned the hills around the station. But there was no sign of movement out there, no indication of anything amiss. Nothing but shadows and soft moonlight splayed on the snowcapped fields.

His attention drifted back to the cash and cocaine transfer near the middle of the station house where the advance teams from both sides met. Danillo was studying the contents of the gym bag the Colombians held open before him. His hands were in the pockets of his brown leather jacket and he looked totally at ease, just another customer looking over the goods his supplier brought to him.

Patricio was doing the same, idly scanning the bundles of currency stacked neatly in the suitcases the Garrison soldiers held open for his inspection. His practiced eyes had swept over so many similar packages that it only took him a few moments to know that the money was all there.

Both sides were satisfied.

Patricio and Danillo spoke quietly, giving the okay to their subordinates to release their respective packages.

While the handoffs were made, Danillo and Patricio spoke a few last words of false and lasting friendship to each other.

The shrieking wind caused members from both sides to

shiver involuntarily from the cold. Most of them hadn't really dressed for the weather. They were in their regular coats and jackets, some in shoes instead of boots. Everyone was eager to make the transfer and get on home.

Gaultieri felt himself relax. He had nothing to worry about except the cold. And even that would be a memory when he climbed into the car and drove his people back to Manhattan. Nothing to worry about at all.

Suddenly blood splattered the ground near Danillo's feet.

It took Gaultieri a second to decipher what had happened. Danillo toppled over like a chopped tree, landing on the ground with his hands still in his pockets. His bloodied head crunched into the gravel beneath the soft layer of snow, bouncing once and coating the ground with a thickening pool of blood.

A rail-thin Colombian enforcer standing behind Patricio made a strange gargling sound, then flew off his feet as if he'd been slapped by the hand of God. He, too, landed in a pool of blood.

And then Gaultieri heard the sound of subsonic slugs cutting through the air, striking soft targets all around him.

The wheelman's head snapped left and right, looking all around in a split-second recon that brought too many images for his brain to decode: guns whipping out of holsters and staccato bursts of flame cutting through the darkness; footsteps pounding and sliding through the snow; men falling, screaming; ravens flushing through the tops of bare trees, awakened by the battle in their territory.

His gaze was drawn up to the distant woods. Instinctively he knew the kill fire came from the high ground, from somewhere up on the ridge that hemmed them in. But knowing that didn't necessarily mean he could do anything about it.

Especially when everyone around him suddenly went mad.

Gaultieri's panicked gaze settled on Patricio, shouting something to his men, then to the vice detective both sides thought they owned.

"No, that's not it!" the stunned detective shouted, raising

his hands in a helpless gesture. He'd been totally surprised by the fire that came out of nowhere and took out Danillo.

Patricio nodded curtly, then surprised the detective one last time. A heavy automatic appeared in the leader's hand and went off inches from the cop's head. The slug knocked the detective to the ground, almost on top of the man in the now bloodied leather coat.

The roar from Patricio's automatic temporarily drowned out the sounds of sniper fire that poured into the station house. Coming just seconds apart, the rounds thwacked into wood, into flesh, into the cars parked haphazardly along the access road and on the grounds of the station.

Bullets were falling like rain, and men were screaming in panic or in pain as they fell into the snow. Both sides had their weapons out and were hastily firing at targets.

The sound was deafening as gunfire rolled up the hill and echoed back to them, punctured by another fresh barrage of gunfire.

Amid the carnage a strange thought occurred to Gaultieri.

Just before everyone started shooting at one another, the ambushers had fired into the ranks of the Colombians *and* the Garrison. It didn't make sense. Why would the drug lords set up an ambush that took out both sides? And he knew for a fact that his crew hadn't planned any surprises for the Colombians.

Who then?

His mind raced back to the Manhattan encounter, to the precise and surgical strike that took out the teams going after Carvaggio. This had the same markings. It was total warfare, and it was being waged by a master.

Even as the answer came to him, Gaultieri found himself caught up in the firefight. There wasn't a chance for him to shout that it was all a mistake, that someone was playing both sides against the other. Whatever ignited the conflict, it was in full force now, and there was no stopping it.

The Colombians were plugging away at Sienna's men, and the Garrison was returning fire in kind.

Gaultieri had already returned fire without knowing it. Only now did he realize that the jackhammer sensation in his hand came from the M-10 spitting fire. He'd already fired half of the clip.

It had been a purely reflex action, caused by the sight of a drug runner who'd been crouching around the corner of the station house to fire at him, even as Gaultieri was trying to seek shelter behind the abandoned building.

Gaultieri's first couple of bursts had chipped away the siding from the railroad building but fell far short of the target. The Colombian enforcer was hit only by a blizzard of splinters or metal chips.

The same enforcer appeared around the corner again, aiming a Heckler & Koch submachine gun at Gaultieri. But this time the man didn't fire—even though he was clearly in position to.

Instead, the gunman tumbled back out of sight for a moment—as if he'd been hit with an invisible sledgehammer—then fell back into sight, tumbling in a bloody heap onto the gravel.

Gaultieri didn't wonder about it. He just counted his blessings and fired toward another cluster of Colombians gathered at the far end of the station house.

Behind him Gaultieri heard familiar voices shouting commands, calling for the Garrison members to pull back and regroup.

He glanced behind him, saw a few of his fellow soldiers lying flat in the snow. And then he realized he was one of the last soldiers standing in the open. He backstepped through the snow, trying to shield himself behind the station house as he rammed another clip into the Ingram and looked for a fresh target to hit.

"Stefan!" someone shouted. "Over here. On three."

Relying on the voice more than the sight, Gaultieri zeroed in on a grove of thick pine trees at the edge of the woods. A few of the trees had fallen, making a natural bulwark.

Now that he knew where they were making their stand,

Gaultieri could make out the figures of the soldiers behind it.

One of them shouted out a three-count, then a fusillade of automatic fire erupted from behind the pine-tree ramparts.

Gaultieri ran at an angle for the fallen trees, staying low in a crouching motion as his crew kept up a cover fire. When he was a few feet away, he dived straight into the snow like a man sliding into home plate.

A hand grabbed his wrist and pulled him into the cover. But there was no time for thanks. Just time for survival. Bullets were smacking into the trees from all angles, and though the barricade was thick, there were plenty of spaces for stray slugs to slip through.

Gaultieri studied the ridge, wondering if the Ingram M-10 would do him much good against the heavy firepower pouring into them from above.

THE EXECUTIONER RAISED his head to scan the killing field below. As he peered through the green screen crosshairs, he saw Gaultieri reach the relative safety of the pine tree fortification where another Garrison soldier had pulled him in.

Good, Bolan thought. If only the man kept his wits about him he might get out of this alive yet.

Earlier in the battle the Executioner had taken out one of the Colombians who'd drawn a bead on Gaultieri. Carvaggio had taken out another.

Gaultieri was one of the men they wanted to stay alive. The other one was Jacob Patricio. Both men could be turned into weapons to use against Victor Sienna—Gaultieri because he was a weak link in the Garrison team; Patricio because he could be a dangerous enemy to have on the streets of New York. Along with his Manhattan-based cartel group, Patricio could call upon the clans back home if a full-scale war broke out.

Those were the only two members of the criminal bands below who had a free pass during the ambush. There was no guarantee either would make it out alive, but neither Bolan or Carvaggio would take them down.

At least not today.

Bolan picked out a crewman in a hooded black parka who was kneeling beside Gaultieri.

The man was attracting too much attention from the Colombians, emptying clip after clip into the enforcers on the far side of the station house and burning off the 9 mm loads. The guy was a regular one-man armory, Bolan thought. He really wasn't doing much damage with his clips, but the flash and chatter of his machine pistol was drawing heavy fire in return. It gave the drug cartel something to focus their anger on.

The man kept moving in jerky motions as he changed clips, giving himself a few more seconds to live.

Bolan didn't want to risk hitting Gaultieri who was ducking for cover just a few feet away. He waited a few crucial moments until the man paused again and peered above the fallen trees. His dark hood gave him some cover in the forested stand, and except for the subgun in his hand, it also gave him the look of a monk.

A monk about to experience last rites.

The Executioner breathed out softly and squeezed the trigger with an easy pull.

The 7.62 mm round bored a third eye through the man's skull and sent him crashing into the brush. It also convinced the rest of the men gathered there that the stand wasn't so safe after all. They backed away toward the woods.

Bolan swiveled the barrel about ninety degrees to his left and fixed the crosshairs on a crouching Colombian shooter who was still chopping away in Gaultieri's direction with an M-16.

One pull of the Accuracy International trigger and the man fell silent, weighted down with a 7.62 mm round in his chest.

Another sniper rifle coughed far off to his right. Down below on the station house one of Patricio's gunmen was driven face first into the snow by a silenced round.

Bolan was on his second box magazine, and from the counts he'd made, Carvaggio had done the same.

There were still a good number of targets to choose from.

Instead of making a break for it after the first several rounds of sniper fire as the Executioner expected, both groups dug in right away. Only then did they realize there was nowhere safe to go. Bolan and Carvaggio had all the angles covered.

Now some of the gunmen began firing up into the woods, realizing that was where the greatest danger came from. A few of them were either lucky or had figured out Bolan's latest position.

Automatic bursts raked the hillside, climbing round by round as the gunners found their mark. Then the bursts ripped through the air over Bolan's head.

It was time to move again.

Ever since he'd dropped the cowboy in the leather coat, the Executioner had been changing his position every five shots or so. Not only did it keep him from being found out, it made it seem as if there was a small army of snipers pouring gunfire from every direction.

Bolan slid back down the ridge, crouching to get enough leverage to push off from the snow. His legs pistoned through the snow as he headed toward the east for one of the stands he'd picked out.

He was careful not to silhouette himself against the sun that filtered through the sparse trees atop the ridge. When he was several feet away from his selected spot he dropped forward, his legs spreading out to anchor him while his hands cradled the white-coated sniper rifle.

During Bolan's brief transit, Carvaggio had fired off another few rounds down below, just to keep the gunmen from paying too much attention to Bolan's white-shrouded figure.

Now, while Bolan dug in, Carvaggio went on the attack.

The Executioner triggered two shots toward a Mafia marksman zeroing in on Carvaggio. The first shot missed him; the second dropped him into the snow.

By now the fatal lesson was sinking in to the scattered pockets of Mob soldiers and cartel enforcers. They knew there was no way they could win this battle. The only victory left was the faint hope of escaping with their lives.

Some moved across the tracks toward the overlook, while others ran into the woods just to get out of the lead rain for a while before planning their escape. Several raced for their cars, figuring that was their best chance to make it out of there even if they had to run a gauntlet of gunfire.

No one wanted to stick around and trade shots with the kill team in the woods.

A fast moving shape suddenly drew Bolan's attention as it sprinted across the snow. Instinctively he swiveled the barrel toward the running man, taking only a second to get him in the sights of the scope. Then the Executioner recognized Patricio's tall form and dark coat silhouetted against the snowy backdrop.

Patricio was running down the access road, accompanied by a trio of enforcers, including the two men who'd conducted the trade with the cocaine couriers just a short time ago. Neither of them was carrying the contraband now.

Bolan and Carvaggio had poured so much fire into the transfer zone that both the cocaine and the suitcases of cash were left on the ground. To go near them was the same as committing suicide.

But Patricio's enforcers were carrying weaponry.

One of the hardmen cut in front of Patricio and leveled his Heckler & Koch MP-5 before him, reconning by fire as he triggered several 9 mm bursts. The muzzle-flashes traced a small arc in front of him as he fired at everything and anything in his way.

The other two enforcers sprayed lead at both flanks, using controlled bursts from their Heckler & Koch machine pistols.

The three gunners produced a stream of automatic fire that effectively cleared a safe path for Patricio.

But the danger wasn't coming from in front of him or from off to the sides. The danger came from above, and no matter how frantically the enforcers burnt off their 9 mm clips, there was no protection from it.

Bolan factored in the lead enforcer's speed and distance as he tracked him through the crosshairs.

The man was moving fast, taking erratic strides across the snow-covered road, perhaps tiring from his initial efforts. The Executioner aimed his rifle in front of the man's chest before squeezing the trigger, letting him run into his subsonic fate.

The gunman staggered from the impact of the 7.62 mm slug, but kept on running for a few more seconds until finally his momentum died, dropping him into the snow.

As he went down, his clutching trigger finger blew off the rest of his clip and sent a 9 mm spray into a black Ford sedan.

Carvaggio fired from his position off to the right, taking out one of the other gunners just before Patricio reached his Mercedes-Benz. The Colombian headman grabbed the door handle to slow himself, yanked open the door, then jumped into the car.

Bolan and Carvaggio wanted him to get away, but they didn't want to make it look too easy.

With blood spraying the air around him, Patricio had no reason at all to believe he wouldn't be next.

He clambered behind the wheel, turned the key, then floored the gas pedal. The car shot forward while the remaining enforcer was jumping into the front passenger seat.

The Colombian gunman fired off several bursts through the door that kept opening and closing as the high-performance vehicle skidded left and right across the road.

The Mercedes swerved sideways across the inclined access road and narrowly avoided a ditch before Patricio regained control and gunned the car forward once again.

With a crazy spinning of tires, it whined up the road and vanished from sight.

NICK CARVAGGIO JOGGED downhill with the sniper rifle slung over his shoulder. His white hood flapped behind him, shaken loose by the speed of his descent and by the harsh wind that shrieked across the ice-bound river and coiled through the forest.

It keened like a banshee up and down the hills and battered at his face with surprising force. But the cold didn't bother him. Like Bolan, he wore layered clothing and insulated boots with Gore-Tex water repellant gaiters. He was at home in the elements.

Halfway down, Carvaggio's feet caught on a shelf of ice running beneath the snow. He tilted sideways until he regained his balance, then slid the rest of the way downhill in a skiing motion.

To keep from tumbling face forward into the snow, the ex-hit man jumped just before the hill leveled out. When he came down into the packed snow, he bent his knees, planting his feet to break his descent. Then he trudged toward the road with his Steyr machine pistol in his right hand leading the way.

He stopped at the edge of the woods and glanced around a thick oak tree at the midpoint of the steep access road. A pair of headlights speared the night from below, angling up into the darkness as they zigzagged across the trees behind him.

Echoes of slamming car doors drifted uphill as remnants of Sienna's Garrison and the Colombian team rushed toward their cars.

Ever since Patricio made it out of the ambush, it had been every man for himself—not that there were many men left.

After Patricio's escape, a car with a lone driver had also made it out, followed closely by Gaultieri at the helm of a forest green five-speed Saab.

Gaultieri had a couple of Sienna's soldiers with him as he gunned his way out of the ambush site, keeping the Saab in second gear as it wound up the serpentine road toward freedom. They'd rolled down the windows and peppered the forest with full-auto bursts until they reached safety.

Now that Patricio and Gaultieri were out of the zone, everyone else was fair game.

Carvaggio took a position behind a C-shaped cluster of gray rocks and waited for the rear guard to approach. He heard two more shots from Bolan's stand, followed closely by the shattering of glass. The headlights from below suddenly blinked out, and a crashing sound tremored uphill as two cars wrenched into each other, then rolled off the road.

For a few seconds the drivers spun their tires in icy ruts until they realized there would be no more escape by car.

Once again car doors slammed as the panicked gunmen jumped out. Their angry and frightened voices carried uphill as they started to move out on foot.

Carvaggio waited behind the rocks with the barrel of his Steyr machine pistol trained on the curved ribbon of road where he expected the enemy to approach.

He'd loaded the weapon with an extralong clip this time, which extended far below the pistol grip, giving it a bit more weight. Along with the 30-round magazine of 9 mm ammo, the TMP had a sound suppressor threaded on that gave it a well-balanced feel.

With his left hand on the extra finger grip below the barrel, Carvaggio could control the in-close weapon.

Designed for short-range combat, the machine pistol could still do a lot of damage with the right attachments and the right man holding it.

THE EXECUTIONER SIGNALED to Carvaggio across the road to let him know he was in position, waited for the return signal, then fell back beneath the boughs of a huge Douglas fir.

Bolan pulled down on the branches to make the gathered drifts of snow fall to the ground now so they couldn't ruin his aim later.

The white powder fell heavily at his feet, enough to raise a cloud during battle. With his path clear, Bolan trained his

Beretta 93-R on the access road and the killing fields around it.

He heard them first, men crunching through the snow, slashing through the branches of the trees that lined the roadway.

Finally one man stepped into view. He was moving cautiously, acting as point man for the others. He'd step into an area, seeking whatever cover was available while conducting a 180-degree scan with his subgun cradled in his arms, then he'd signal to the rest to follow.

Highly trained troops, Bolan thought, judging from the careful but confident way the point man moved. The man had done this on other killing fields, perhaps even serving his country well before drifting into the underworld. But now he was treading softly onto his last battlefield.

Bolan let him go another ten yards, long enough for him to signal the all clear for the others.

As soon as they stepped forward, looking like big city dowsers following the slanted barrels of their rifles, Bolan took out the point man with a 3-round burst.

When he went down, the others turned toward Bolan's position and concentrated their fire on him. But they were firing uphill and by the time their first rounds were loose, Bolan was lying flat on the ground with his head down.

Their full-auto volleys thwacked into the tree behind him and sliced through the branches of the forest beyond.

The gunners kept up their sustained fire until another sound sliced through the cold winter air—the silenced hush of Carvaggio's 9 mm Steyr.

He hosed down the roadway with a deadly rain of lead that ripped into the staggered line of gunmen. The staccato bursts from the TMP caught them totally off guard as they concentrated on Bolan's position.

Even as the bullets whipped into them, they turned toward Carvaggio and sent a few bursts his way. That's when Bolan opened up again and emptied the Beretta 93-R.

The cross fire took every last man off his feet, and with a few choking gasps their lifeblood trickled onto the snow.

The Executioner came out of cover first. He carefully stepped closer to the road, zigzagging from tree to tree until he had a clear view downhill. He saw a collection of bullet-riddled cars scattered along the road. Two more vehicles were slanting sideways toward the field, and one was lying on its roof.

Past the cars, out into the fields, were clusters of fallen men in dark pools of blood.

It looked safe—at least to the naked eye. The Executioner took out his handheld thermal imager and scanned the field for any sign of moving targets. But all he saw were the signatures of the fresh corpses who would soon chill in the winter's night.

Carvaggio also scanned the area with a night-vision imager before coming out of hiding, sweeping the field with the small periscope-like device.

Then both soldiers hurried to the field, covering the ground quickly until they were behind the station house where the aborted transfer had taken place.

Carvaggio fell silent as he studied the devastation. It wasn't his first time in an extended battle, but it was his first waging war against people who used to be his friends. Almost half of the newly dead had been his comrades-in-arms only a short time ago. But he had no false regrets about the situation. Any man among them would have taken him out first chance he got.

"This is where it leads," he said. "It stopped being a matter of honor and became a matter of money to them. Whatever respect they had went up in smoke and coke."

Carvaggio had never been happy with the Garrison's occasional involvement with the drug trade and had stayed away from it. But to the rest of Sienna's soldiers, it was just another way to turn a buck.

He lifted one of the suitcases and threw it on a scarred and splintered bench next to the station house. Lifting the lid, he looked at the bundles of cash. There were packets of pressed fifties and twenties, the kind of money that could be moved around without attracting much notice.

Bolan threw the other suitcase next to it. Blood money in stereo.

"What do we do with these?" Carvaggio asked, lifting one of the currency packets and balancing it in his hand.

The Executioner studied Carvaggio's eyes and his manner. The ex-hit man wasn't overwhelmed by the sight of the money like many of Sienna's regular soldiers would be. As the top assassin for the Garrison, he'd come into a considerable amount of money from carrying out legitimate hits against targets who had it coming.

No, Bolan thought, Carvaggio already had more than enough money. What he needed was a lifetime to spend it. These suitcases full of cash wouldn't tempt him to stray.

"We'll add it to the war chest," the soldier said. "We can use it against Sienna. Maybe we can even use some of it to buy an audience with Patricio."

Bolan slipped off his hooded white shroud and laid it flat on the ground. Taking two bundles at a time, he transferred the contents of the suitcase into the parachute-like cloth. After folding the shroud several times and binding it with stretch straps, it was manageable.

A few moments later Carvaggio fashioned a similar package.

That just left the gym bags of cocaine bricks.

"And them?" Carvaggio asked as he nodded toward the bricks.

Bolan shrugged. "Any suggestions?"

"Yeah," Carvaggio said. With a flash of his hand he pulled out a matte-black knife and flicked open its four-inch blade. He cut into the corner of one of the bricks and gashed through the plastic, pouring a stream of white powder onto the ground. Picking up the gym bag, he walked down the tracks several yards, then faced the river.

He cocked his arm and threw the spilling brick of cocaine

in a high arc toward the Hudson. It tumbled in the air until finally it came down on the slow moving ice floes that cracked and crushed against one another.

The brick hissed as it cracked open on the ice, then seeped into the dark waters. A few seconds later another brick sailed in the air with the same result.

As Carvaggio continued throwing the opened bricks, Bolan jogged down the tracks with the strapped parcels of confiscated currency and the other satchel of powder to join him.

They had to hurry now before any local agencies responded to the firefight in the woods. Though the area was isolated, there was no way the battle would go unreported for long.

Bolan and Carvaggio had a good trek over the mountains before they reached the stashed Ford Explorer to take them out of the area. Instead of going south to Manhattan, the Executioner figured on driving north at first, then swinging over to Connecticut where the gadget-laden Explorer wouldn't attract too much attention. The comm gear and scanners installed in the dash would help them evade any official presence in the area.

But first they had to get out of the kill zone.

Bolan dropped the cocaine satchel next to Carvaggio, who dug into the contents with the same brutal efficiency he'd shown before.

One after the other he tossed the punctured bricks into the river. Carvaggio savored each brief flight, eyes glinting with satisfaction as they burst like bombs upon the dark ice of the Hudson and the thin ice of Sienna's crumbling empire.

6

Hal Brognola tugged open the window on the fourth floor of the unofficial federal building on Lower Broadway, allowing fresh air to waft into the overheated room.

Like many other buildings in the downtown area, it had a staid gray facade and enough glass to keep an army of window cleaners in style. But unlike the neighboring buildings, which mostly housed prestigious brokers or law firms, this building served as a base for covert Justice Department operations.

The Special Services Unit had taken over most of the fourth floor, leaving a small corner office for the big Fed when he was in town. He didn't need much space or any of the perks that went with his position. He just needed a safe place to touch base with Bolan and some of his other key operatives.

Still cradling the phone on his shoulder when Bolan first walked into the office, Brognola sat on the edge of the metal desk. He listened intently for a while, then spoke to the other party in the gruff, authoritative tone that Bolan knew so well. No false dramatics. Just the voice of a man who knew when to give and when to take in order to get the job done.

With an idle sweep of his hand, Brognola pushed aside a stack of folders that contained volumes of depressing and often degenerate facts of life and death in the underworld. He'd brought along several major-league cases to study on the shuttle flight from D.C. to New York that he caught earlier in the morning.

The Big Apple was only an hour from Washington, but these days Brognola was never far from the paperwork war, grabbing whatever time he could to study dossiers and files, hoping to build a trail toward organized crime figures and U.S.-based terror groups.

Most of the cases would be handed over to the aboveground arms of the Justice Department. But special cases, like the one involving Nick Carvaggio, went to Mack Bolan, who was now sitting at a government-surplus utility table crammed against the opposite wall with his long legs stretched onto one of the wooden ladder-back chairs.

The table was laden with radio gear, beepers and cellular phones, magnetized car-tracking beacons, high-tech cameras—all the usual spook gear used by the SSU surveillance squad.

Amid all the electronic gadgetry were a couple of monitors with built-in VCRs. It looked like a TV repair shop, but the mechanics who used this gear were quite a bit more deadly.

Bolan cleared a space in front of him and flipped off the foam lid from one of the two large cups of coffee he'd picked up at a shop around the corner. Steam rose into the air, spreading the scent of fresh roasted coffee through the drafty office.

"Good God, Striker," Brognola said after hanging up the phone. "You didn't have to bring your own coffee. We got our own damn machine out in the hall."

"Yeah," Bolan said. "I remember from the last time we talked here. That's why I brought you one, too."

Brognola laughed, then flipped off the coffee lid, tossed it onto the middle of his desk and took a sip. "Large too."

"I figure we might be here awhile," the soldier said.

"That we might," Brognola agreed. He took a couple more sips, then slipped into the roller chair behind his desk. "Where do we stand with Carvaggio?" he asked. "Can we still trust him?"

"No reason not to," Bolan said. He swung his feet to the floor and briefed Brognola on his activities with Carvaggio, bringing him right up to the attack on the station house. "I imagine you heard a bit about that already."

"Just about every news report in the country's running with it. Fortunately they're all playing up the angle we want."

"Gang war's good for business," Bolan said. "The New York papers probably doubled their circulation."

Brognola nodded. "What concerns me is the TV coverage. So far the local stations are playing it up—but they're not digging too deep."

"I noticed," Bolan said. "Announcers all sound like sports reporters, keeping score with the body count."

"I think the real problem might come from the networks," Brognola said. "Right now the story's just a blip on their newscasts—a sixty-second sound bite between all the political scandals and celebrity gossip that passes as news these days…"

"But?" the Executioner prodded.

"But I'm afraid the networks will start cranking up their teams—and actually do some investigating—if we make many more splashes."

"That's hard to control, Hal," Bolan said. "We have to strike where and when we can. If we want to come out of this alive, we're bound to make some noise."

"I understand, Striker. I'm just saying we have to keep this contained. If the networks decide it's a major story and send in their heavy hitters, they might get lucky. Or get in the way. There's a chance they could tumble onto our connection. Suppose we end up on a prime-time special. Where does that leave us?"

"Exposed," Bolan replied. "Probably out of business. But I'll still go on doing what I have to do, Hal. You know that. I expect you'll do the same in whatever way you can."

"Whatever way's left to me."

"Settled," Bolan said. "We know what we'll do—if we have to. But I don't think it'll come to that. One thing is

certain, though. Eventually this operation's going to end up
on a Rupert Sawyer special.''

''There's nothing we can do about that, except control the
content. Is that doable?''

''When this is all over,'' Bolan said, ''we've got to give
the guy something to run with. Some inside stuff. In turn
he'll go with a cover story that'll get the essential truth out
about these people, but leave out what we want him to. Until
the last shot's fired, he promised to keep us out of it.''

''You think he'll keep his end of the bargain?'' the big
Fed asked.

''He's grateful to be alive,'' Bolan answered. ''And he
thinks I'm as dangerous as the guys hunting Carvaggio.
Yeah, he should toe the line and will probably help us out
in the long run.''

''Unless Sienna's boys catch up to him and decide to use
him as target practice,'' Brognola pointed out.

''Until that happens, I'm assuming he's doing exactly what
he promised me.''

''According to our people, he is,'' Brognola said, reaching
for the remote control on the corner of his desk. ''At least
on the surface. Here, take a look for yourself. This is some
prepared footage and raw tape he's getting ready for the future broadcast.'' He pointed at the monitor behind Bolan and
clicked on the power button.

Bolan pushed his chair away from the table and turned to
look at the monitor.

A blue screen came on, followed by some time cues and
a commercial placement insert, then the image of Rupert
Sawyer filled the screen.

''Fortunately Sawyer's still running a loose ship,'' Brognola said. ''These are copies of some tapes our people got
hold of.''

Brognola tapped the volume button on the remote until
Rupert Sawyer's resonant voice filled the room. ''This is Rupert Sawyer, retracing the last bloody steps of an underworld
hit team that itself came under the gun...''

On-screen Sawyer was in his best newsman's trench coat as he walked past the wreckage of the midtown office building where he'd met up with Carvaggio for the covert rendezvous that so many people knew about.

The producer's narration omitted the fact that he'd actually been there while the shootout went down, and he was careful not to mention any details that would give away his insider's knowledge. In that regard he kept to the same details that the rest of the print and broadcast media had.

But Sawyer's re-creation of the shootout was a lot more convincing and insightful than any of the pieces the competition had done.

"It began here right where I'm standing," Sawyer said, looking straight into the camera while gesturing behind him at the shattered doorway. "According to my sources, a highly paid assassin attempted to breach the security of his target's hideout, only to find the tables turned on him. Without even knowing what happened, the hit man was taken out with one shot to the middle of the head."

The camera zoomed in for a close-up of the somber broadcaster as he said, "He was but the first member of the hit team to die that day in the early-evening hours when the hunters became the hunted, lured into a trap by someone more proficient at execution than they were. An unexpected assassin was also at work that day."

Sawyer moved around the corner, letting his cameraman lead the way as if the camera itself were the eyes of the unexpected assassin.

Bolan shook his head. "The guy's got a way with a camera," he said. "Almost makes you feel like you're there."

Though Bolan and Brognola both regarded the man as an opportunist, there was no denying the talent they saw on-screen. The producer of *Case Closed* mixed cinema verité with the high-tech voyeurism mastered by the tabloids. It was definitely an audience grabber.

After a brief jaunt down the sidewalk, the camera suddenly turned toward the road, as if sensing a predator. A van was double-parked in the road, practically the same color as the one Bolan encountered.

Accompanied by Sawyer's voice-over, the camera zoomed in on the van, as sounds of explosions and gunfire overpowered the image. And then the tape cut to a grainy black-and-white newspaper photo of the real van wreckage with bodies and blood scattered all around it. The photo slowly morphed into a full-color image highlighting bright red blood on the bodies.

Several other images followed, showing a close-up of each corpse from a different angle, lingering on the shotgunner who still looked dangerous in death. The screen image dissolved into a mistlike background, making the corpses fade like digitized ghosts.

Sawyer's pontificating voice provided more narration as the camera did a jump cut to the alley in back of Carvaggio's building, showing the other casualties that the Executioner and the hit man had left behind.

The producer's image came back on-screen as he stalked toward the camera. "The human wreckage behind me is among the first victims—no, let's call them soldiers—who fell in a war started on the streets of our city. But as far as the underworld is concerned, there's no geographical limit to the arena where they confront one another, as witnessed by yet another battlefield in an idyllic upstate area that also found its solitude shattered by slaughter."

The next shot showed Sawyer standing behind the station house where Bolan and Carvaggio had carried out their sniper attack. In the background were the fields of snow covered with dead bodies, blood staining the ground. Shattered vehicles rose up from the snow like tombstones.

"Enemies in life, comrades in death, the soldiers of competing Families met similar ends here on this snowbound cemetery," Sawyer said as he walked toward the field.

The camera swept over the corpses and the cars, then pulled back for a long panoramic shot of the scenic woodlands rising in the distance. "Once again the deadly roll call featured reputed underworld mobsters. But this time there was yet another faction on the field of death—Colombian enforcers from one of the cartels bringing powdered death to our city. Perhaps it's only fitting that they met their deaths here in the pristine powdered backdrop of a winterland..."

There were several more shots that showed where the battle raged, then came the closing sequence with Rupert Sawyer slowly moving closer to the camera. "Some troubling questions still remain. Who is behind this wide-ranging war?"

Sawyer resumed his trademark stalking of the camera, moving in for a tight close-up. "And this brings us to an even more critical question—Who is winning this war? These questions and others will be answered in future editions of *Case Closed.*"

"That's what we've got so far," Brognola said, switching off the VCR with the remote control. "I understand there's more on the way."

Bolan turned away from the fading screen. "Does he have an air date yet?"

Brognola shook his head. "Nothing definite. You can bet when it does air he'll pull out all the stops. Lots of media coverage, lots of promos. He knows what he's doing."

"Sure looked like it," Bolan said.

"What did you think of the package he put together?"

"It's got me hooked," the Executioner said. "I'll be watching to find out what happens."

"You'll be the one making it happen, Striker," Brognola said. "Except for the intel and logistics support the SSU can give you, you'll continue to be pretty much on your own."

Bolan understood. If he got in a tight situation and really had to, he could call on the SSU for some emergency backup. Other than that, the Justice Department covert operatives would act strictly as the intelligence branch of the New York mission. But the military end of it was up to Bolan.

Brognola couldn't risk having Justice Department operations compromised by official direct intervention. The last thing he needed was to have the media latch on to a "secret army" of federal spooks running rampant through America.

"Sorry to throw so much on your shoulders this time," his old friend said. "Sienna's bigger than we first thought, but when you get back out there, I'm afraid you'll still be fighting a one-man war."

"Two-man war," Bolan said. "Carvaggio knows how Sienna operates and where he's most vulnerable. Besides, Hal, I knew what it was like going in. It'll work out. With your guys handling the spook side of things, it leaves me free to concentrate strictly on executive action."

"Fair enough," Brognola said. "So let me do my part for a while. Let's get back to Rupert Sawyer and another angle he's working on this Sienna thing. Carvaggio wasn't the only underworld source he was cultivating. Are you aware of that?"

"Somewhat," Bolan said. "Nick told me there'd been others who approached Sawyer."

"He tell you any names?"

"Nothing specific, Hal. So far we've been pretty busy just staying alive."

"Her name's Ambrosia Lyons," Brognola said.

"Sounds real," Bolan said.

"About as real as the figure that first attracted Victor Sienna," Brognola said. "Showgirl type, a trophy to display on his arm now and then. He kept her as his mistress, just long enough for her to learn some not too flattering things about his activities. When Ambrosia figured she knew too much for her own good, she took off. The person she turned to was Rupert Sawyer."

"Is the girl a threat to Sienna?" Bolan asked.

"Hard to say. She was bound to pick up something, but who knows what she really saw? These guys don't let women get too close to their business. But you know the story—she wants to do an exposé, go public with her story and make some money in the bargain."

"And maybe she'll make herself a target in the process,"

Bolan said, shaking his head. "Don't these people know who they're dealing with? Sawyer almost gets his butt shot off with me and Carvaggio, and now he's doing the same number with her."

"He's being reasonably safe about this," Brognola said. "He keeps her in one of the apartments paid for out of the *Case Closed* budget, hidden under operating expenses. No one really knows about it except him."

"Sounds like he's got more experience with girls than with gangsters," Bolan said. "Even so, the girl could be in danger."

"I thought you'd want to know about it. Add her to the equation."

The Executioner considered the girl's role. There was no way Sienna could know how much she'd tumbled onto. "Maybe we can use her to put out some stories on Sienna, throw some more heat on him. But only if we can guarantee her safety."

"I'll post some people around her. That'll also help us keep an eye on Sawyer. Apparently he's debriefing her quite regularly these days."

Brognola gave Bolan the address of the apartment, then moved on to some harder intel.

Justice Department operatives across the country had picked up on a "talent scouting" trip that Sienna's right-hand man was making—Chicago, Kansas City, L.A.

"Apparently this guy McNeil is lining up some replacements for the soldiers who went down," Brognola explained. "He's also hiring a couple of specialists to come after you and Carvaggio. The Families aren't too happy about McNeil poaching in their territory, but the guys he's going for aren't attached to anyone yet so that makes them fair game."

"Free agents," Bolan concluded.

"And right now no one wants to openly confront Sienna. He's grown pretty strong over the past few years."

Bolan knew most of the background on Sienna, but listened as Brognola filled him in on a few more details the

SSU had assembled on the Mob strongman. Apparently Sienna had taken over a number of Mafia operations that used to be run by other Families. He still kept some figureheads from the old clans as fronts, but he was the power behind the operations.

Sienna's rise began with the influx of the Russian *mafiya* into the U.S. After the cold war ended, KGB-trained assassins and Spetsnaz troops found themselves out of work and drifted into the underworld, where they could continue plying their trade. When the *mafiya* expanded its operations to America, it brought in combat brigades and simply executed anyone who got in the way of their enterprises—legitimate or criminal.

To stay in the game, the Sicilian and Colombian clans working the East Coast also had to follow suit. They started building small private armies.

And when the local Families needed more protection than they had on hand, they turned to Sienna's Garrison. He'd come along at just the right time. His growing crew of military veterans was more than capable of standing up to the Russian soldiers.

Though Sienna initially put together his military strike teams to provide muscle for other Families, he eventually became as powerful as some of the Families he worked for.

As Sienna did more and more work, he used unheard-of amounts of cash to bring in even more soldiers. Inevitably he'd grown from an up-and-coming soldier to an underworld warlord.

Now there was a delicate balance of power in place.

The other Families liked having Sienna's services available if they ever needed them, but they disliked the idea of perhaps having to face Sienna if he decided to come after them one day.

It was inevitable. Soldiers needed wars to fight and territories to conquer. The Garrison would either continue to grow or run into a force stronger than itself.

Bolan and Brognola spent another hour figuring out ways

to be that force. The SSU would keep tabs on the Garrison recruits as well as provide some more intel on Jacob Patricio, another weapon Bolan wanted to turn against Victor Sienna.

The small fourth-floor office had become a war room, and though he had other fires to put out, Brognola knew that if they didn't take care of Sienna now, he might grow beyond their reach.

"All right, Striker," Brognola said, signaling that the meeting was over, "that's all we can do for now. I've got some other people to deal with, including a few who are calling for the head of Nicholas Carvaggio. Any suggestions on what I should tell them?"

"Yeah," Bolan said. "Without Carvaggio, we don't get Sienna."

7

Stefan Gaultieri lived in Brooklyn Heights on a street of row houses, many of them with identical stoops and wrought-iron gates. He'd lived in the neighborhood for years, enjoying the closeness of the delis, bakeries and pizzerias lined up next to one another one avenue south of his apartment.

A block and a half in the other direction was a subway stop that could take him into Manhattan. Or if he had to drive, it was just a quick trip across the bridge.

The Garrison conducted operations all over the five boroughs of New York City, but its main base was in Manhattan in one of several apartments, lofts or warehouses that Victor Sienna maintained in the city.

Gaultieri preferred to keep a reasonable geographical distance between himself and Sienna. That way he could also keep his home life separate from business.

Here in the neighborhood, Gaultieri was just one more guy who seemed to have a lot of time on his hands and a lot of money to spend. No one asked what he did or who he worked for. He felt safe and anonymous—until the moment he saw Nick Carvaggio walking down the street.

It was about ten in the morning, and a cold spell had settled in from the harbor. There were only a couple of other people on the street, but they were farther down the block. No help there, Gaultieri thought.

Carvaggio was alone, but he was directly in Gaultieri's path.

The wheelman had been on his way to the newsstand near

the subway stop. He'd planned on a brisk morning walk to pick up a couple of papers, then to linger over breakfast in one of the coffee shops. But now his routine was shattered, along with his former belief that he was destined for a long life.

Carvaggio had slipped out from between a couple of parked cars halfway down the street, obviously waiting for Gaultieri.

He headed for the Garrison driver in that straight ahead, no-nonsense gait of his. He was totally at ease, unworried at the prospect of a shootout in broad daylight. That was Carvaggio's attitude—take what comes, but take it first.

Gaultieri couldn't turn, couldn't run. He stopped in the middle of the cracked sidewalk and waited for him. He felt the holstered Colt weighing heavily inside his jacket. Any other time, with any other man, he would have pulled out the weapon without hesitating.

The ex-hit man kept moving in a decidedly unhurried manner. Their eyes met from a good distance away, each man scoping out the other. Gaultieri knew he had a shaken look on his face. He'd seen Carvaggio in action too many times to look otherwise.

Carvaggio had a relaxed gaze about him, as if Gaultieri were just some harmless threat that had to be taken care of.

"What do you want?" Gaultieri asked as the man they'd all been trying to kill came to a stop five feet in front of him.

"Not you," Carvaggio said.

"Why should I believe that?" Gaultieri asked. His voice was too quick, too high-pitched. Instead of a belligerent challenge, it sounded like a squeak of terror.

Carvaggio pretended not to notice. "I have no quarrel with you, Stefan Gaultieri," he said. His voice was calm and had a measure of respect. He'd ridden with the Garrison soldier before and knew that was his real strength—he was a better wheelman than gunman. "My quarrel is with the man you work for."

The reference to Victor Sienna was enough to put Gaultieri

on the alert. He was already on the outs with Sienna. If he failed him again, there would be no more chances. His hand reached for the slightly open zipper of his jacket, but his fingers paused there, unable to continue.

Carvaggio watched his hand, not moving, not saying a thing until Gaultieri's fingers fell away from the jacket.

"Good man," Carvaggio said as a thin smile appeared on his face. "This jacket's loaded."

"I kind of figured that," Gaultieri replied. "I've seen it go off enough times. Back when..."

"Back when we were on the same side," the ex-hit man finished.

"Yeah."

Carvaggio took a few steps closer. "We should still be on the same side. I did nothing to be ashamed of. You do know why Vic put a bounty on me, don't you?"

"I know what I been told," Gaultieri said.

"You believe it?"

Gaultieri shrugged. "Sometimes you got to believe things you don't want to."

Carvaggio nodded. "Guess so. But I'm thinking you know what really went down. You know about the woman Sienna wanted hit. She had nothing to do with this thing of ours, Stefan. Nothing at all."

"That's not for me to say."

"Then let's move on to the other thing," Carvaggio said. "You must know about the hit on the Fed. I figure Vic's saying that the whack brought a lot of heat on the Garrison. But that wasn't me. Not my style. Hey, if I got to take someone out, I go right up and do him. You know that."

"Like you are now?" Gaultieri asked. He thought of the glory that would be his if he made a move on Carvaggio, but it was tempered by the thought of lying in a coffin if he tried.

"Stefan," Carvaggio said, "come on. You and me always got along. I got no reason to take you out unless I have to."

"Easy to say," Gaultieri replied, "hard to prove."

"Not this time. I had you in my sights at the station house." He crooked his finger in the air and mimicked pulling a trigger. "That's all it would've taken, Stefan."

Gaultieri stared hard at him, stricken by the revelation that more than luck was on his side that day. "It was you."

"Hell, yeah."

"That's what everyone figured," the wheelman said. "You or a SWAT team. But hey, who can tell in this business? I mean, lots of people might want to take credit for that bang-up."

"Count on it," Carvaggio said. "I was there. But instead of taking you out, I made sure you survived the cross fire."

"How's that?"

"I took out one of your Colombian friends, remember? The shooter at the station house who stopped being friendly and started being dead. You were as good as gone—but I thought it'd be better if you stayed around a while longer."

Gaultieri was getting jittery. So far he'd managed to keep up appearances, like he and Carvaggio were a couple of old friends catching up with each other. But having this man so close was like looking at a six-foot, hawk-eyed omen of death.

Gaultieri looked around, not really expecting to see any of his fellow soldiers on the street. They hardly ever came to this place. But what if they'd been closing in on Carvaggio? And even now they were watching him talk to enemy number one—putting two and two together and coming up with a dead Gaultieri as the result. No, the wheelman thought, that was just his nerves getting to him.

"Suppose I believe what you're telling me," Gaultieri said. "What difference does it make? What can I do?"

"You can go on living," Carvaggio replied. "Help me out with some information."

Gaultieri laughed. "I can't believe this! Every trigger man in town's looking to put you away, and you're asking me to join you. What chance would I have?"

"It's not just me," Carvaggio said.

Gaultieri remembered the ambush that had sprung on them at the station house, shots from all directions at once. Controlled extinction. "Who's with you on this?" he asked.

"The kind of guy who can bring in as many people as he wants," the Mob fugitive said. "Where and when he wants." His voice was casual, but Gaultieri could tell that Carvaggio admired whoever was helping him out.

"Why's he helping you?"

"Maybe I'm helping him."

Now Carvaggio was starting to look around, as if he were worried about being shadowed.

"I don't see what I can do," Gaultieri said. "I'm in the middle here."

"Just think about it," Carvaggio said. "Maybe you'll make the right move. Help me figure out who did the hit that Sienna blamed on me."

"I don't know about that, Nick. I'm out of the loop."

"Maybe you can find out anyway," Carvaggio suggested. "And there's probably a few other things you could do to make yourself useful if you want." He reached into his pocket and took out a card with a number scrawled on it. "When you want to talk call this number and leave a message."

Gaultieri reached out slowly, as if the card were booby-trapped, then looked suspiciously at the number.

"What is it?"

"It's one of the answering services I use."

"Who do I ask for?"

"Professor Riley."

Gaultieri laughed. "You're moving up in the world, Professor."

"Some move up, some move down," Carvaggio said. "And some just stop moving. Call me, Stefan. You don't have to die for Sienna."

Gaultieri held the card out in front of him, like the numbers were part of a lottery. "I don't know...I don't think I can, Nick."

"Think of this, Stefan," Carvaggio said as he took a step closer. "There's me on one side and Sienna on the other. Who you think is going to be standing when this is all over—me or him?"

Gaultieri looked at the hard-edged face of Nick Carvaggio and saw death in his eyes. But whose? "Nick, there are so many guys gearing up for you."

"Doesn't matter how many soldiers he has," Carvaggio said. "I'm getting to him, Stefan. Play it smart and make sure you're not in my way."

He turned and walked away, unconcerned. All Gaultieri had to do was take out a weapon and shoot him.

But Carvaggio knew him too well.

Gaultieri wouldn't make the play. Not that he was above shooting someone in the back. Death was death. What held Gaultieri back was the suspicion that Carvaggio would somehow sense the moment his hand touched metal.

Some guys were like that, he knew. He remembered his time in the Army, how out of the blue someone would turn—not hearing a sound but knowing they were in someone's crosshairs just the same. It was almost supernatural. Carvaggio had that ability. The instant Gaultieri made up his mind to shoot, Carvaggio would turn and cut loose with that shotgun-tailored coat of his.

Gaultieri looked at the phone number on the card before shoving it inside his jacket pocket.

He would have to memorize the number another time, then destroy the card. He was too numb to concentrate now. Instead, his mind was doing a number of calculations, involving the various ways he could be killed and the different factions that would do it.

Sienna's people could be quite creative in the way they would take care of him if they found out he was dealing with Carvaggio.

With Carvaggio it would be a clean kill. But it could come any time—if Gaultieri happened to be in the way of a bullet meant for Sienna.

He kept walking toward the corner, intending to follow his routine as best he could. But somehow the thought of sitting down with coffee and a newspaper no longer held the same appeal.

Stefan Gaultieri had been approached. Sooner or later he would have tell Victor Sienna what happened or he would have to call the professor.

THOMAS LIEGE FLEW into JFK International Airport on a Boeing 767, arriving shortly before noon.

Like many other businessmen who'd taken the morning flight from Chicago, he brought a laptop with him and spent a considerable amount of time staring at the screen.

Unlike most of the businessmen who pored over spreadsheets and pie charts, Liege spent his time playing video games. War games mostly, the kind that required deft maneuvers, fast reflexes and a high aggression factor.

He was a natural.

Though outwardly he appeared to be a somewhat young and successful corporate executive, Liege's real business was war. He had been studying and practicing it ever since he enlisted in the Marines at age eighteen.

He'd spent nine years in the U.S. Navy, seeing considerable action in a UDT special warfare unit before moving on to a SEAL team.

When he finally left official government service, he toured the world as a paramilitary specialist, fighting undeclared wars in unmentionable ways. Depending on the side, he was labeled a mercenary or a murderer.

He prospered in the early days of the Bosnian conflict, but there his talents weren't so singular. Soon everyone was at war, and armies of former civilians became proficient at killing. Just after he'd decided it was time to leave the country, Liege's team of mercs was ambushed and driven into a minefield. A good portion of his right foot and his right cheekbone were blown off, but he came out with a considerable bank account.

Skilled plastic surgeons and prosthetics had restored his looks, as well as his gait. The recuperation depleted his hard-earned bank account, but a man of his talents didn't have to look too far for work.

Five years had passed since he left his mercenary days and became a freelancer for the underworld.

He was highly trained, highly paid and fortunately for the Garrison, he was currently highly motivated to leave his apartment on the shores of Lake Michigan.

Liege's presence on Chicago's Gold Coast was becoming an embarrassment to the very people who most often used his talents. Though the publicity surrounding him had died down somewhat, Liege was no longer the hitter of choice in Chicago.

A number of feature articles had connected him to an underworld assassination, which normally was a welcome piece of information to the newspapers and police departments alike.

But Liege had also been connected to the deaths of two witnesses who had the misfortune to be on the scene while he plied his trade. They'd been considering testifying against him.

Their minds weren't quite made up when they were killed in an accident—an explosive accident that had the signature of Thomas Liege all over it. For nearly a week running, the citizens of Chicago were calling for Liege's head. So were the police and the Organized Crime Task Force.

But without witnesses there wasn't enough evidence against him. That was a common situation surrounding cases involving the specialist. Not only did his targets go down, but a lot of innocents went down at the same time.

Until the heat died, Liege was going to be blacklisted for a while.

Some of his employers had already grown wary of using him, even before he took out the witnesses. He was good, but he was becoming too reckless. Give him a name and that guy was gone. But sometimes he took out his targets a bit too loud, drawing too much unwanted attention.

Like with the latest witnesses.

There was talk in the underworld that his past employers were considering performing a public service to put Liege on a hit list. That was what made him ripe for recruitment by Drew McNeil. This also made his surveillance by SSU teams relatively simple.

The Justice Department was interested in both McNeil and Liege, so much so that the department had a couple of people on the flight from Chicago, as well as a mobile surveillance team waiting at JFK.

When Liege picked up his baggage, he was never far from an SSU operative or a camera recording his moves.

When he stepped outside the terminal, a Garrison associate was waiting in a late-model Lincoln with lots of chrome and lots of engine. An SSU operative discreetly followed him out of the building. She stowed her gear in a small Buick that was waiting for her farther down the queue of cars.

Liege put his baggage inside the trunk of the Lincoln and then, a bit too casually, took out a small canvas bag that had been waiting there for him. It was large enough to hold a camera or a firearm. Later the Garrison would have more specialized weapons available to him, but for now this would do.

The SSU knew he had no other weapons.

Back at the Chicago airport, shortly after Liege had checked his bags with the airline, his luggage was taken to one of the small security rooms set aside for such purposes and carefully examined by SSU operatives. There'd been no weapons, just some computer games for his laptop and enough clothes for a week's stay. Long enough to get acquainted with the town.

Long enough to find the man he'd been hired to assassinate.

Liege slung the canvas bag over his shoulder, adjusted the

strap, then climbed into the front seat of the Lincoln for the short drive into Manhattan.

The Buick fell in behind him, the lead car in a shifting convoy of SSU vehicles keeping it in sight at all times.

Following a bit farther behind the official convoy was Nick Carvaggio, who appreciated his tinted windows when so much federal heat was around.

He was driving Bolan's Ford Explorer, eager to get a look at the man who'd been brought into town to kill him.

Carvaggio hung back all the way into Manhattan until Liege's car pulled up in front of the Trentmore Hotel on 37th Street.

It was no surprise.

The hotel was once elegant and upscale but had briefly fallen into a state of neglect and then into the hands of Victor Sienna. Now it was in a state of limbo, trading on its former reputation to keep up the occupancy rate. More money would have to be pumped into it, or it would come down several notches in the guidebooks.

Like he'd done with many of his other holdings, Sienna stayed in the background as a very silent partner.

Though it would have been smarter to put Liege up somewhere else, Sienna couldn't resist playing the grand baron and housing the imported assassin in one of his midtown fiefdoms.

In Sienna's twisted scheme of things, it was perfectly safe. He would have Liege nearby, an assassin on hand who was ready to be sent into action the moment the Garrison located Carvaggio. It never occurred to him that his operations outside the city could be of interest to anyone or that the Justice Department was closely following his recruiting efforts.

Carvaggio hung back in the traffic on 37th Street until he saw Liege walk through the lobby of the hotel.

He picked up the Explorer's car phone, then called Bolan to let him know the target had arrived.

THE EXECUTIONER PICKED UP the phone on the first ring, knowing it would be Hal Brognola or Nick Carvaggio. They were the only two people who knew he'd checked into the hotel directly across from the Trentmore the night before. They'd been playing a hunch that Sienna would stay true to form. He'd housed several other associates in the hotel, and there was a good chance he'd do the same for Liege.

"Yeah?" Bolan said.

"Yeah," came Carvaggio's simple response. It was enough to let Bolan know that the man he'd been watching get out of the Lincoln was the same one the SSU had tracked from Chicago.

Bolan had seen the man through a magnifying scope, and it appeared to be the same man from the dossier Brognola provided to him. But it was good to have face-to-face confirmation.

"I'm ready," Bolan said.

"I'll stay in touch," Carvaggio replied, then broke the connection.

It was going to be a long haul. Bolan didn't want to move against Liege until some of Sienna's crew stopped by, giving the SSU operatives the chance to track members of the Garrison after they met with Liege. It would also make things a lot more confusing in Sienna's empire. After Liege was taken out, Sienna would suspect that leaks were coming from his own crew, that somebody from within his own ranks was helping Carvaggio. It was a simple equation. If Liege was whacked a short time after Sienna's own people saw him, then there could be another Judas in the ranks.

Aside from Sienna's real enemies, Bolan wanted him to have a lot of imagined ones. Soon Victor Sienna wouldn't feel safe no matter how many soldiers he had around him. He'd be wondering if any of them would turn their weapons on him.

There was another reason for waiting. Bolan didn't want any personnel from the SSU to be around when the hit went down.

He settled back into his post in the curtain-shrouded hotel

room. He was sitting on a desk chair he'd pulled by the window. On the counter running below the sliding glass windows was a row of soda cans and empty coffee cups.

Next to the counter was a bedside table the Executioner had rolled into position. It was sturdy enough to hold the binocular he'd attached to a night-vision telephoto lens. Mounted on the tripod, the rig looked like a blunt-nosed bazooka. It was heavy and cumbersome, but when broken down into separate components it could easily fit into a suitcase.

It was definitely worth the trouble. The rig allowed him a clear view of every window on every floor. With the almost six-inch wide eyepiece on the binocular, Bolan could survey the hotel across the street without having to peer through a tiny scope all day.

For a long duration surveillance, there was no other way of doing it. One man simply couldn't stare through a scope for hours on end without losing his edge or his vision. But this way, it was like watching a small portable television.

The surveillance scope was hidden by the curtains, and there was no chance anyone would detect the passive night-vision device.

Also hidden by the curtains was the sniper rifle. Bolan had been expecting Liege. Even without the intel from the SSU, he'd sensed that he would soon encounter the man from Chicago. But even if the man hadn't shown up, there was a chance some other gunners from Sienna's crew would end up at the Trentmore.

But now it was settled. Soon Thomas Liege would meet his end. It was just a matter of waiting.

Bolan turned on the radio and trolled through the New York stations, moving through the jazz, reggae, news and talk shows. He changed the channel every now and then to keep his mind occupied. Even with the wide screen binocular, it was possible to trance out.

He waited through the afternoon, undisturbed except for the phone calls that came from Hal Brognola every two hours on the scrambler unit Bolan had jacked into the hotel phone line. The SSU was sending its intel directly to Brognola, who in turn fed the summaries to Bolan. So far a number of Garrison elite had stopped by the hotel and gone up to Liege's room on the twenty-second floor.

Bolan had recognized some of the visitors. The SSU had photographed all of them.

They'd been followed closely ever since they left.

Liege stayed in the hotel room. He was like a fireman on call, waiting for the fire to put out.

Instead, the fire was waiting for him.

At ten o'clock that night Bolan made two calls. The first was to Hal Brognola, who sounded tired when he picked up the phone. Though he was temporarily based in downtown New York, he was still carrying a full Washington workload.

"Looks like he's in for the night," Bolan said.

"Right."

"So it's a good time for *everyone* to turn in."

"Right," Brognola said. "Give me ten minutes. If you don't hear back by then, figure everyone's punched out. The field will be all yours."

Bolan waited. There was no call from Brognola, which meant it was last call for Thomas Liege.

He crunched the soda cans and foam cups and threw them in a plastic bag, which he dumped into an open suitcase on the bed. He didn't want to leave any sign of his observation post.

Bolan clicked off the night-vision binocular and carefully packed the components into one of the suitcases, which he locked and positioned by the hotel-room door.

He rolled the bedside table back into place, then took up his selected sniper's post by the wall. He'd opened the window enough to give him a clear field of fire at the hotel room across the way.

Ten o'clock.

Liege was continuing the routine he'd established—smoking a cigarette; pouring a drink from the small liquor bottle on the desk; flipping through the channels of the hotel cable system; opening the window now and then to let the cool winter air suck out the smoke that filled the room.

It was a routine that Bolan knew by heart.

The Executioner took in the scene opposite, studying it to see if anything was amiss—if perhaps somewhere out there in the checkerboard windows of the skyscrapers someone was waiting for him to show his face.

He scanned the buildings on both sides of the hotel, then looked beyond them at the Empire State Building, with its upper stories serving as a brightly lighted backdrop for the white snow falling on the dark city night.

Then his eyes swept back down to the hotel. He knew where Liege's room was from memory. Maybe he knew it too well and had neglected signs from other windows where other Garrison shooters might be.

For a moment he considered the possibility that maybe this had all been part of an elaborate trap, that Liege was the sacrifice and the real assassin was out there right now, thinking to himself how easy a target Bolan was. But he dismissed the thought. His senses told him there was no danger to him now. In fact he was about to remove the greatest danger the Garrison could pose to him.

Bolan let some more time pass to make sure that any SSU operatives near the hotel had more than enough time to leave. He didn't want an incriminating trail leading to the SSU. Though the unit was a covert entity and the operatives were all dedicated to secrecy—and would certainly shed no tears over Thomas Liege—the Executioner thought it was better to let as much time pass as possible.

Their job was done; his was just starting.

He waited in the darkness until his own battle sense kicked in and told him it was time. Then he reached Carvaggio on the car phone in the Explorer. There was a bit of hiss, but he could hear the man's voice clearly through the static.

"Listen," Bolan said, "it's almost checkout time. So I'll be getting ready in the next few minutes."

"Got it," Carvaggio said. "You'll be needing a ride."

"Yeah. Pretty soon. I have to do a bit of last-minute packing, then I'll be ready to go."

"I'll be looking for you."

Bolan hung up, then turned his attention back to his target across the road and held the stock of the sniper rifle close to his cheek. Since he was so familiar with the feel of the rifle—and had acclimated himself to the view across the street—it took only an instant for him to zero in on Liege.

It was an almost subconscious maneuver. The rifle had once again become an extension of the Executioner, and the barrel was drawn to Liege as if his body were a magnet.

The rifle had a full 10-round magazine, but Bolan figured on using just two shots. The hotel room's glass window might offer a bit of distortion and perhaps interfere with the trajectory of the first bullet. The second would be a direct hit.

Either slug would probably do the job. Even with the built-in suppressor, the sniper rifle still had a range of several hundred yards and Bolan was simply firing across the street at a downward angle.

"Okay," the soldier said softly to himself as he fell in sync with Liege's routine, "here we go."

The hit man was stubbing out a cigarette in an ashtray on the desk, waving his hand through the cloud of smoke. Next he would open the window to let the cool air disperse the smell of stale tobacco. And he would also linger a bit to look out at the city he'd come to conquer.

Liege walked slowly toward the window, looking completely relaxed. The sleeves of his white shirt were rolled up as he leaned against the glass. He looked totally unaware and unconcerned. In his mind, no one knew that he'd come to New York except Sienna and his crew. The main thing occupying his thoughts was his ascendancy to a high position in the ranks of the Garrison.

As soon as he added another body or two to his résumé.

The crosshairs of the sniper rifle drifted across Liege's head, resting on his forehead.

Bolan eased his trigger finger back against the metal.

Liege frowned suddenly, as if he'd heard something that displeased him. His subconscious had picked up some cue that he was in danger. Or maybe it was the preternatural radar that most predators and prey felt. Whatever the cause, Liege felt it.

He looked up suddenly, his arms tensing and ready to push away from the window.

Bolan pulled the trigger.

The 7.62 mm subsonic round smacked through the glass and into Liege's head, driving him back from the window so he tottered on his feet. Even as the shattered glass fell like blood-specked diamonds, the Executioner triggered another shot.

This one caught Liege in the chest, adding to the momentum of his falling body and driving him flat on his back as if it were nailing him to the floor. His arms flopped onto the rug.

Bolan studied him through the scope long enough to confirm the kill. He was no longer moving, no longer breathing.

Thomas Liege was gone, checked out of Manhattan and the earth all at the same time.

The Executioner pulled the sniper rifle back into the room. He closed the window, removed the bipod, then broke down the weapon into its separate components and packed it in the suitcase that was still open on the bed.

Bolan double-checked the room and dropped the key into the checkout envelope on the desk. He left a few dollars as a tip for the maid, bolstering the illusion that the room had hosted just another out-of-town visitor.

Bolan stood in front of the mirror and carefully fixed his tie, then smoothed the lapels of his business suit. He didn't want anything to look out of place, making sure that he seemed like a businessman with a late appointment. Someone who had his display gear packed up in attaché-like suitcases. After all, New York was a twenty-four-hour town where business was conducted at all hours.

Passing his self-inspection, Bolan picked up his suitcases and stepped out of his room.

Taking the elevator down to the second floor, he headed for the stairway that led to the first floor. The stairwell door opened close enough to the hotel exit for him to breeze by unseen and unquestioned by the desk staff.

As soon as he stepped out of the hotel, Bolan saw the Explorer prowling slowly along the row of parked cars.

He avoided looking across the street, nodded slightly to the right, then started walking down the sidewalk. A half block farther the Explorer pulled over, front passenger door swinging open as Carvaggio brought the vehicle to a stop.

Bolan opened the back door, flung his suitcases inside, then climbed into the front passenger seat.

Carvaggio swung the Ford casually into the flow of traffic and drove away from the site of the hotel where Victor Sienna had extended his welcome to Thomas Liege—and Bolan showed the underworld just how dangerous Sienna's welcome could be.

8

The last time Bolan saw Jacob Patricio it had been through a night-vision scope when the Colombian and two of his enforcers were fleeing from the station house ambush.

Now he was seeing him through an opaque glass wall that separated Patricio's private office from the rest of the third-floor exhibition space of his Tribeca art gallery.

The industrial-chic atmosphere and the soft lighting system made it seem part-cathedral and part-warehouse. High white walls held dramatically oversized paintings, mostly by South American artists. Many of them conflicted—either pastoral scenes or scenes about war and its aftermath. Stationed here and there were pedestals with modern sculptures and jade figurines.

Finely worked gold headpieces and helmets sat in glass cases on obelisk-like columns. Long display cases held rows of weapons and relics allegedly handled centuries past by Aztec and Mayan rulers.

The dark hardwood floors were polished to a mirrorlike finish, like a glassy racetrack that wound from exhibit to exhibit. The place was moderately busy for early in the afternoon. There were about a dozen people milling around who seemed to know a bit about art. They also looked like they had the money and considered this the right place to acquire it from.

Bolan didn't know that much about art, other than it was nice to look at on occasion. He also knew that some people considered it a better investment than gold. He'd seen fine art in corporate boardrooms and cartel bedrooms as well as in homes of war criminals and psychopaths around the world. He had the feeling that the owners didn't know much more about the pieces other than what they could be insured for.

To many of those art lovers, it was just one more way to launder money. And considering Jacob Patricio's other business, it was quite convenient for the Colombian importer to own an art gallery.

Though Bolan wasn't a master of the ins and outs of the art world, the attractive woman standing by his side knew quite a bit about the subject. Her black hair was cut short, and she wore a navy blue skirt and jacket over a white blouse, giving her the look of a professional.

Though her career was spent mostly as an undercover operative for the Justice Department, she knew enough to pass herself off as an informed patron of the arts. Denise Fairmont could hold her own in the esoteric conversations so common to galleries.

Brognola had assigned the SSU operative to Bolan after a good deal of thought. He'd selected her for two reasons. The SSU was conducting deeper surveillance of Jacob Patricio, and this would put her into a good position to learn more about his operation. The other reason was that she was an accomplished field agent who had seen a considerable amount of action.

No matter how limited her role was supposed to be, Bolan and Brognola wanted someone who could handle herself in case the elegant art dealer discovered her identity.

Bolan was also dressed for the undercover role. His black suit was tailored to his lean frame and there was a brushed leather attaché case slung from a strap over his shoulder that looked heavy with a businessman's workload.

"Now?" Fairmont asked, glancing around the gallery.

Bolan stepped back from the painting he'd been pretending to look at. There were only a few other couples around. "It's worth a shot," he said. He walked over to the sleek desk in front of Patricio's office, which looked expensive enough to be part of one of the displays.

Patricio's bejeweled aide had been sitting behind the desk studying the gallery visitors like they were entrants in a pageant and she was a judge.

"Yes?" she said.

"I'd like to see Mr. Patricio," Bolan stated.

"I see." She smiled as if that were a wish that everyone had, but few were granted it. "And you are?"

"I'm the guy he'd like to see," Bolan said in a bored and somewhat annoyed tone. "*If* he knew I was out here."

She gave Bolan and the woman by his side another brief inspection, which they seemed to pass, then she pushed away from her desk. "I'll mention it to him," she said, obviously used to dealing with clients who wanted discretion. "But what shall I say it's about? He'll want to know."

"Tell him it's about his upstate property," Bolan said.

Patricio's aide looked confused. "I'm not aware he has any upstate property."

"I'm sure there are a lot of things you're not aware of," Bolan said. "With this particular property there were some losses involved." He idly patted the leather case at his side. "Losses that could be reversed."

With a brief nod, she stepped away from the desk and slipped into Patricio's inner sanctum. She returned a couple of minutes later and said, "Mr. Patricio will be with you shortly."

"Thanks," the soldier answered. As he and Fairmont drifted through the gallery, he could almost feel the well-placed security cameras tracking his moves. Patricio would be studying him, trying to determine if he was friend, enemy, or customer.

Five minutes passed before the tall, imposing figure of Jacob Patricio stepped out of his office. He spoke briefly to his aide in a hushed voice, then walked toward Bolan and Fairmont. He nodded politely to her, then fixed Bolan with a speculative gaze.

"I was intrigued by your comments to my assistant," Patricio said. "But I'm afraid you have me at a disadvantage. You seem to know quite a lot about me, but I have no idea of the possible connection between us. Nor have I any idea who you are."

Patricio's voice had been neutral. He wasn't about to back away from anyone or dismiss an approach from someone who might become a potential ally.

"Call me Michael Blasco," Bolan said, using a variant of one of the backstopped identities Brognola set up for such occasions. If Patricio had the right connections to law-enforcement agencies and did some checking, he would find out that the Blasco name was connected to a number of unsolved cases. Major hauls all of them. The Blasco legend would also have links to a couple of Manhattan Families and give him a reputation as an underworld fixer.

"Michael Blasco," Patricio said, testing out the sound of Bolan's nom de guerre and not quite liking it. "I haven't heard that name before. In this business I know everyone."

"I'm not in your business yet," Bolan said. "Not completely."

"I see."

"But I'm learning," Bolan said, nodding toward Fairmont and introducing her as his adviser. "I've enlisted her services to help speed things along."

"Ah," Patricio said. "You plan on making some investments in art?"

"I plan on making an investment in you."

Patricio smiled. "Some investments involve a great deal of risk."

"Without great risks there's little reward," Bolan responded. "I think you and I share the same beliefs on that."

Patricio glanced at the leather case. "You mentioned to my assistant an upstate property and some trouble connected with it. What does that have to do with you?"

"I make troubles go away," Bolan said, patting the leather case for discreet emphasis.

"Perhaps, Mr. Blasco, we should continue this discussion in my office where we'll be safe from interruptions. In the meantime—" he turned to Fairmont, gesturing at the gallery "—your adviser can continue her appraisal of our exhibits. If you have any questions, feel free to ask my assistant." He waved at the formerly brusque assistant, who now sat at her desk beaming love and affection.

"Thank you," the agent said.

"What do you think of it so far?" Patricio asked her.

"Some stunning authentic pieces," Fairmont answered.

Patricio smiled but seemed a bit disappointed.

"And a few exquisitely rendered fakes," the operative continued with a smile. "They could fool most people—with the right provenances attached."

Instead of taking offense, Patricio smiled. The crime lord was obviously impressed with her. "You've chosen well," he said to Bolan. Then he bowed slightly toward Fairmont. "Now if you'll excuse us."

Patricio led Bolan into his office, which was as plain as the gallery was ostentatious. The Spartan look was a subliminal cue to Patricio's guests to let them know that they could get down to business now that they were removed from the glitz of the gallery.

There was a large desk in the center of the room and a table full of fax and videophone gear against one of the walls. On another table were a couple of security monitors with several split screens, presenting a dozen high angle views of the gallery.

A stocky man in an expensive white shirt and shoulder holster sat in front of the security monitors. He turned toward the Executioner and regarded him with the same impassive gaze Bolan had seen on some of the ancient statues in the exhibit.

It was also the same gaze Bolan had seen back at the station house when he'd been scoping out the Colombian enforcers. This was one of the two men who had shepherded Patricio away from the shootout.

"Leave us, Heberto," Patricio said.

The man straightened his tie and put on his jacket to cover his weapon. He glanced at Bolan on the way out, fixing him in his memory, then went out into the gallery.

Patricio gestured at the chair in front of his desk, then dropped into the leather armchair behind it. He wheeled it forward, eager to get on with the mysterious business Bolan had brought to him.

"In here, Mr. Blasco, we can talk freely and completely," Patricio said. He leaned on the desk and cradled his chin above the clasped steeple of his hand. "You apparently possess some knowledge—or think you do—about some of my activities. That can be dangerous knowledge."

"In the wrong hands, yes," Bolan agreed.

"But yours are the right hands," Patricio said.

Bolan shrugged. "That's what I'm saying."

"And that may be true," the Colombian said. "But I have no way of knowing. In fact, Mr. Blasco, other than your little exhibition out there and the admirable way you handle yourself in a safe area like my gallery, I don't know a thing about you."

Now it was Bolan's turn to lean forward. They stared at each other, hard-faced men who could be enemies or allies. "The only thing you really have to know about me," the Executioner said, "is that I'm an enemy of Victor Sienna."

The mention of Sienna's name brought a look of disgust to Patricio's face. It also brought a lot of interest.

"The Garrison is a good thing," Bolan continued, using the most common name that Sienna's crew was known by, "but Sienna has outlived his usefulness."

"You're a friend of his?" Patricio asked.

"Never a friend. My people have used his services. But lately Sienna has lost sight of his place in the scheme of things. He's either creating trouble for people or letting things get out of control."

Patricio unclasped his hands and drummed his fingers on the table as he let Bolan's words sink in. Then he leaned back in his chair, appearing at ease for the first time since he'd encountered Bolan. "When you say he creates trouble, do you mean he was actually behind the ambush we experienced at that desolate train station?"

"We're not sure of that," Bolan said. "All we know is that he lost his edge. Maybe his ability. These days he's not so much a soldier as he is a sellout. He's involved in too many fields aside from the one he used to excel at. He's undependable, unpredictable, and that makes him just as dangerous as if he's at war with us."

"Is he?"

Bolan shook his head. "He's not aware of it yet. But very soon we're going to war with him—not the Garrison. We want that enterprise to continue. In these times we need to have such a force available. We just want it to continue with someone else leading it."

"Someone like you?" Patricio suggested.

"That's always a possibility," Bolan said. "If my people want me to."

"Who exactly are your people?" Patricio asked.

"The ones who wish to inaugurate change," Bolan said. "Sienna is on his way out. If not voluntarily, we'll give him a push."

"He'll never go voluntarily."

Bolan smiled. "We're counting on that."

"That is welcome news," Patricio said. "But it surprises me that such news comes from an unknown quarter. Surely if you are of sufficient stature to move against Sienna, I would have heard of you."

"I make it a point not to be heard about until the right time or the right person comes along."

"That I can understand," Patricio replied. The reason he'd prospered so long in his businesses was the different faces he presented to the parties he dealt with. To some he was a world-class art dealer. To others he was a preeminent supplier of cocaine. Sometimes the two overlapped, but to most of his clients he kept his businesses separate. Jacob Patricio was living proof that it was possible to keep the real business secret from the world at large.

Patricio's gaze fell to the leather case Bolan had at his side, which was the real purpose of their meeting and the ticket into his inner office.

"Oh, yes," Bolan said, as if the case had slipped his mind. He gently slid the case onto Patricio's desk.

The Colombian's face softened as Bolan started to unzip the case, giving the cartel leader a glimpse of the contents. Christmas had come early for him.

Bolan lifted the lid all the way back so that it rested on the desktop and displayed the slip-cased green stacks of fifties and twenties.

"What's this for?" Patricio asked.

"The upstate deal that went sour," Bolan explained. "Half of the money for the deal came from my people."

Patricio nodded. It wasn't unusual for different Families to bankroll a share of the deal. By pooling their funds they limited their own risks but still had a chance to make a great profit. "The money was recovered by your people?" Patricio said.

Bolan sensed the man's sudden wariness and knew that the Colombian was running various scenarios through his mind. Patricio had to be wondering if the Family that Bolan supposedly worked for was behind the ambush that took down members of Sienna's Garrison—the same ambush that wiped out several of Patricio's own people.

"Not my people, no," Bolan assured him. "Those few soldiers of Victor Sienna who made it out alive also had the presence of mind to bring out the money. They returned our investment."

"What about the powder?" Patricio asked. "Did they take that with them?"

Bolan shook his head. "As far as we know, the powder melted away with the other kind of snow. It's gone. Who knows how? The Garrison was responsible for the money. Your people were responsible for the coke." The Executioner was careful not to speak in an accusing tone, just giving the Colombian his matter-of-fact interpretation.

"We didn't expect a war up there," Patricio said. "We were lucky to get out alive. None of my people were thinking of the powder at the time. And now you say you don't know for sure what happened to it."

"Maybe the ambushers took it," Bolan said. "Or maybe it was confiscated by the first cops on the scene and they forgot to mention it to the reporters. Or maybe some of your people salvaged it, and, uh, didn't get around to mentioning it yet?"

Now Patricio shook his head. "Too many good men died in that field that day," he said. He seemed genuinely stricken at the thought of the families in his clan who had lost their sons. "The only ones who survived came out with me. They had nothing with them but the weapons needed to fight their way out."

"Sienna did no one any good that day," Bolan said. "Except the undertakers."

The look of sorrow on Patricio's face was quickly replaced by anger and suspicion. "Tell me something," the South American said. "Is it possible that these same levelheaded men who managed to take the money with them also took the powder?"

Bolan acted as if the thought was entirely new to him. "That's beyond my information. All I know is what the Garrison told my people."

"I, too, spoke with Sienna. His answers gave me no satisfaction."

"That's a common thing these days," the Executioner said as he slid the case of currency toward Patricio. Now that he'd sown enough suspicion with the Colombian dealer, it was time to move in for the kill.

Patricio didn't refuse the leather case nor did he accept it right away. Instead, after a few moments of deliberation he gently pulled the case to the side of his desk, then tapped his fingers on one of the currency stacks. "What is this for?"

"You lost men up there," Bolan said, "and a substantial amount of product through no fault of your own."

"The fault wasn't yours, either," Patricio said. "Nor is the debt. If anything, the make-good money should come from Sienna."

"It should," Bolan agreed, "but Sienna doesn't see it that way. He's throwing the blame on your people."

Patricio's face reddened. Not only had he been ambushed, but now his reputation was being slandered. He looked at the case. "The money is meaningless."

"In the larger scheme of things, yes," Bolan agreed. "But it's not just the money, it's the message that goes with it. You suffered losses on a deal my people were involved in. This is half the money meant for the exchange. If we give it to you, it means that you're only out half of the product. We both assume the same loss."

"And what do you want in return for your generosity?" Patricio asked.

"Goodwill. So we can do some more business in the future." He paused and added, "And perhaps in the meantime you might be able to help us in some small way."

"How small?"

"Nothing really," the soldier said. "Just spread the word to your associates about what happened. Let them know Sienna gave you no satisfaction—but other people made it good."

Patricio nodded. "And you wish me to mention who made it good?"

"Don't mention any names," Bolan said. "For now we want him to think the whole world's against him."

"And are they?"

"They will be soon enough."

"And then?"

The Executioner rose. "Then it won't be an issue if someone takes Sienna out."

"If?" the dealer asked.

"When."

"You have my blessing," Patricio said as he zipped up the leather case and set it behind his desk. "And my full cooperation. Consider us partners."

As Bolan shook the man's hand, he noticed that Patricio could barely conceal the pleasure he felt at the deal they'd struck. From the Colombian's point of view he had nothing to lose and everything to gain. Here was Sienna's competitor who'd come to him out of the blue, paying tribute and promising to remove Patricio's enemy for him.

In return all Patricio had to do was say a few words to the right people about his misfortune at the hands of Victor Sienna, words he probably would have said on his own.

Bolan felt the same way about the deal but hid his pleasure behind a mask of indifference as Patricio escorted him to the door like an old friend.

The negotiation had gone better than Bolan had expected. The art and cocaine dealer had just become another weapon to throw into the fray.

And sooner or later, Bolan thought, their partnership would be very limited. When Sienna found out that some of his money for the station house deal ended up in the hands of Jacob Patricio, the Colombian could become a permanently silent partner.

9

Most of the Garrison soldiers who'd been unlucky enough to see Bolan up close were currently stationed six feet underground, but the Executioner took precautions on this latest recon just the same. He wore a pair of nonprescription glasses, a black felt hat with a turned-down brim that shadowed his eyes and a staid business suit.

There was always the chance that a few of the survivors who'd seen the Executioner face-to-face were shadowing Rupert Sawyer at the same time Bolan and Carvaggio were. But the soldiers would be looking for a man in a leather jacket, knit cap and a handful of high-caliber weaponry. Not a businessman with an attaché case.

Bolan doubted the Garrison was tailing the producer this day. Victor Sienna had more pressing things on his mind. Now that his empire was under siege, the underworld chieftain was probably circling the wagons and calming the troops.

But there was no guarantee that scouts weren't there somewhere, checking out Sawyer. According to Brognola's intel, a few underworld types occasionally kept tabs on the *Case Closed* producer in case Sienna felt it was time to reach out for him.

That time was approaching fast.

"Let me out here," Bolan said, satisfied that the area was clear.

Carvaggio wheeled the Explorer to the curb and let Bolan out about a half block behind the producer.

Sawyer was walking down West 57th Street like a man without a care in the world. The producer was laden with his usual assortment of video gear and recorders, but on him they were practically a uniform. They gave him the illusion of safety, a shield against the world that proclaimed him an observer not a participant.

There was another reason the producer had a carefree attitude. He was playing the covert operative game and had convinced himself that no one could possibly know where he was.

Sawyer had taken a circuitous route from his production studio and actually managed to slip out of their sight every now and then. The producer had ducked in and out of shops, going in one door and out another. He'd also suddenly crossed streets at stoplights only to cross back in the middle of the block. They were beginner's tricks but effective just the same.

It was a good sign, Bolan thought. It meant that Rupert Sawyer was taking things seriously and just might have been able to shake any of Sienna's people who were following him.

Bolan had been around Mob operations long enough to know how they worked. A Mob surveillance team would troll about for their target. If they lost him one day, fine, they'd pick him up another day. The underworld crews were master opportunists. They knew that sooner or later the right time would come along and they'd get their man.

But even if Sawyer had become an expert at evading shadows, this day it still wouldn't have worked on the Executioner and Carvaggio. They already knew Sawyer's ultimate destination.

Walking quickly through the afternoon crowd, Bolan caught up with Sawyer just as the producer reached an apartment building.

"Sawyer," Bolan called out when he was a few steps behind him.

The silver-haired producer wheeled, a look of total shock

on his face. The astonishment of discovery turned to fear, as if he were expecting a Garrison soldier to draw on him. And then the fear turned to confusion.

Sawyer didn't recognize Bolan. Not with the business suit on, not with the attaché case.

"Yes?" he finally stammered. "Who are you?"

Bolan tipped his hat back enough for him to see his face.

"Oh my God," Sawyer said.

"No, just me. Striker."

"Yes, of course, I remember our...our arrangement. Our collaboration in the...investigative piece...but, uh, I'm afraid it's not possible for me to talk right now."

Bolan smiled. "Not only is it possible, it's inevitable. We have to talk, Rupert. Now."

"What about?"

"About you staying alive," Bolan said. "You interested?"

"Of course. Where should we talk?"

"Walk with me. We'll find a place."

As Sawyer fell in beside him, Bolan headed for the corner. His peripheral vision caught sight of the Ford Explorer slowly trailing behind them. Carvaggio would be nearby in case Sawyer and Bolan became targets.

Less than a block away Bolan found the right kind of place. It was a two-story restaurant with a glass-enclosed terrace that looked down on the street below. The glass was tinted just dark enough to offer privacy for those inside without ruining the view.

The corner table that Bolan selected on the second floor had a view of the street, so he could see anyone who came through the main entrance. At the same time it was far enough away from the street so Bolan wouldn't be surprised if anyone stormed the gate.

"Now what?" Sawyer asked.

"Now you order," Bolan said, nodding toward the menu the waiter had placed in front of them.

"I'm not hungry," the man replied, almost whining.

"That's not the point," Bolan said. "This is supposed to

look normal, like we're having a meal here, not planning a survival strategy.''

Sawyer shook his head. "You're too much. What happens if I don't want to order anything? You gonna pull a gun on me? How normal will that look?''

"Suit yourself," Bolan said. "I just thought you'd want things to look nice and relaxed when Ambrosia Lyons joins us.''

"What?'' The producer did a double take, then slowly sat back in his chair, staring wide-eyed at the Executioner.

"You know," Bolan said. "Ambrosia. Victor Sienna's old flame. Ex-Mob mistress who came to you awhile back? The one you're doing a story about that you didn't mention to me.''

"Oh," he said. "That Ambrosia.''

"That's the one," Bolan said. "Listen, Rupert, you're backsliding on me here. For a while I thought you were playing along with us. Now I see you're just playing along with this ex-actress.''

"I'm not," Sawyer protested. "She's a source.''

"More like a sorceress," Bolan said. "From what I hear, she's got you under a spell or something—the amount of time you spend with her. But who knows, maybe you really do plan on doing a story with her.''

"Sure I do," he insisted. "It's a special project.''

"Yeah," Bolan said. "Special project that might get terminated. You're putting her in danger.''

"I've been real careful—''

"Not careful enough," the Executioner said. "She has a right to know what you're getting her into. So after we talk things over, you'll make a call and tell her you've got a surprise for her. She can join us for dessert and we'll all work things out together.''

Sawyer looked hesitant. "Thanks for the invite," he said, "but I don't think so—''

"It's not an invite," Bolan said firmly.

"But it's too hard getting us together on such short notice. She lives pretty far from here—"

"Yeah," Bolan said. "At least a block away."

"What are you talking about?"

"Ambrosia lives at the apartment building you were about to go into when I caught up with you."

Rather than deny it, Sawyer simply shook his head in amazement. "How do you know all this?" he asked.

"It's our business to know. You know film and TV, we know people. What makes them tick. What they're likely to do under given circumstances. But most of all, Rupert, we know how to find people and how to catch them."

"What are you getting at?" Sawyer asked.

"The truth, Rupert. If we can find you and Ambrosia, other people can too. That will be extremely unpleasant for her. And for you."

"But that won't happen," Sawyer protested.

"Why not?"

"It's too risky for them," the producer said, dismissing the notion. "I'm in the media!" He spoke about it as if it were a sacred calling. "The Mob knows that if something happened to me, other broadcasters would step in and do an even bigger investigation. It just doesn't make sense for Sienna. He'll fear reprisal from my peers."

Bolan gave him a look. Several suggestions about the caliber of Rupert Sawyer's peers came to mind, but he kept them to himself. Sawyer needed handling, not goading. "These guys fear no one and nothing," the soldier said. "The idea that they're afraid of journalists has gotten a bit too much currency in the past few years."

The producer's cherished beliefs were beginning to weaken, but like a cultist indoctrinated for years, Sawyer couldn't let go of the myth just yet. It was all that sustained him and the crusading reporter act he'd played all these years.

"The truth is, reporters get whacked all the time," Bolan said. "Mob hits, spook interventions, whatever you want to call it, it happens. And it's not just something that occurs in third-world countries, Rupert. If reporters are perceived as real trouble, they're the first to go. They may be good at digging out facts, but they're also good at digging their own graves."

Sawyer needed no more convincing. He followed Bolan's cue and ordered a light meal from the menu. And then he listened like a chastened man as the Executioner filled him in on what was happening with Victor Sienna and what was going to happen to some of his enemies.

The Garrison chief was at the end of his rope, tired of getting hit without being able to strike back. That meant he'd go after whatever targets presented themselves. It was a long list: the Colombians, suspected traitors within the Garrison, any allies of Nick Carvaggio, which, at least in Sienna's view of things, included Rupert Sawyer.

Anyone who could possibly bring down heat on Sienna. Like Ambrosia Lyons.

"But those are just possibilities," Sawyer said.

"They're probabilities," Bolan corrected him. "And the odds of them occurring are going to skyrocket pretty soon." He and Carvaggio were gearing up for another move against Sienna that could push him over the edge. Instead of sitting back, he would have to go on the warpath.

Without getting into specifics, the Executioner hinted that Victor Sienna would soon become a very angry man. Along with the military assault led by Bolan and Carvaggio, there was going to be a media blitz against the Garrison.

Highly placed unnamed sources in the Justice Department and intelligence community were going to flood the media with inside information on Victor Sienna. There would be enough hard information to paint a picture of him as a threat to the public, and more importantly, to the underworld itself. Sienna would probably figure that Sawyer and Lyons might be the source for that information.

"It could get very dangerous for you both," Bolan said.

"Sounds like this could be dangerous for you, too."

"It always is," Bolan said. "But that's expected and I

know how to deal with it. But I don't think you do, Rupert. Neither does Ambrosia.''

''What do you want us to do about it? You said they could find us if they want to. We can't hide from them.''

''You can be hidden—both of you—until this whole thing is over and Sienna's out of the way. Then you get the inside story. You can keep it to yourself or use it to put yourself all over the map, Rupert. It will be big and it will be all yours.''

Rupert was nodding, entranced at the vision of the future which not only included Ambrosia but an Emmy or two.

''Where do we hide out?''

''We've got hotel rooms, apartments, safehouses all over the city,'' Bolan said. ''And we have access to more.''

''Who's we?''

''You know the type,'' Bolan answered. ''Unnamed sources. Top government officials. Intelligence insiders.''

''Is there protection with this?''

''Around the clock,'' the soldier said. ''You and Ambrosia will be looked after every minute of the day. There will also be a discreet watch placed on the staff at your production studio.''

''This is pretty heavy stuff,'' Sawyer said. ''Lot of money and manpower involved. What are we supposed to do for it?''

''Maybe fashion a few stories that'll help us maneuver Sienna where we want him. Maybe not. It might not come to that.''

''That's it?'' Sawyer asked. ''Just cooperate?''

''There is something else.''

''There always is,'' Sawyer replied. ''What do you need?''

''Do you have a summer home?'' Bolan asked. ''A country retreat somewhere? Isolated place you go to relax?''

The question took the producer by surprise, but he answered quickly. ''Matter of fact, I do. It's in Connecticut.''

''Are you attached to it?''

''Of course I am,'' Sawyer said. ''Why do you ask?''

"It might need considerable repairs at the end of this thing."

Sawyer looked intrigued. "There's always insurance, if something happens to it. But what do you need my place for if you've got these other places around the country?"

"It's like this," Bolan said. "Sienna will come after you sooner or later. It's only a matter of time—and a matter of prodding. We can make sure he finds out about this summer place of yours. He'll be suspicious, expecting a trap, so he'll check it out to see if it's really been yours for a while."

"Then what?"

"And then he'll come after you there."

Sawyer blanched.

"You won't be there," Bolan said. "We will."

The Executioner saw the wheels turning. It was the best of both worlds for the producer. Not only would he be with Ambrosia, but he would also be covering a story from the inside. In fact he'd be part of the story. "I don't know, Striker. It's a big decision to make."

"It's already made," Bolan said. "You either go along with it or you go it alone."

The producer raised his hands in appeasement. "I'm not saying I'm refusing. Just that it's a big decision. And I'll have to talk to Ambrosia and convince her to go along."

"I'll talk to her," he said. "The deal starts now. Go call her and ask her to come down for coffee, dessert. And a surprise."

"You're one hell of a surprise, all right," Sawyer said. "Every time I think I've got you figured out, I find out you're a couple of moves ahead of me."

"Like I said," Bolan replied. "I'm in the people business." Saving some of them, saving the world from the others. "I have to know what they're going to do before they do. Now call Ambrosia."

Sawyer made the call.

About fifteen minutes later a very low-key Ambrosia Lyons joined them at the table. She, too, was into the under-

cover game. Instead of the flamboyant beauty Victor Sienna
had known, she had transformed herself into a demure creature. Still beautiful, but without the glitz. Her long hair was
pulled back into a ponytail. She wore a dress that compli-
mented her abundant physique but didn't make a display of
it. But her eyes were still striking. Green and catlike.

Sawyer made the introductions and after a moment of
small talk, Lyons's green eyes bored down on Bolan. He saw
why first Sienna and then the producer had fallen under her
spell.

"I'm not completely clear on this, Mr. Striker," she said.
"I mean, of course Rupert's told me that you're working with
him on a project. But what are you? A producer? Director?"

"Actually, Miss Lyons," Bolan said, "I'm more like a
subject."

"Oh really," she said. She stiffened slightly and glanced
at the producer, wondering if he'd brought yet another mobster into her life.

"It's not what you're thinking," Bolan said. "I'm not on
the same side as Sienna or any of the other Families. I'm
against him. Very much against him."

"I see," Lyons said. "At least I think I do. I mean, I
believe you. But I don't see what you're doing here." She
turned toward the producer. "Rupert? Care to fill me in on
what's going on?"

Sawyer leaned forward. "Yeah. Uh, he's here to, uh, help
us out. Things are going to get dangerous, uh, with the story
we're doing and the kind of people we're covering. They
might get angry…real angry—"

Bolan raised his hand to cut off Sawyer's roundabout ex-
planation of how the producer had placed both of their lives
in jeopardy. "The reason I'm here, Miss Lyons, is to save
your life."

10

Donovan Schole, a Treasury agent who'd been recently attached to a Justice Department task force, was stunned by the message from Washington, D.C., that reached him at two in the afternoon.

The call came in on the secure transceiver built into the dashboard of his surveillance vehicle, a five-year-old pale green delivery van. It was parked halfway down the street, across from the Lower East Side restaurant he'd been watching for the past three days.

The call was from Frank Moore, a legendary field operative who used to work side by side with Schole in the currency investigation unit of the Treasury Department's Special Operations Division, but now rode a desk full-time. Moore told him to stand by for orders to pull out.

That didn't make a whole lot of sense to Schole, nor did it make him very happy. Not after the intense watch they'd conducted or the intelligence they'd gathered. Their targets were getting ready to move, and it was going to be an incredible score.

It was exactly the kind of operation they were supposed to shut down. *And they were getting ready to call it off!*

Incredible, he thought. But not really. Nothing surprised him these days.

He understood the reasoning for the standby call. The team leader wanted to make sure all units were within reach before giving the final order to pull out. That way no one would be left behind, a lone gun against the Mob.

But three days of intelligence gathering was a lot to throw away, Schole thought. For three, sixteen-hour days he'd alternately sweated or froze his ass off in two different surveillance rigs.

Schole knew he'd have a cold when this was over. He'd also have a lingering suspicion that he and the other undercover operatives could have done more if only they'd been allowed to see it through.

The Fed was aware of at least three other government teams who were monitoring the traffic around this restaurant. Like his team, they were studying the customers throughout the day. They listened to the tapped phones and deciphered the wise-guy code words that were never that hard to figure out.

A good number of the Garrison calls had been made to upstate phone numbers. Evidently the operation was going to take place there. Schole didn't know the exact location or the time frame. He just knew that something was going down soon between the Garrison associates and another clandestine group the Treasury Department was extremely interested in.

So why would they walk away from it at this point? Schole's unit was watching Sienna's crew. Other units kept tabs on a shadowy network of former Syrian and Iranian intelligence officers who were operating in the New York City area. There was no official name for them yet, but informally the Treasury Department called the collection of former Mideast spooks the "green team."

The green team ex-operatives still had links with their respective intelligence services. But they were operating in deep cover, so there could be no official flare-up if they were caught. They also had substantial links with the Mob Families.

It was a symbiotic relationship. And the host body for both the Garrison and the Mideast crew was the restaurant he'd been watching. Over the past couple of days representatives from both groups had developed appetites for the restaurant's Mediterranean fare.

A gathering of the clans. It wasn't hard to figure out how it came about. The Garrison was affiliated with Mafia Families in the heroin trade. In turn the Families got their product from harvesters in the Bekaa Valley and other Mideast sites known for the quality of their narcocrops and the protection the traffickers received from their governments.

The drug trade had spawned several complementary enterprises like money laundering and gunrunning. It also set in motion a criminal and terrorist bazaar that never stopped growing or changing. And now that underworld alliance was evolving into a loosely knit network that posed an even greater danger to the United States.

Counterfeit currency was flooding the U.S. in unheard-of numbers and quality. And it wasn't the detectable fakes of old. This currency was just like government-made U.S. dollars—but it wasn't being made by the American government.

Almost perfect fifty- and one-hundred-dollar bills were being churned out in clandestine Mideast mints. The high quality greenbacks were printed on expensive machines and paper, embedded with all of the high-tech codes and imprints that were formerly impossible to reproduce.

The latest crop of phony bills, called "superdollars" by the Treasury spooks, duplicated whatever safeguards the Bureau of Engraving had developed—multicolored threads with microscopic words printed on them, holograms, watermarks. Whatever they came up with, the counterfeiters analyzed and adopted with record speed, proving that it wasn't just a rogue operation but a government-sponsored operation.

The Treasury Department had traced the emergence of the bills to the former intelligence operatives from Iran and Syria but had no clear-cut proof of either government's direct involvement. One problem facing the Treasury Department was that it didn't have enough agents stationed overseas. Another was that even if there were more agents, there was little they could do until the phony money reached the shores. Hostile governments weren't about to welcome them with open arms.

Not only was the counterfeit currency used to fund terrorist and underworld operations, but it was also a weapon aimed directly at the United States. If enough of the counterfeit currency made it into circulation, it could destabilize the dollar.

The duplication scheme was frightening enough. What Schole had picked up from his briefings was even more terrifying. New York was the number-one entry point for the bogus money that the green team smuggled in through diplomatic collaborators. And the Garrison was one of the major recipients. In exchange for the counterfeit, they provided sophisticated weaponry from one of their armories.

Sienna's crew had its own arms caches in the city, but there was also a more clandestine depot upstate where they stored weapons stolen from military bases and National Guard armories. Other weapons were bought at fire-sale prices from South American arms merchants who were re-selling the arms the U.S. flooded the continent with during the Contra hysteria days.

The Garrison armory was another link in the terror chain, Schole thought, but as the second call from Washington came in, he knew he wasn't going to be on the team that actually broke that chain.

He picked up the receiver and listened to the command from his superior that he didn't want to hear.

Frank Moore told him it was time to leave the area. Further surveillance was no longer needed. The operation was over.

"But I don't understand, Frank," Schole said. "I mean, how can you tell us to move out now? We've got these guys right in our sights. Something's going to happen soon. They're meeting with the currency brokers. It's not a social function."

"The order stands," Moore said. "You are to withdraw immediately."

"How high's this order?"

"How high do you want it?"

"Give me a name."

"No names. How about titles?"

"Give me what you can."

"Okay," Moore said. "Here it is. The guy behind this handles intradepartmental task forces. Army. Justice. Agency. Our field teams. Whatever he wants he gets. Word is that if he has to, he can get the President to back him up. You want to get through the White House and argue with him?"

"No, sir."

"Wise choice," Moore said. "Now vacate the area, then turn in your report."

"Why bother with that?" Schole asked.

Moore's voice took on a harder edge. They were long-term friends, but even friendship had its limit. "Intelligence will be collected as usual," Moore ordered. "And it will be acted upon. Your part is done. Understood?"

"Understood."

"Then I'll see you when you get back," Moore said.

"Right." Schole signed off, then turned the defroster up a notch to melt the sheet of ice that was starting to creep up across the windshield.

The White House, he thought. At least that part was re-assuring. It meant that the green team and the Garrison were ultra high-priority targets. So high that from here on in, Schole was out of the loop. It was time to forget what he knew about the case.

It wasn't the first time this sort of thing happened. He'd been on similar missions before, psyching himself up to close in on a target when for one reason or another he was called off the case. This was just the first time he'd been called off when he was so close to the kill.

But now a full-scale covert operation was underway with-out him. As he drove the van into traffic, he couldn't help wondering who'd carry it out. And if he should envy him or pity him.

Whoever was doing it, was going to war.

FROM THE PACKED-SNOW bunker on the perimeter of the Gar-rison's upstate armory, the Executioner scanned the freshly plowed entrance leading up to the gates of the fenced-in warehouse complex. Razor-wire spirals covered the full length of the fence.

Snowbanks lined the furrowed path, which was wide enough to fit only two vehicles.

Just inside the gates stood a wooden guardhouse with small boxlike windows looking out from all four walls. A guard peered out into the night from within the small warm sanctuary, waiting for their expected guests to arrive.

From Bolan's last communication with Brognola, he knew that a green-team caravan was en route from Manhattan—three late-model vans, chromed up and crammed with fake currency.

They were due anytime now. It was only about a two-hour ride to the Catskill region, where the Garrison maintained its armory in an isolated rural industrial park. At one time the warehouse complex had been a thriving operation, drawing in workers from the nearby hamlets and villages. But now it looked almost abandoned.

A couple of trailers and cabs were frozen in place near one of the warehouse loading platforms. The bays still held inventories of outdated appliances and electronic goods, enough to maintain its cover as a genuine storage depot.

But a closer look at the place revealed that its real business wasn't warehousing.

A couple of office buildings were situated close to the back gates that ran parallel to the ice-blocked Hudson River below. Even the back fences by the river were covered with razor wire.

It was a fortress, plain and simple. Sienna's crew was taking no chances this time around. It was happening on the Garrison's territory, and it was going to be totally in its control. No uninvited guests could spoil the deal.

Bolan had no intention of going into the complex. That was suicide. He and Carvaggio were there to make sure no one got out.

They'd each dug bunkers out of snowdrifts in the woods that flanked the entrance road to the warehouse. They were once again covered head to toe in white shell clothing to keep their silhouettes practically invisible.

They'd carried enough weaponry into the woods to see them through the night. Their high-speed escape machines waited nearby in case the siege backfired on them.

They'd reconned the complex from all angles while preparing their strike plan. Now all they had to do was wait for their targets to seal themselves in.

The Garrison team was already intact, housed in one of the long flat buildings inside the complex where the gunners kept their crated weapons. From the observations Bolan and Carvaggio had made, the crew inside the gates was comprised strictly of soldiers. That confirmed the intel that Brognola had forwarded to him. The usual caretaker who looked after the place had been sent away a couple of days earlier. Since then familiar faces had been arriving at the armory.

Now there were about fifteen soldiers gathered inside. Enough to make the exchange with the green team and provide security. Except for a couple of hardmen who stepped out into the cold to patrol the inside perimeter, most of Sienna's crew stayed out of sight.

The subzero wind was keeping them inside. During those times when the wind wasn't shrieking through the woods and across the icy plain, the temperature wasn't hard to handle at all. But when it came up it could be murder. Without face masks and insulated mats to lay on, it would be impossible for Bolan and Carvaggio to tough it out this long. But the bunkers were sealed off, except for observation slots carved out of the snow wall.

This night the danger wouldn't come from the wind. It would come from the combined firepower of the Garrison and the green-team gunners.

Bolan lowered his thermal imaging scope and dropped back into the white cocoon and waited.

Another half hour passed before he heard the sound of an engine. Then headlights bounced up and down in the night.

When the van rolled up to the gates, the guardhouse soldier stepped out of his shack. While he started to unchain and unlock the gates, a four-man team of Garrison soldiers appeared from the shadows of one of the warehouses.

As soon as the gates opened, the soldiers stepped outside and looked over the occupants of the van before waving it through. The vehicle rolled inside the complex, the gates were closed and chained, then the entire process was repeated ten minutes later when the second and third vans arrived.

The vehicles drove up to the office buildings, and the traders quickly filed out.

Inside the vans was counterfeit currency, so well made that in some cases it sold for almost fifty percent of its face value. But according to Brognola's intel, the Garrison was paying twenty percent face value plus a lot of weaponry the green team was interested in—rocket launchers, smart mines, Special Forces handguns and suppressors.

Whatever the Garrison could get its hands on, it would sell. The fact that the weapons would probably be used against the U.S. didn't bother the soldiers, nor did the fact that the fake currency Sienna would start spreading around could ultimately destabilize the dollar.

It was just business. Just money.

But enough to bring the wrath of the U.S. government down upon Sienna in the form of Mack Bolan.

The Executioner waited for two full minutes after the gates were closed—the agreed upon time that he and Carvaggio had established earlier—before he emerged from the bunker with the tools of war strapped to him like talismans.

Like a nocturnal creature coming out of hibernation, he slowly trod through the snow, feeling the circulation returning in the leg and arm muscles that had stayed dormant for so long.

Carvaggio moved in from his position on the other side of the road. Even though Bolan knew where he was, it took a few seconds for him to decipher the white-clad shape from the snowy backdrop.

It was slow going at first. There was a bit of crust on the snow, and the last thing they needed was for the guardhouse soldier to hear the crunch of their footsteps.

Soon it wouldn't matter what he heard, Bolan thought, as he raised the silenced Colt Model 635 submachine gun before him and walked quietly through the snow.

The Executioner moved at an angle that kept him out of the direct line of sight of the guardhouse window. He could hear a radio playing inside, as well as the soft footfalls of Carvaggio off to the right. The man was laden with explosive packages that would be placed at the doorstep of the warehouse. There were also the hushed voices of a two-man patrol coming from the left. They were still far enough away so they wouldn't interfere with Bolan's approach.

He stepped close to the fence, pausing as he saw the shadow of the man moving about in the guardhouse below an overhead caged lightbulb.

He moved to his right until he was almost in front of the window.

The man was looking out the window, not toward Bolan, but at the road, as if he were expecting an attacker to announce himself. At the last second the soldier glanced Bolan's way, perhaps acting on instinct and realizing the enemy was at the gate.

The Executioner eased the barrel of the silenced Colt through the wire fence and triggered a 3-round burst.

The 9 mm rounds crashed through the small glass window and into the man's temple, removing a considerable amount of bone as the triburst dropped him.

He thudded against a wall and vanished from sight.

Carvaggio moved closer to the gate, crouching on the ground while he unloaded his white canvas kit of plastic explosives and went to work setting the charges.

The ex-Garrison hit man concentrated on the task at hand but couldn't help hearing the voices from the two-man patrol who'd been alerted by the execution of the man in the gatehouse.

"Got them?" he called out to Bolan.

"Any second now," the soldier said. "Stay put and stay low."

The Executioner crept slowly along the fence, watching for the arrival of the Garrison patrol. He, too, could hear them but until now they'd stayed out of sight.

So far the two soldiers couldn't be sure of what happened. They'd heard the glass breaking and the cough of the suppressed 9 mm rounds. But then came silence. It was impossible for them to know if their man had been taken out in an attack or if he'd done the firing and was lying low and waiting to engage the attacker.

And if it was an attack, why had it stopped?

One of the patrollers stepped into view. The other man emerged from the shadows about ten feet behind him. They were going the silent route, figuring that in a few more seconds they'd get the drop on whoever was in control of the gatehouse.

Instead, they just got dropped.

Bolan slowly rose to his full height and rested the barrel of the Colt submachine gun on a V-shaped crook in the wire fence, using it to balance his weapon.

It took only an instant before his eyes adjusted and he had the first man in the sight of the Model 635. It was a continuous motion, as normal and instinctive to Bolan as breathing. Balance, sight, shoot.

The burst caught the first man in the chest and knocked him back into the second who spent a furious half second trying to escape the deadweight before flinging him down and shouting, "Get back. Get away from me." As the first man's dead body dropped into the snow, Bolan triggered another burst into the one who was still standing.

The second gunner managed to get off one shot before he died. Staggering on his feet without enough strength left to hold the gun upright, he squeezed the trigger by reflex. His long-barreled automatic fired straight into the ground, scorching the snow.

The sound of the heavy-caliber slug echoed across the compound, waking everyone inside.

A half dozen Garrison gunmen ran out onto the dock from one of the warehouses—a half dozen men Bolan hadn't counted on. Somehow he and Carvaggio had missed them.

Perhaps the squad had been camped out in the darkened warehouse as a reserve unit to throw against the green team in case things got out of hand. Or maybe they'd been staged there as a counterstrike team to keep Sienna's crew from being taken by surprise one more time.

For whatever reason they'd been waiting there, they wasted no time in springing into action.

"The gate!" shouted one of the men from the squad. "Take the gate." But it was an unnecessary command. All six men had already jumped to the ground, a rifle team of like mind, advancing toward the gate with automatic rifles and submachine guns paving the way.

Streams of autofire ripped through the darkness, spreading in a wide and blazing arc. Six men raced across the compound, firing full-auto bursts, filling the air with lead.

The heavy metal volleys scythed across the gatehouse and the fence, splintering wood and ricocheting off metal links.

It was a one-sided firefight.

No return fire came from the white fields outside of the fence. The only source of gunfire was Sienna's crew, spitting clip after clip into the night.

The fusillade would have been deadly if their targets had still been near the gate. But Carvaggio and Bolan had withdrawn, angling away from the barrage of the counterattack.

Carvaggio had set his charges in place. His work was done.

Now all they had to do was wait for the team to reach the gate.

It would have been suicidal to return fire. A few flashes from their automatic weapons would give away their positions to the enemy. Bolan and Carvaggio could have taken a few of the soldiers, but if they were pinned down in an open battle and had to trade shots with the enemy, sooner or later reinforcements would arrive. Then they'd come under fire from the entire Garrison.

This way they only had to deal with the six men who were now pounding the air with unreturned fire.

There was an undeniable bravery in the counterattack of the Garrison soldiers. Like shock troops, they just kept advancing toward the gate, reloading fresh magazines on the move, drawing pistols and revolvers if their subguns jammed or clicked empty.

The only thing on their mind was obliterating anyone who stood outside the gate.

As the rifle team neared the gatehouse, the gunners spread out along the fence, peering into the darkness. During the temporary lull in the firing, two of the soldiers ran up to the gate at full speed and started tugging on the lock and chains.

A third man dashed into the guardhouse, stepping over the body on the floor to pull down a key ring that was hanging on a nail. "They got Leonard, too," he said when he came back out and tossed the keys to one of the men at the gate.

The three remaining soldiers weren't about to mourn the dead. Not while the killers were on the loose.

The largest of the three men had a submachine gun slung over his shoulder and an over-under shotgun cradled in his hands. It was an expensive hunting shotgun with a gleaming finish that looked like it was the man's pride and joy.

He was in a hurry to use it but couldn't see any targets. "Come on, move it," he shouted to the men who were fumbling with the lock and key. "Before they get away from us."

As soon as the lock clicked open and the chains snaked free, both men pushed on the gates.

The gates opened up—so did the earth beneath them.

Volcanic masses of snow, ice, mud and metal erupted from the ground. The explosive charge cast both men in a fiery halo that swept over them in an instant, nearly incinerating them before they had a chance to cry out.

The shock wave rolled inward and knocked the other men off of their feet. Two of them stayed down, too dazed and wounded to move. A third man raced back to the complex and shouted for help.

The man with the shotgun stood in the middle of the ex- ploded gate and fired into smoke-filled nothingness.

He triggered both barrels before the second explosive charge mowed him down in a sea of flame. One of the shat- tered and twisted gates flew into the air and landed on his face and chest, branding his dead body with the white-hot fencing.

Heavily armed men poured out of the office buildings at the back of the compound, running around like hornets in search of the invaders who'd stormed their kingdom.

But the invaders were nowhere to be seen—just plenty of dust, smoke and a swirl of snow in the air. Flames licked at the shattered boards of the gatehouse.

There was no one moving out there, adding to the eerie feeling that fell over the armed men. They'd been more than willing to fight, but the enemy had withdrawn.

First they'd heard the sounds of the firefight and the gates had been breached by explosive charges. And now a stillness settled over the compound as the gunrunners and counterfeit brokers milled about in the freezing wind.

Soldiers from both factions looked at their respective lead- ers, waiting for orders. Death was just a second away for the soldiers on each side if they decided they were enemies.

Freddy Marchonne was Sienna's lieutenant in charge of the armory crew. He was a new breed of soldier. His hair was long in a well-kept ponytail, and he dressed like he'd seen one too many fashion magazines. But beneath the slick garb he was still a man to be feared. A man who knew how to handle himself.

Malik Kusa was the leader of the green-team commandos. A veteran officer in Syrian military intelligence, he'd held regular army commands and irregular ones. He'd worked with guerrilla fighters, narcotics dealers, terrorists, and ultimately with the international who's who of the underworld.

A total professional, Kusa knew the Garrison had no reason to ambush them and risk the enmity of the powers behind the green team. Sienna's men already had enough problems of their own without igniting another war front.

Marchonne instinctively felt the same as his green-team counterpart. There was no reason why the counterfeiters would want to upset the relationship they'd so carefully developed. It was strategic and profitable for both of them.

That meant the threat facing them now was coming from an outside source, most likely the same source that had been chipping away at the Garrison's defenses since Nick Carvaggio fell out with Sienna.

Marchonne and Kusa shared a look and read each other's thoughts as their own. There was no conflict between them, just a mutual interest in survival.

The deal was aborted.

The vans still had the currency and would leave the compound. The Garrison would stay in control of the weapons—though for how long was uncertain. Even though the armory was in a wilderness area, it wasn't totally unpopulated. With explosions and gunfire shattering the night, eventually the law would descend.

That meant they had to leave immediately.

The drivers of the vans switched on the engines and roared toward the gates.

Some groups of Garrison soldiers headed for the front of the compound on foot while others clambered into Jeeps and late-model cars parked around the warehouse docks.

As THE FIRST VAN approached the sundered gate, Nick Carvaggio ran in a crouching motion along the outside of the fence, relying on the white shell clothing to camouflage his movement.

The driver was going about thirty miles an hour by the

time he reached the shattered metal fence. He figured his speed would carry him over the bloody debris and the splintered metal fence posts out into safety. At the last moment he saw how deep the trench actually was. Too deep for the tires to cross.

With all of the ice and snow on the ground, it was too late for the van to stop without losing control. The driver slammed on the brakes, obviously unused to driving in these conditions. The brakes locked and the white van skidded forward.

With a groan of crunching metal, the front end of the van jackknifed into the trench caused by Carvaggio's explosives.

The front wheels bounced once, then chopped down into the jagged well of the crater. The tail end of the van stuck up in the air, wheels spinning uselessly as the driver's panicked foot stomped on the gas pedal.

The driver had braced himself against the fall by gripping the steering wheel, but his passenger wasn't so lucky. The green-team gunner was propelled headfirst through the windshield.

For a split second his bloodied face hung there like a jack-in-the-box, then the necklace of cracked glass around his head spiderwebbed into further cracks. His side of the windshield disintegrated around him, causing his upper body to slide halfway out of the van. The gun that had been clutched tightly in his hand dropped into the snow.

The driver bailed out of the front door and landed feetfirst in the ditch. "This way," he shouted to the disoriented green-team commandos who'd been thrown around like loose baggage in the back of the van. He had one foot out of the ditch and both hands on a submachine gun when Carvaggio rose up from the whiteness and stitched a 9 mm line of bullets across the driver's neck.

Even as Carvaggio triggered the short burst, he heard the side door of the van start to roll open.

One of the commandos had been ready to follow the driver but saw what happened just in time to avoid following him to his death. Instead of jumping out, he nosed the barrel of his automatic weapon through the half-open door and sprayed gunfire toward Carvaggio.

But the ex-hit man hadn't stopped moving. The volley of lead singed the air and kicked up spouts of snow behind him. As he ran in front of the van, Carvaggio triggered two more bursts to keep the occupants more interested in ducking for cover instead of shooting back at him.

Using both hands to control the bullet stream of his subgun, left hand hooked around the forward finger stop and right hand working the trigger, he carefully placed two more short bursts into the van.

Carvaggio couldn't afford to waste any ammo, not with a van full of gunners on his hands—and a line of Garrison soldiers who were running toward the battlefield.

The ex-hit man strafed the full length of the front windows with another series of bursts, providing cover for his movements and doing whatever damage he could to the gunmen inside.

Figuring he was just about empty and had poured about twenty-four or twenty-seven rounds from the 30-round clip into the van, Carvaggio kept moving toward the other side of the gates where the Executioner was closing in.

Bolan held an M-16/M-203 over-and-under assault rifle-grenade launcher combo close to his shoulder and aimed at the van, where one more gunner was trying to pull himself up through the open side door.

The time for a close-quarter machine pistol was past. Now it was time for some heavier ordnance.

Bolan waited until Carvaggio was airborne and diving out of the blast zone before he pulled back on the launch tube trigger. The low-velocity armor-piercing grenade thumped into the van.

The 40 mm bomb shredded the light metal and ignited the gas tank, turning the van and the occupants inside out.

As the tin can wreckage rolled in the air and spilled its once human contents onto the sizzling ground, the Executioner stepped away from the fiery blizzard. He slid the aluminum barrel forward and popped another low-velocity grenade into the weapon.

There was no way out for the enemy now. The gate was closed, sealed shut with smoldering wreckage. He aimed for one of the Jeeps near the office and trigged the M-203 once again. The high-explosive round flew through the air in a lazy arc, landing on the roof of the Jeep. The blast punched through the thin metal ceiling, slicing right through the gunmen inside.

The white hot rain blew out the windows.

Carvaggio had joined the bombardment, tossing phosphorous grenades over the fence into the compound. One after the other the high-powered explosives went off, spreading shock and confusion through the troops who'd been trying to reach the gate. They'd concentrated so much on making the compound impossible to get in, they never realized it would be just as hard to escape.

And for that reason, only a few of them would make it out.

"CUT THE FUCKING WIRE," Marchonne said.

"I'm going as fast as I can," the man said, grasping the wire cutters. He was a heavyset Garrison soldier, and the tool he wielded was equally large. But the blades had dulled and rusted from years of disuse.

His hands were red from the below-zero wind, as well as scratches from the portion of the fence he did manage to cut through. The dull blades kept mangling the wire instead of making a clean cut. Only with his bulk and a considerable amount of swearing was he able to make any cuts at all.

Marchonne fell silent. It was that or scream at the top of his lungs and that was out of the question, not if they wanted to make a quiet exit and get out of this thing with their lives.

The Garrison crew chief shook his head and waved his Heckler & Koch MP-5 in the darkness. They were at the back of the compound, intent on cutting through the fence and climbing down the concrete river wall onto the ice-filled Hudson.

Marchonne no longer thought about salvaging the counterfeit money that was burned and blowing in the wind like confetti. By the time he managed to gather up any of the money, the place would be an inferno.

Whoever was leading this assault knew what he was doing. For all purposes, the battle was over. If they stayed any longer, they'd be picked off by the attackers or rounded up by the authorities.

It was definitely military, Marchonne thought. Carvaggio had hooked up with some of his old Special Forces pals, and they were playing games with the Garrison, turning the armory into a regular shooting gallery.

First they bottled up the crew and dropped grenades on them like mortar fire. Then they'd fallen back, waiting in silence and holding their fire until one of Marchonne's teams scouted out the inside perimeter. That's when the unmistakable sound of machine-gun fire cut through the night and through the crew.

The man had been right outside the fence, covered in white camouflage, less than twenty yards away when he opened up. And bodies fell. The two men who'd survived had caught a brief glimpse of him before they took off, chased away by another blizzard from the guy's Steyr TMP.

Marchonne had sent another squad out there to patrol the inside perimeter, reconning by fire. So far they'd made a lot of noise but no confirmed hits.

The green team—what was left of it after one van and a Jeep were blown to bits—had tried to scale the fence at a dark corner. One of them ended up tangled in razor wire, a dangling and screaming target calling out for help from his compatriots.

When they ran to help, they were met with a full-auto burst from the enemy gunner.

Marchonne didn't know who was left from the green-team

crew. All he knew was that if he didn't get out of here soon, there wouldn't be anyone left alive.

He cursed Carvaggio and whoever was helping him.

He cursed Victor Sienna.

And he cursed the man with the wire cutters who spun angrily, looking like he was ready to crack open Marchonne's skull.

But instead the man threw the cutters at the leader's feet. "It's done," he said, then barreled into the fence like a half-back breaking a tackle. The sheared ends of the broken links scratched and clawed at the huge man's face and arms like fish hooks, but he was more interested in long-term survival than short-term pain.

After he bulled his way through, the opening was large enough for the rest of the crew.

Marchonne waited for two more soldiers to climb through before he followed them onto the snow-covered walkway. The path was about five feet wide and in good weather provided plenty of room to navigate. But now, covered with a sheet of ice, it was treacherous.

It was a fifteen-foot drop to the river, the ice-covered route that led to freedom.

One by one they slithered over the river wall, holding on to the weathered crevices and climbing down as far as they could before they had to make the jump.

Finally all of them were on the icy surface.

It felt as thick as a roadway, solid enough to support their weight. There were no patches of black ice to worry about. That was one good thing about the hellish weather. The Arctic cold front had swept over the Catskill for several days now and hardened the surface of the river. If they had to, they could make it all the way over to the other side without the ice cracking.

"Okay, Freddy," said the man who'd used the wire cutters. "You got us to the river. What do we do now? Skate to New York? Leave everybody behind?"

"No," Marchonne said. "We deal with Carvaggio and whoever's with him the same way they dealt with us."

"How's that?

"We outflank them. Spread out, move through the woods…"

"I don't think that's gonna work out," the big man stated.

"Why not?"

"Take a look."

Marchonne glanced up at the river wall. Off to the left he saw a momentary shadow. A white-caped figure was there for a moment, then gone. He looked to his right and saw another shape, which was also in winter white.

"Oh shit," he said.

"What are we gonna do?"

"We're gonna die," Marchonne said, "unless we take them out first." All thoughts of flight were gone. He raised the Heckler & Koch and fired an extended burst skyward.

Two gunners stepped alongside him and fired in the same direction. The rest of the crew moved toward the right and peppered the sky with lead.

And then the sky fired back.

WHILE CARVAGGIO WHIPPED a picket line of slugs toward Marchonne's cluster of soldiers from the right flank, Mack Bolan inched his way through the snow at the river's edge on the left. He'd dropped to the ground after Marchonne's reflex volley and moved a good distance up the bank.

The Colt submachine gun was slung over Bolan's shoulder, its light weight barely noticeable as he lay prone on the edge of the riverbank and aimed the heavier M-16/M-203 combo at the ice.

He didn't need to use the quadrant sight on the grenade launcher. His target was the entire river.

He waited until Marchonne's crew moved away from Carvaggio's kill zone—and into Bolan's.

Then he fired an HE round down to the ice.

The grenade exploded in a sheet of flames, ripping huge chunks from the frozen surface.

Bolan followed with a full-auto burst from the M-16. As Marchonne's people fired in the Executioner's direction, Carvaggio let loose with the Steyr again.

Caught in the cross fire, the Garrison began to fall. Some had lead in them, some just slipped on the ice as they panicked from the explosive barrage that seemed to followed them wherever they went.

Gouts of water fountained in the air as the grenades punched huge holes in the ice, forcing them to constantly seek new cover. The river was opening up all around them. Soon there wouldn't be much ice left for them to stand on.

It was too much for Marchonne to take.

While there was still room to maneuver Marchonne double-timed it across a strip of ice. He lost his balance and his control, screaming at the top of his lungs as he held the Heckler & Koch in front of him to fire off one last clip.

The moment of rage finally brought Marchonne into the open. Bolan stroked the M-16's trigger.

The first rounds dug into the ice at Marchonne's feet. The next dug through him.

The Garrison lieutenant dropped onto his back with his lifeless arms flung over his head. As he slid, he painted the ice red with a streak of blood before slipping out of sight, sinking in the dark icy water, floating downriver.

A few seconds later Marchonne's soldiers followed him, laden with rounds from the M-16 and the TMP.

It was time to move out.

Enough damage had been done to the armory and to the counterfeit currency. Whatever was left could be dealt with by the local authorities who would soon descend on the battlefield to sort things out.

Bolan headed back toward the final rendezvous point they'd selected earlier, a thick gray fallen tree trunk that offered a lot of shelter and stood out from the rest of the landscape. If one of them had failed to show, then the other would go back for him.

But Carvaggio showed up a couple of minutes later, lugging his battle gear, still in one piece.

They looked back at the flaming compound, then scanned the area outside the fence to make sure there were no war parties out looking for them.

Then they trekked to the ravine path they'd first followed when they set up their observation posts. A half mile away were the two white snowmobiles they'd rode into the woods.

By approaching the armory from the ravine, they were able to cover the sound of the machines. But just to be on the safe side, they'd stopped well out of earshot and walked the rest of the way.

Now there was no longer any need for stealth.

They secured their gear in the back, started the machines, thumbed the throttles and headed out as fast as the terrain allowed.

The powerful machines had come directly from an Army base, courtesy of Hal Brognola, and had been waiting for them at a rented hunting lodge along with a wide-bed pickup with enough space for both machines.

They were the same kind of snow machines used by the Army's Arctic Scouts. War machines. Sleek, fast, sturdy and capable of crossing great distances in rough terrain. But they had only about five miles to go before they reached the lodge.

As the snowmobiles headed south, they heard sirens all around them. The local law was on its way.

Soon the media would be full of stories about another battle between rival Families. And just as soon, the underworld would be thinking about how dangerous it was to be a friend of Victor Sienna.

11

"This has been Rupert Sawyer reporting for *Case Closed*. Until next time—"

With a click of the remote-control button, Victor Sienna made the televised face of Rupert Sawyer disappear. "There won't be a next time," he said, tossing the channel flicker onto the coffee table. He looked up at Drew McNeil, who'd been idly pacing the hotel suite while they watched the latest instalment of the producer's series on the underworld. "Right?"

McNeil shrugged. "Maybe."

"No maybe," Sienna said. "I want him gone. He's doing too much damage to me."

"He's not doing the damage. He's reporting it. Big difference."

"Not really," Sienna said. "The guy's killing my reputation. Christ, that whole show about this so-called underworld war was nothing but propaganda against me and how I'm losing control of my people. Makes me look weak, makes me look like fair game to anyone with half a notion to take me on. You see it any other way?"

McNeil shrugged again. "Let me think it over." He had no argument with Sienna's feelings about the show, just with his conclusion. The special program had been promoted these past few days as an inside look at the battling Mob Families. Instead, it had been mainly about the erratic performance of the Garrison and how their reckless actions were breaking an underworld truce that had been in existence for years.

The producer had called the once-feared Garrison an underworld army of misfits and murderous thugs instead of a top-notch outfit of military veterans. He'd referred to Victor Sienna, the alleged leader of the army, as a one-time mastermind who'd apparently lost his mind. It was almost as if he were trying to get a reaction from Sienna.

It was up to McNeil to make sure the Garrison leader reacted the right way. Now Sienna was acting out of anger. In his frame of mind, who knew what command he would give? And once he gave it he wouldn't back down, even if he knew it was wrong. He had too much pride to admit to such a mistake.

He'd been stung by Sawyer's cleverly arranged sequence of video clips that blamed the rash of massacres and murders on the poor judgment of Sienna. Sawyer had then displayed a bit of TV bravado by calling the Garrison leader a jackal in hiding, afraid of his own people and the enemies he made in the underworld.

Shortly before the piece ended, the producer hinted that Sienna's own worst enemy was himself, and it was only a matter of time before the other Families took the matter in hand and cleaned up the mess themselves.

Someone had to be working behind the scenes guiding Rupert Sawyer, McNeil thought. After weighing the *Case Closed* piece, and Sienna's state of mind, McNeil drifted back to the couch.

"Well?" Sienna said. "You had enough time to think or you want to take the day off?"

McNeil ignored the dig and returned to Sienna's earlier comment. "Okay," he said. "You want to call it propaganda, sure we can call it that. But you can't let your emotions get caught up in that stuff, Vic. Otherwise you let someone else call your shots. You've got to stick to your own game plan."

Sienna laughed. "Game plan? What's that? Sitting around waiting for the news guys to tell me how many more people I lost? Sitting around while my hired assassin is taken out in my own hotel? Sitting around watching Rupert Sawyer tell the world what a fuck-up I am?"

"He's not your real enemy, Vic."

"He's got too much inside detail on me. Carvaggio's feeding him everything he knows. Fucking producer's also got his hooks into Ambrosia—you can tell by some of the things he's said. Things only she knows. Christ, Drew, we've got to act, and it's gotta be fast. I can't take any more hits like this."

McNeil looked at the coffee table, which held an ashtray overflowing with cigarette butts, and a half-empty bottle of expensive whiskey. Normally Sienna wasn't that much of a drinker, but in the past few days he was relying on the bottle instead of the battle.

"All right, Vic," McNeil said. "What do you want to do?"

"Get Sawyer. Get the girl. Get Carvaggio. Get anybody," he shouted. "Just so we can prove you don't go against me and get away with it." He reached for the bottle.

"Let's talk outside," McNeil counseled, pointedly looking at the bottle. "Go for a ride. Check things out."

Sienna looked at the fifth of whiskey, almost surprised to see it in his hand. He nodded, realizing he'd been reaching for it by reflex lately. "You're right," he said. "Besides, we been here too long already."

The hotel on Broadway had been just one more in a succession of anonymous high-rise hotel rooms where Sienna and his crew camped out. He'd taken a lesson from his deceased opponents who'd stayed too long in one place.

It was time to move. McNeil picked up the hotel phone and made a few calls.

WITHIN A HALF HOUR several of the Garrison security teams were milling about the street near the hotel. Some checked out the cars double-parked near the entrance. Others patrolled the underground hotel parking garage, reconning the area before giving Victor Sienna the all clear. These days he moved about like royalty with his own secret service protecting him.

In groups of twos and threes the soldiers climbed into the four-car convoy and drove onto the streets of Manhattan. There were two forward cars, a car with Sienna and McNeil, and a backup car.

Any other time the military-style movements of the Garrison could have been written off as paranoia. But after the events of recent days, Victor Sienna had good reason to fear for his life. So many people were eager to take it.

He felt safe moving around. If nothing else, he wasn't sitting, waiting for someone to hit him. Now at least he was a moving target as the heavily armed convoy prowled the streets.

The city was covered with white. Another storm had come in from the ocean and dumped several inches of snow on the ground already, giving the brightly lighted shops and the streets an almost holiday feeling.

But the man who sat in the third car of the convoy wasn't looking for a holiday feeling. He was looking for blood. He sat in the back seat of the Lincoln, gazing at what used to be his town. Now he felt like a stranger.

Worse, he felt like a fugitive.

McNeil sat by the other window, tracing a line through the condensation with his index finger. He looked calm, not bothered by the world that was caving in on Sienna, and seemed content to listen to WABC while the convoy moved randomly through the streets.

Sienna looked over at him and shook his head. "Dammit, Drew, how can you just sit there? Not even breaking a sweat."

McNeil shrugged. "Why not? No one's shooting at us. Not yet, anyway. There are a lot of people standing between us and Carvaggio."

"For how long? With these kinds of casualties, no one's gonna want to sign on with us. The new guys you brought in, who knows what the hell they're thinking."

"They're thinking they're getting paid pretty well, and that sooner or later they have to earn that pay."

"Make it sooner. It's time to close out the producer of *Case Closed.*"

Satisfied that he'd made at least one important decision, Sienna leaned back against the cushion and contentedly lighted a cigarette, filling the Lincoln with a cloud of smoke. As a man used to action, he couldn't bear the thought of just sitting back and waiting for something more to happen to him. "Time to close him out," he said, having discovered a mantra to get him through his time of troubles.

McNeil sighed. He looked out the window as the Lincoln glided up Park Avenue alongside the narrow median that was covered with small conifers and shrubs. The parklike strip between the north-south avenues was blanketed with snow, and to the suddenly melancholy man it looked like a haven, a refuge from war that was worth exploring.

For a moment McNeil wished that he could see New York through civilian eyes, as a place to live and not a territory to kill for. But there was no other trade left open to him. McNeil had left military service behind him and had simply traded it for service in the army of Victor Sienna.

There was no retirement from that service, nor was there any escape from Sienna's snap judgments.

McNeil was beginning to think that maybe Rupert Sawyer's propaganda wasn't so far off the mark. The man that Victor Sienna had to fear the most was himself.

The Garrison leader had taken McNeil's silent reflection for agreement. "So it's settled," he said. "It's time we take out Sawyer."

McNeil shook his head. "Even if it was time, there's no way we could do it now."

"Nothing to it," Sienna said. "He's a walking bull's-eye. Guy like that's always dying to be in the limelight. You said so yourself. Our people see him all over the place."

"Not anymore," McNeil said. "Rupert Sawyer is a very hard man to find these days."

"How hard can that be?" Sienna demanded. "The guy's on TV, isn't he? He's putting those shows out, isn't he? That takes a studio. A crew. People who can be reached."

"Afraid not," McNeil said. "Sawyer hasn't been seen anywhere near the studio lately. And if you noticed, whenever he was on camera, it was against a different backdrop. Like they're splicing it in from somewhere. Remote camera patching into the main studio, whatever. These days they can do anything."

"What about his people?" Sienna asked. "His staff is still around. They got to run the place."

"Yeah, they're around," McNeil said. "But so are a lot of white hats. Feds, cops, who knows what they are, other than they're suddenly all over the studio. Taking notes, taking photos. Any time I had one of our people on watch, they saw a lot of heat."

"Put some of our people on Sawyer's associates," Sienna ordered. "Feds can't watch them twenty-four hours a day. Tell them to nose around a bit, find the right people to buy some information from. Somebody's got to know where Sawyer is. Hey, where could he go?"

"Maybe he's hiding," McNeil suggested. "Or maybe he's being hidden."

"Witness Protection Program?"

"Could be."

"Find out before he hurts us any more."

McNeil nodded. Then he listened to Sienna as the chieftain went on about other targets.

First among them was Carvaggio. But his whereabouts were even more difficult to find than Rupert Sawyer's.

"I admit it, Drew," Sienna said. "I don't know how we can find that guy."

"Maybe we should stop looking," McNeil suggested.

Sienna's face hardened. "What are you saying?"

"I'm saying the Families want this to come to an end."

"What Families are you talking about?"

McNeil didn't feel like mentioning any names. "All of

them," he said. "Anyone with a stake in the city. It's bad business all around."

"You talking face-to-face with them?" Sienna asked. His voice was tinged with paranoia, sounding like he thought McNeil was another candidate for defection. "Listen, Drew, I already got one Judas on my hands. I can't take another."

McNeil raised his hands. "Relax. I'm not talking face-to-face with anybody. What I'm doing is hearing from a lot of people concerned about us. Lot of messages are getting back to me. Friends of friends are thinking we grew too fast, took on too much. They're wondering what's going on with us."

"War's going on," Sienna said. "And it's going on until I get Carvaggio. If I'm the last one—if I got to kill him myself—I'll do it. I got no other options."

"You could cancel the contract," McNeil said. "Lie low for a while. Let business get back to normal."

"You kidding?" Sienna said. "If I cancel the contract, I cancel us. If I don't swat that betrayer, people'll start thinking they can get away with anything."

"It's worth considering," McNeil said.

Sienna shook his head adamantly. "Out of the question. I know what you're saying, Drew. It looks bad to our friends. No one will want to deal with us anymore...unless we come up a winner for a change. We need someone we can take out. Someone who deserves it."

That brought the conversation around to a target that was deserving of Sienna's wrath and, more importantly, was within striking distance.

Jacob Patricio.

Word had reached them that Patricio was making a lot of noise about the ambush that took out a lot of his people. He was making sure that all of their mutual associates heard about it. Patricio had placed the blame for the massacre squarely on Sienna's shoulders.

If that wasn't bad enough, word had also reached Sienna that Patricio was spending some Garrison money that had been recovered from the ambush site.

At the very least, that made Patricio a liar. In Sienna's last conversation with the Colombian, Patricio said the only thing he brought away from the rendezvous was his life. There wasn't any time to spend looking for money. So he said.

But maybe he got some of the money. Maybe he was even in league with the ambushers. Maybe he was double-crossing a bunch of Colombians he wanted out of the way. What better way to do it than have it look like a third party killed them?

It was hard to figure if the man was guilty or not. But either way, Sienna was determined to put an end to Patricio's career.

McNeil knew there was no way he could stop it from happening. Sienna needed a target to strike at so he could show the world he wasn't a patsy.

Patricio was available.

McNeil gave the word to the driver of the Lincoln to take them to the Tribeca district where Patricio ran his gallery.

The four-car convoy cruised the streets to get familiar with the layout of the terrain for when the battle came.

There would be more recons of the area, McNeil knew, but psychologically this was the most important one. It gave Sienna a chance to go on the offensive. If the Garrison was to survive, Sienna had to see himself as a master of war, not a victim.

THREE NIGHTS LATER McNeil rode through the streets of Tribeca once again. This time he was sitting in the back seat of a recently stolen Cadillac.

It had been taken from a lot in a suburb of Parsippany, New Jersey, shortly after the dealership closed, then driven to a garage where it was gassed up and fitted with New York plates. It was delivered to a Garrison soldier who paid in cash.

A slightly different arrangement had been made for the heavy-duty Ford pickup truck that the Cadillac was following on its circuit through the triangle of West Broadway, Canal

Street and Hudson Street that gave the lower Manhattan area the Tribeca name.

The pickup had come directly from a reliable chop shop in Brooklyn, where it had been put together from several different stolen parts and outfitted with reinforced armor and a snowplow.

Two gunners rode in the cab of the truck, one old hand and one of the new soldiers McNeil brought in from his last recruitment trip. A few more soldiers were riding in the flatbed under a green canvas tarp.

Three other men rode in the Cadillac with McNeil.

Two more Garrison vehicles trailed the Cadillac. All of them were tasked to the same assignment: the elimination of Jacob Patricio.

Normally McNeil wouldn't take part in an operation like this. Usually after he set up the planning stage, he left it up to the squad to carry out the hit. But Victor Sienna was tired of losing. He wanted McNeil to personally oversee this one. He wanted a victory.

During the past forty-eight hours, McNeil had done his best to insure a triumph this time out. He'd visited the gallery off Hudson Street a number of times, conducting surveillance on Patricio's operation and seeing if he kept to any kind of timetable. Twice he'd actually gone inside, posing as a potential customer so he could learn the number and type of people Patricio had around him.

Patricio's staff was made up of two distinct types. The first was the professional salespeople, who exuded culture and a discreet but detectable craving for high commissions.

The second type was the harder sort, men who might have known the difference between an abstract portrait and a fingerpainting, but were there for a different purpose. They were the ones who stayed after closing, guarding Patricio while he conducted business in his office.

Patricio rarely deviated from his routine.

The Colombian art dealer came to the gallery early each afternoon to meet with clients and artists, and stayed there until exactly eleven o'clock. That was when his security cars drove down the alley alongside the gallery and parked outside the unmarked metal door at the side of the building.

The first car held three enforcers and always parked just beyond the door. The second car was a white Jaguar driven by Patricio's personal driver, and it always stopped exactly parallel to the door.

The third and final car of the entourage had only the driver, leaving enough room to transport the remaining bodyguards who'd been stationed at the gallery.

Like any man of his standing, Patricio had plenty of enemies back home in Colombia. And now that he had some serious enemies in the U.S. as well, Patricio always took maximum precautions.

When it was time for him to leave the building, Patricio made sure that he was visible for only a few moments before ducking into the Jaguar and speeding away.

Then he would go for a late dinner, a night on the town or return to his high-security apartment complex on the Upper West Side.

Once he left his workplace he was unpredictable. But until then he followed a precise timetable, giving McNeil the chance to predict Jacob Patricio's time of death within a few minutes.

"Let's get in position," he said to the driver of the Cadillac when they were on Varrick Street. They still had time to spare, but McNeil didn't want to risk getting delayed in the late night rush of traffic. It was nightclub time, and though a cold winter rain was falling, the streets were still busy.

The Cadillac driver picked up the car phone and rang the men in the pickup. "It's going down," he said. "Head over to the gallery."

As the four-car hit squad rode toward Patricio's, McNeil picked up the Ithaca shotgun lying on the seat beside him. It was a Model 37 Stakeout version, a modified weapon used by special police and military units. The barrel was chopped and it held a smaller magazine, just four rounds instead of the customary eight.

The short barrel made it easier to conceal, and it also added a kick to the volcanic spray of the special cartridges McNeil had brought along.

JACOB PATRICIO WAITED inside the main floor of the gallery as one of his men unlocked the gray metal door that led to the alley. His bodyguard, a slight but wiry man with graying hair and a suspicious mind, pushed the door open suddenly and stepped onto the small concrete stoop.

He looked up and down the alley, hand under his jacket and resting on his holstered weapon. But the gun didn't come out. Both sides were clear.

A moment later headlights from Patricio's security detail splayed across the brick buildings as they drove toward the door.

The bodyguard looked over the gunmen in the first car, then studied the faces of the driver in the Jaguar and the car behind it. The bodyguard nodded, then waited at the gallery door.

Patricio appeared in the doorway a moment later. He ducked his head to cover his face from the driving rain, then headed for the door of the Jaguar that his bodyguard held open for him.

Before he could climb in, Patricio heard the roar of a pickup truck gunning down the alley.

He snapped his head to the right and saw the truck's heavy steel plow rising off the ground, clanking and shuddering until the driver levered it up to window height.

Not only was it a bulletproof shield, but the plow was now also a battering ram aimed straight at the lead car.

Patricio shouted a warning, but the men in the lead car had already seen it coming. Two of them were out of the car, raising their submachine guns at the portable guillotine heading their way.

FIFTEEN 9 MM ROUNDS pounded into the front of the pickup truck, imploding the reinforced armor and pocking the hood. But the bullets didn't pierce through to the engine block.

The man who'd fired the first full-auto burst threw down his emptied submachine gun and flattened against the wall.

The second man's full clip bounced like rivets off the curved plow.

"Hold your fucking hat," the pickup driver said, slamming the pedal to the floor and aiming the plow at the lead car's windshield.

Crumpling like tin, the front end of the car collapsed inward. As the truck lurched forward, the curved lower rim of the plow scooped up the windshield and peeled back the roof of the car.

Glass flew like snow, a thousand small pieces dropping through the air and falling onto the alley. Some of the glass was specked with blood from one of the men who'd been trapped in the car.

The momentum of the pickup pushed the wrecked car back into the Jaguar and spun it sideways.

As the pickup continued straining forward, the three gunmen hidden in the bed of the truck flung off the tarp and aimed their Heckler & Koch MP-5s at the remnants of Patricio's security team.

The chatter of the machine pistols echoed down the alley, followed by the death cries of Patricio's bodyguards. They didn't have a chance.

And for a moment it looked like Patricio would join them. The cab of the pickup was right by the door and the driver had one hand on the wheel, the other on an automatic that he waved at Patricio.

The Colombian headman didn't lose his cool, and for that, he didn't lose his life. He stood his ground for the split second it took to fire a .45 round into the driver's head.

The steering wheel spun from the dead man's hand and his foot fell off of the gas pedal, causing the racing, droning engine to drop to an idle.

Patricio ducked back inside the building as the gunners from the back of the truck swerved his way, slapping fresh clips into their submachine guns.

Before they could squeeze any bursts, the counterattack began.

It came from above and it came heavy.

High-velocity lead projectiles rained on the pickup, knocking all three gunners off their feet. They were leaking like sieves by the time they hit the metal bed of the truck.

Gun barrels protruded from half a dozen windows that ran along the second floor of the gallery, spitting yellow flame into the alley. With the truck disabled, the automatic fire drifted toward the second Garrison car that had trolled down the alley.

Two Garrison soldiers had already jumped out of the car and were running for the pickup when the heavy fusillade began.

When they saw the effect of the firepower on the pickup, they turned and ran back to the car, firing their weapons blindly overhead to protect themselves.

Only one man made it back to the car. The other guy fell flat on his face with a thick red line of blood running down his back from head to toe, looking like he'd been cut by a chain saw.

McNEIL WATCHED his certain victory disintegrate before his eyes. One moment everything looked perfect, a clean and quick kill that would get them out of the kill zone in less than a minute.

He'd stepped out of the Cadillac, after it was parked just past the mouth of the alley, to watch the hit go down and confirm the kill.

It was working just like he'd planned—until the firestorm fell on them from above. He realized that Patricio's team had also been planning for this night, as if someone had tipped them off.

And now chaos reigned.

McNeil's Cadillac was parked just ten yards away. All he had to do was run back, hop in and get out of there with his life.

But his people were being cut down, people he'd recruited especially for this operation, people who expected him to know what he was doing. McNeil couldn't walk away.

He crept down the alley, staying close to the shadows by the wall as he raised the pump-action shotgun toward the tier of windows.

The incandescent Starflash shell shrieked down the alley, filling it with a blinding nova. While the men in the windows were stunned by the sudden white brilliance, McNeil fired another shotgun round. This time the round burst through one of the windows, taking off the upper body of a Colombian gunman.

Behind McNeil came a Garrison gunner with about twenty pounds of machine gun in his hand. The Squad Automatic Weapon had a heavy box magazine of 5.56 mm NATO assault cartridges. And in ten seconds about a fifty of those devastating rounds had strafed across the second floor windows.

Like magic, the Colombian gunmen disappeared, some wounded, some ducking for cover.

McNeil continued moving until he was halfway down the alley, firing off two more brick-busting rounds at the windows. When he saw the back of the pickup truck he figured there was no one left to save. The bodies were pulped with lead.

Suddenly the passenger door of the truck swung open and a soldier stepped out. He aimed a Colt automatic at the windows and squeezed off six rounds as he ran back toward McNeil and the machine gunner standing beside him.

"Patricio?" McNeil shouted. "Did you get him?"

"He's inside," the man shouted.

McNeil scanned the upper windows. The Colombians were holding back, but he had no doubt they still had several gunners alive.

Then he looked down the alley. A half-dozen Garrison soldiers were standing there, weapons covering the windows while they waited for a sign from McNeil. He shook his head.

It would take too long to get inside, and if they did, they didn't know what they would find. The police would be here any second now. The hit-and-run had turned into a pitched battle.

Patricio had obviously expected this and was safe now. He had a guardian angel somewhere. A guardian with teeth.

McNeil signaled that it was over. They piled into the cars and screeched out into the street.

TWENTY-FOUR HOURS LATER, after spending most of the day and part of the night in a police station answering questions from homicide detectives and federal agents, Jacob Patricio received a call in his Park Avenue penthouse, which now had the atmosphere of an armed camp.

It was an unlisted number, but Patricio wasn't surprised that the caller was able to get in touch with him. He wasn't surprised by anything this man could do.

The caller was the man who claimed to be Michael Blasco, and he was asking Patricio about the art gallery incident.

"It happened just as you said it would," Patricio replied. "A most accurate prediction."

"I had good sources."

"Frightening sources. They appear to have an extensive intelligence capacity."

"Unlimited capacity," Bolan answered.

Bolan had warned him that one of the wealthy looking art lovers who'd come to his gallery was actually Drew McNeil, Victor Sienna's military planner. The presence of McNeil in his gallery meant that Patricio was included in Sienna's latest plan.

Though Patricio had welcomed the warning, it was unsettling that this kind of intelligence came from him. It meant that Blasco or someone else had the gallery under constant surveillance.

Too many people were aware of his business these days, people he didn't know enough about.

But Patricio had taken the advice and prepared himself for the attack from the Garrison. Obviously he hadn't prepared well enough. He'd almost bought it in the alley.

"I thank you for your warning," Patricio said, "but I'm afraid it came too late and at too great a cost. Some of my best people were killed."

"Yeah," Bolan said. "Hard to make a living in your field. Sometimes its harder to stay alive."

"Especially since I got involved with the Families. It almost seems like I'm fighting a war here. And I'm beginning to think I'm fighting your war for you."

"That sounds about right," Bolan agreed. "So far your luck's held out. But I don't think it'll hold out much longer."

The coolness of the man on the phone didn't anger Patricio, though any other time it might have thrown him into a rage. But this night Patricio's instinct for self-preservation was at work, picking up whatever cues it could from this man named Blasco. He recognized a certain detached quality in his voice, something in his tone that made it clear he'd done this kind of thing several times before.

Michael Blasco was a professional operator who knew how to maneuver allies and opponents alike. Patricio had encountered that type in some of the military and intelligence people he'd dealt with in South America. But the question still remained—who was Blasco operating for?

"I don't know who you are, who you work for or what you really want," Patricio said. "All I know is that in some way I've helped you. And I think in some way you've helped me. My advisers tell me that under normal circumstances, I wouldn't have been released so easily." Patricio paused for a moment.

"Your advisers are right on the money."

"They also advise me that it's time to leave your country. I intend to do so. But not until I spread the word to the other Manhattan Families that there will be no more dealings with them because the Garrison has created too dangerous a climate for us to work in.''

"That sounds like a good idea," Bolan replied. "I can almost guarantee your luck wouldn't hold out much longer."

"Are you certain of that?"

"Let me make another prediction for you. I predict your luck will hold out for twenty-four hours more. Longer than that, who knows what will happen to you."

Patricio hung up the phone and looked at the somber faces of the gunmen sprawled around the luxurious quarters. They were wondering what kind of fate Patricio had decided for them.

But someone else had decided that fate for them. They wouldn't die in New York—as long as they left immediately.

Instinctively Patricio knew that Blasco would keep his word. That same instinct told him that if he ever came back, he would be fair game.

12

At ten in the morning the two men walking down Lower Broadway looked like average businessmen who would be at home in any of the prominent and lofty skyscrapers in New York's financial district.

But they were far from average and so was the building they were heading for.

When they reached the steps of the government building, Nick Carvaggio looked up at the gray stone edifice like it was the Bastille, a dungeon from which he'd never return. But he shrugged it off and didn't miss a step as he accompanied the Executioner into the operation center for the Justice Department's covert task force.

The fiftyish man at the main desk, whose dark suit, tie and owlish glasses gave him the look of a bank officer instead of a covert officer, nodded at the Executioner. Bolan had become a familiar face in the building. No one knew his real name or title, just that he had the ear of Hal Brognola.

After Bolan signed in, the deskman buzzed him and Carvaggio through the glass door that led to the elevators.

They rode up to the fourth floor where the Special Services Unit had set up its temporary shop, then headed for the corner office where Hal Brognola waited for them.

Brognola was on the phone but when he saw them standing in the doorway, he cut the call short and gestured them in.

"Good to see you again, Striker," Brognola said, shaking his hand and closing the door behind him.

Then the big Fed looked at Carvaggio, who was returning the same kind of level look.

There was no fear, no friendship, no hatred in either man's stare. It was a totally neutral gaze until Carvaggio laughed and said, "You don't look so glad to see me."

Brognola laughed. "It's more of a shock than anything else. But the fact that Striker vouches for you and what you've done for us, yeah, that makes me glad to see you. Thing is, half the guys on the next floor would like to see your head stuck on a pole outside this building. They've been after you since—"

"Since someone else took out your man," Carvaggio said. "Not me."

"That's the assumption we're operating under. For now it's just the three of us thinking along those lines. We could still use some proof about the murder of Agent Prescott."

He turned to Bolan. "Any chance of getting it?"

"Maybe," Bolan said. "We're working on it. That's what we've got to talk about it."

"Start talking, then," Brognola said. He sat behind his desk while Bolan and Carvaggio pulled a couple of chairs up to it.

"We got a guy in the Garrison who's just about ready to switch sides," Bolan said. "He doesn't know it yet, but it's going to happen real soon. Nick's going to make a final approach to him tonight. Guy's current name is Stefan Gaultieri."

"Current?" Brognola prodded.

"It might take some serious convincing to bring him in," Bolan said. "Witness Protection Program. New identity. Maybe money."

"What can this guy do for us?"

"Two things," the soldier replied. "First, he can give us Sienna."

"You mean he'll take him out?"

Carvaggio shook his head. "That's not his style. He won't

go directly against Sienna. But he might play along with us if we dangle the right kind of carrot in front of him.''

"Gaultieri can help us set up Sienna once and for all," Bolan said. "Lure him out into the open. There are other ways of doing it, but we figure Gaultieri's the best bet."

"You said there were two things he could do for us," Brognola said. "What else is on the plate?"

Bolan leaned forward. "Gaultieri probably knows more than most about what happened to Agent Prescott. Same deal as before. If we give him the right package, he might confirm what we already know."

"This Gaultieri," Brognola said. "How clean is he? I've seen the logs and know he's been with Sienna awhile, but not much more than that."

"He's no worse than some of the people who made it into the Witness gig," Bolan said. "Better than a lot of them. But Nick's the authority on that."

Carvaggio shrugged. "Gaultieri's a straight shooter. Unlike some of the Garrison guys, he wouldn't go out of his way to hurt anybody. Warring against other Families, other crimies, yeah, he saw nothing wrong with that. He got dragged along on some of the dope deals, but that wasn't his thing. So, bottom line, he's no saint and he's no hero. But he can do what we need."

The big Fed thought it over for a while. Finally he clapped his hands together. "Okay. Go after him. The deal is this— we'll give him what he wants if he gives us what we need. If he backpedals once this is over, then he's locked up for keeps."

"Good," Bolan said. "That gives us something to work with. But before any of that happens, we've got to work things out with Nick."

"I'm listening," Brognola said. He turned toward the ex-hit man. "What do you want?"

"My freedom," Carvaggio said. "That and a new name, one of those backstopped IDs you keep handy. Something that'll hold up if someone looks close."

"That's it?" Brognola asked. "No traveling money? You'll need something to set yourself up."

"No money. I can get by with what I've got put away."

"You've got it," Brognola said. "If this works out."

"Thing is, Hal," Bolan stated, "the way this is going down, there won't be any time to hang around afterward. We need to get that in motion now. Can you do it?"

"Yeah. I'll get some people started on it."

"One other thing," Carvaggio added. "If Gaultieri can't prove someone else killed your agent, is that a deal breaker?"

Brognola shook his head. "No. I'll probably have to take a few hits, but it won't be the first time. I'll get by."

"All right," Bolan said. "Here's what we need." The Executioner laid out the scenario.

He and Carvaggio would handle the ground war, turning Gaultieri and setting up a final confrontation with the Garrison.

Brognola would handle the media war and feed intel to Rupert Sawyer so the isolated producer could shape another program about the underworld, this time ridiculing the Garrison for their mishandled massacre at the art gallery.

One more broadcast of *Case Closed* would probably be enough to put Victor Sienna over the edge and make him ready to grab for the bait they would offer.

RUPERT SAWYER HAD NEVER felt self-conscious in front of a camera.

Until today.

That afternoon he felt outclassed by the crew that was helping him prepare the latest taping session, a *Case Closed* segment that would be transmitted to his West 57th Street studio for a broadcast later in the evening.

After decades of reporting, editing and packaging news features, Sawyer had come to think of himself as an all-around expert who could master the ins and outs of any subject.

Sometimes it took only fifteen minutes to grasp the intricacies of a situation. Other times it took an hour or two. And on occasion it took days, months and years of in-depth reporting to become a full-fledged expert.

These days network experts were usually correspondents who knew only the correct spelling of the place they were being sent to cover or had read an article or two on the subject.

Over the years Rupert Sawyer had prided himself on his in-depth knowledge of organized crime. He'd met with criminals and criminologists, detectives, district attorneys, forensic scientists, and thought he knew the score when it came to the underworld.

That trademarked air of authority worked well for a general audience. The problem this day was that nearly everyone who was gathered in the airtight and soundproof basement recording studio knew more about the subject than he did.

The film unit was made up of combat photographers and surveillance experts for organized crime task forces, along with a behavioral scientist from the FBI who helped Sawyer put together the script in a manner calculated to push all of Victor Sienna's buttons and make his loathing win out over his logic.

The director and videographer working on the segment had produced on-site documentaries of wars and revolutions and coups around the world, from Romania to Russia. They had covered Mob activities from Italy, Sicily, Bulgaria, Russia and New York.

Together the crew had about a hundred years' experience covering the underworld arena and the terrorist scene. They knew their subject inside out.

Despite the sudden and unexpected case of humility, Sawyer forced himself to convey the usual cocky and well-informed persona of a dedicated crime fighter, a dauntless investigator who dared to tread where others couldn't follow.

He swaggered toward the camera with his hands deep in his trench coat pockets and began his intro for the segment on the Garrison's latest humiliating defeat.

It felt hotter than usual, and the lights seemed brighter than ever on his eyes, but he somehow managed to come on like a gangbuster as he said the first few lines of what they all hoped would be Victor Sienna's eulogy.

After the usual introductory remarks, Sawyer spoke in that somber voice that was one octave away from parody, but still conveyed the seriousness of his subject.

"Like many immigrants," Sawyer said, "Jacob Patricio came to the United States to build a future for his family. But unlike many fine upstanding immigrants who had a lot to offer this country, Patricio's family turned out to be a cartel, a cartel engaged in flooding the shores of our country with cocaine, crime and corruption."

Sawyer paused for a few beats, maintaining his rock-jawed gaze all the while. At this point in the script a montage of inserts would be spliced in for his voice-over narration, which would be dubbed in later.

The first series of insert scenes would be too familiar to American audiences: streets in Colombia, red with the blood of rival cartel gunmen; prisons with cartel kingpins lounging around in their Jacuzzi whirlpools, while servants waited on them and their concubines.

The second series of inserts would show similar scenes, but this time the streets running with blood were in the U.S. And instead of plush prisons, the video footage would show luxurious American estates guarded by gunmen.

The last images on-screen would be stock footage of Patricio's art gallery, featuring the opening night from one of his exhibitions when the street outside was full of people anxious to get inside.

"Patricio was a well-respected man," Sawyer continued, "both by his high-society clientele who patronized his fashionable art gallery—and by the underground crime Families who were interested in making different kinds of deals with the Colombian trafficker. Patricio's underworld associates paid incredible sums for unprecedented shipments of cocaine he imported into the United States. And the gallery was the perfect place to launder the money.''

Sawyer fell into another one of his meaningful pauses, then did a voice-over for the next series of inserts, which featured grisly footage of the carnage outside the gallery after the battle between Patricio and the Garrison.

''It was here at this unfortunate juncture of art and commerce that Jacob Patricio learned a crucial lesson—he was not willing to die for art or for the other enterprise he brought to our country.''

Sawyer outlined the details of the bloody encounter between the Garrison and Patricio's cartel security team, then said, ''Shortly after this battle, Jacob Patricio left the country for good. And this is what he left behind.''

The script called for a series of shots that transformed the blood-dried faces of the dead men on the ground into black-and-white mug shots. The first shots were of the cartel enforcers who'd lost their lives outside the gallery. The next were of the Garrison soldiers who died on their latest mission, all of them known associates of Victor Sienna.

For legal reasons Sawyer had to keep referring to Sienna as the *alleged* head of the Garrison. Though everyone knew it was his organization, there had been no concrete proof yet. At least not the kind of proof that would hold up in court.

''Obviously the Garrison crime family had a major falling out with Patricio's cartel,'' Sawyer said. ''Was it over a deal gone bad—a common occurrence in its activities these days—or was it a personal vendetta? The answer eludes us for now.''

Sawyer continued the narration that would accompany several shots of Victor Sienna from his military days throughout his reign with the Garrison. ''Though authorities are looking for the alleged leader of the Garrison crime family, he is nowhere to be seen.''

Sawyer raised his eyebrows. ''Perhaps it's because he's afraid to show his face. Or perhaps he realizes that he has become a pariah among his own kind.''

Sawyer closed in for the kill, reciting failure after failure of the Garrison soldiers and how they were being sent to their deaths instead of being led to their deaths because the leader couldn't be found. "Is he the power behind the throne—or is the throne empty of a real leader?"

Sawyer went on to pay a backhanded compliment to the Garrison for creating a constant state of turmoil in the New York underworld. Not only had a major cocaine supplier been shut down, forcing the buyers to cultivate new sources, but there was a growing distrust between the Families as they wondered who was really behind the attacks.

Before signing off, Sawyer twisted the knife a bit more by featuring an on-camera interview with Ambrosia Lyons. He introduced her as the former mistress of the alleged Garrison boss, who left him for personal reasons.

The camera lovingly captured Lyons in silhouette, keeping the lighting just dark enough to hide her face but not her figure. "I was with Victor Sienna for a long time," she began in a plaintive voice. "Too long. He was a dangerous man who put all of his efforts into violence and greed."

The camera moved in for a close-up as she continued her breathless confessional. "The reason I had to leave him was his obvious mental imbalance. It was impossible to know what a man in that dangerously unhinged state of mind would do next."

Sawyer nodded as if the words had come from on high, yet another unimpeachable source. "Dangerous, yes," he said, sagely nodding at the camera. "But fortunately this time he appears to be more of a danger to his associates than to the God-fearing citizens of this city."

The director yelled "Cut," and Sawyer walked off the small sound stage, shaking his wrists to get rid of some of the adrenaline burst that always swept through him after a stint on camera.

While he was doing his standard cooling down routine, Sawyer almost ran right into the behavioral expert from the

FBI. The blue-suited man looked down and smiled at the producer.

"What do you think?" Sawyer asked.

"I think you managed to cast doubt on his manhood and convince the underworld that the Garrison is a sinking ship," the FBI headhunter said. "I also think that Victor Sienna will very much want to find you."

13

Two days after the latest *Cased Closed* broadcast, a succession of black cars pulled up in front of the West 44th Street restaurant to drop off their underworld ambassadors.

The cars pulled up to the curb and stayed there just long enough for a driver or bodyguard to open the door for the passenger to get out.

They looked more like frequenters of a men's club than the powerful advisers of half-a-dozen crime Families.

Most of the ambassadors were men in their forties and fifties, members of the new Mob who liked to conduct their affairs like corporate executives. To them it was all a matter of numbers and of territories. There was room and money enough for everybody these days. No need for the bloody wars of old.

It was true that even in the new regime people still got killed now and then, but only for good reason. Lately there'd been too many people killed for no reason at all. That was why these men had come together today—to bring back the age of reason.

They'd arrived within minutes of one another and were ushered into the restaurant. From the outside, the restaurant looked like a small, drab and deservedly anonymous place.

The narrow window front was curtained off from the street. A small doorway zigzagged into a cramped alcove, opening into a long dining room with uniformed wait staff and elegant tables.

The tables were far enough apart from one another, and

the dimmed lighting was calculated to give each table a cocoon of privacy.

But this day the tables were empty.

The dining room was quiet, with just a bit of light piano music floating through the air.

In the back of the restaurant a few tables were on raised platforms where the bodyguards and drivers would sit for the duration, quietly studying one another in the manner of uneasy allies.

Farther back was a private room set aside for the ambassadors, complete with a long, oval conference table so no one felt more equal than the other. It was a neutral zone, not one of the usual hangouts that were prone to being watched by vice cops or the Feds.

One by one the conference table filled until there were seven men. The last one in was Drew McNeil, the reluctant guest of honor, who had been respectfully invited to attend the sitdown. A refusal to come would have been considered an unthinkable breach of etiquette on the part of the Garrison, an insult that would eventually be settled by breech-loaded shotguns.

McNeil's presence at the meeting meant that there was still a chance to settle things amicably. The Garrison crew still followed protocol and weren't out of control.

It was a low-key meeting, and the subject that had brought them all together wasn't even mentioned until after dinner had been served, the plates cleared away and fresh coffee placed on the table.

Eugene Raimundo, McNeil's counterpart from the Anganese crew, signaled that the inquisition was about to begin by leaning back in his chair and lighting a cigar. As the cloud of ceremonial smoke streamed toward the overhead vent, Raimundo glanced at McNeil.

One by one the other men turned their gaze on him, as if an internal alarm had gone off inside each man.

"So," Raimundo said, smoothing his hands out on the

tablecloth and looking straight at McNeil, "when's it going to stop?"

McNeil looked back at him. "When is what going to stop?"

"What we all want to stop," Raimundo said. "Victor Sienna's reign of error." The warlord from the Anganese crew looked around the table for silent confirmation, then gestured with a wave of his hand to include everyone who was sitting there. They'd obviously chosen him as their spokesman. Obviously there had been another meeting before this one. "Don't tell me you can't figure it out. Your man's making too many mistakes, and we're all paying the price."

Even though Raimundo had little fear that the place was bugged, he still spoke in the roundabout way that he'd developed through years of caution and conditioning.

It was a language they all understood. No explicit threats had to be made, just insinuated.

"The thing is," McNeil said, "Vic's got a lot of things going on. And he's also trying to straighten out a lot of things."

"Trying," Raimundo repeated. "You saying he can't do it?"

"I'm saying he's working on it right now," McNeil replied.

"Doesn't seem to be working too well, judging from the heat coming down on everybody. Just look at the papers with all their crazy headlines and the TV shows with Vic's mug splashed all over the screen every time you turn it on."

"That's one of the things we're working on," McNeil said. "The producer on that *Case Closed* show's got a real hard-on for us all of a sudden. Trying to make his name on us."

"He is a problem," the other man admitted. "But not the main one. We, all of us here at the table, know that the real problem is Victor Sienna. Ever since he started this vendetta against Carvaggio, a good man at that, he's lost his senses. Making deals that go bust, making war when he doesn't have to. Sienna's a time bomb, Drew, and when he goes off he's going to take a lot of us down."

"That's what I came here to tell you," McNeil said. "It's under control."

"Not from our angle, Drew. Just take a look at the body count. It's like a full-scale war going on out there, and none of us knows who's behind it and who's going to get hit next. Could be Feds helping Carvaggio. Or it could be something a lot worse."

"Like what?" McNeil asked.

"Like maybe the Executioner," Raimundo said. He cocked his head and studied McNeil's reaction. "What do you think?"

McNeil shrugged. "It's hard to say. The thought crossed my mind. There's a military angle here somewhere. Lot of hit-and-run tactics. Lot of firepower. But that's Carvaggio's background, too. We're leaning toward some Special Forces outfit he hung with."

Raimundo nodded. "Special Forces. Executioner. There's little difference. The outcome will be the same. Whatever it is and whoever it is, it's too much for the Garrison to deal with."

"We don't have a choice," McNeil said.

"Sure you do. Drop the vendetta against Carvaggio and cancel the contract on him. Then lay low for a while."

"For how long?"

"As long as it takes for things to get back to normal, Drew. We both know there's some wars you just don't start. And there's some wars, even if someone else starts them, sometimes you have to walk away. This is one of those times."

McNeil pushed himself away from the table. He looked from face to face. This wasn't a negotiation. It was a one-sided discussion. They were supposed to do the talking, and he was supposed to do the listening.

"Bottom line, Drew," Raimundo said. "In the old days the Garrison could handle whatever came its way. You guys were the best at what you did. But now, you're spread too thin. Vic took on too much, too fast, and unless he pulls back, he'll have to take on all of us. Whatever private war he's waging, it has to stop now."

"Soon," McNeil promised. "It's going to stop soon. A few more days is all we need. We'll finish it up and things'll be quiet again. We just need a little more time."

The man to McNeil's left pounded the table with a closed fist. He kept it there, anchoring his controlled rage. "For God's sake, Drew, you're not listening to us! We can't take any more chances with this situation. Who knows what'll go wrong next? We lost a lot of business when Patricio went down. We were able to trust Patricio, whatever problem Sienna had with him, but now we've got to bring in some new people, set up new routes. We had a good thing going with him. And it's gone."

"These things happen," McNeil said.

Raimundo shook his head. "Not anymore, they don't. When Vic knew what he was doing, we went to him all the time. We needed guns, we went to Vic. We needed some crews to shepherd a deal, we went to him. That's because we knew what to expect. But now what happens?"

The warlord from the Anganese Family threw his hands up in the air. "Now Vic runs operations into territory he doesn't own. Sometimes he pays his percentage, more often he doesn't. It depends on whether he thinks he can get away with it. We let it go because he used to be someone we needed. But now Victor Sienna is someone we don't need. This business comes to an end, or he does."

McNeil nodded. "I'll see what I can do." But he knew it would be futile. Sienna was single-minded now, especially after the *Case Closed* broadcast. He'd increased the bounty on the heads of Rupert Sawyer, Nick Carvaggio and whoever was backing him up. He wanted all-out war, and it wasn't going to stop no matter who asked, or who told him.

Sienna would just as soon wage war against all the Families than lay down his weapon. He was a wronged man, and he was determined to make it right.

Raimundo was picking up on McNeil's thoughts.

The Anganese warlord sighed and shook his head. Then he stood, walked behind McNeil and placed his hand gently on his shoulder.

"As a friend I'm asking this, Drew. If it comes down to it and Vic won't listen to reason, do us all a favor?"

"What kind of favor?" McNeil asked.

"Remove Vic from the equation. There'll still be a need for the Garrison as long as the right guy's running it. That's you."

"Thanks for the vote of confidence," McNeil said, "but I don't think it's gonna be in the cards."

"It's your hand, Drew. Play it however you see fit. We'll know your answer soon enough."

Raimundo and the other ambassadors filed out of the conference room, leaving McNeil with a few hard choices to make.

He could help Sienna continue his private war, which would probably lead to open warfare with the men he'd just sat down with, or he could "remove" Sienna. The hit had just been sanctioned by the representatives of the other crews working the same territory, so there would be no fallout there. Any fallout would come from the Garrison soldiers, and he knew that many of them would welcome a change in leadership. No one was happy with Sienna these days, most of all his own people.

He shook his head. It was kill or be killed. But it was more likely, kill and be killed. There would be no easy way out of this.

McNeil finished his coffee. He thought of how easy it would be take out Sienna and walk away from this mess. Easy for others, not for him. He'd signed on with Victor and he'd stay with him until the end, which was probably closer than he expected.

AT ELEVEN O'CLOCK at night, Stefan Gaultieri heard footsteps behind him as he walked down the street for his car. They were heavy footsteps that scuffed loudly on the sidewalk.

The pavement was cold but dry, leaving a perfect template for someone to walk silently.

If they wanted to.

Whoever was behind him wanted Stefan to know that he was there, just to notch up the tension a bit.

The Garrison wheelman glanced behind him and saw a familiar shape. Nick Carvaggio. He'd been expecting to see him again, but didn't know under what circumstance.

At the same time, he saw another shape come out of the darkness across the street. The man stood there ready to cut him off if he ran, or cut him down if he fought.

This was the guy who'd been helping Carvaggio, Gaultieri realized. Carvaggio was bad enough to deal with, practically impossible. And from all the reports, that guy was even worse.

"Stefan," Carvaggio said. "Good to see you."

"Yeah, well, it's not good to see you, Nick. And it's not good to be seen with you."

"Street's clear," Carvaggio said, as he caught up to him. "Don't worry, we're always discreet about this kind of thing. Been watching your place for a while. No one's around."

"For now," Gaultieri said. "But things are happening quick. Our people are moving all over the place."

"Then let's get out of here," Carvaggio suggested. "You can take me for a ride."

"What's this about?" the wheelman asked.

"Wait until we're on the road," Carvaggio answered. "We can talk in the car."

"Yeah, we can talk in the car," Gaultieri repeated, shaking his head with resignation. "Can't wait." He resumed walking down the street toward his vehicle, which was parked at the end of the block, much closer than usual. In his Brooklyn Heights neighborhood, sometimes he was lucky to find a parking spot within a half mile.

Carvaggio fell in alongside him and walked with the easy pace of a man who had nothing to fear. Everything was under control, including Stefan Gaultieri.

The man who'd been standing across the street like a sentinel got into his vehicle, a Ford Explorer that was blocking a driveway. He eased the big 4x4 onto the road and prowled slowly behind them, coming to a stop just behind Gaultieri's crimson sports car as the two men reached it.

Carvaggio climbed into the passenger seat, jacket open, hand within easy reach of his gun, in case Gaultieri decided to become a hero. Or if they ran into a roving Garrison crew.

Gaultieri switched on the ignition, turned on the defrosters, then sat behind the wheel, staring straight ahead as the high-powered engine shuddered under the hood.

The ex-hit man looked sideways at the driver. "If you're waiting for a guardian angel, you can forget it. You're stuck with me. Let's move."

"I'm waiting for the engine to warm up," Gaultieri said. "It's cold out there, and this is a sensitive machine." He patted the sleek dashboard. "You want it to conk out in the middle of the street and have a tow truck haul us away? That'll be real discreet."

"Okay," Carvaggio said. "You know your car. Give it thirty seconds more to warm up, and then we'll take our chances, all right?"

About a half minute later, Gaultieri shifted into first gear.

The Ford Explorer fell in behind him as he pulled away from the curb, an unexpected chauffeur for the man he and every last soldier in the Garrison were sworn to kill.

"Where we going?" the wheelman asked.

"Across the bridge."

"Then where?"

"Midtown. Around. Somewhere away from your base of operations here. Don't worry about it. We just want to talk to you."

"That's what I'm worried about. Last time we spoke, you did all the talking."

"Did you think about what I said?" Carvaggio asked.

"Yeah."

"And?"

"I'm still thinking."

Carvaggio laughed. "Don't take too long. This offer's not gonna be on the table forever."

"What offer?"

"The offer we're gonna make when we get to the city," Carvaggio said, sitting back for the ride.

They crossed the bridge into Manhattan. The traffic was more sparse than usual. The hour was late, but not for New York. The cold had something to do with it. The heavy snow that had been plaguing Manhattan had stopped, but now a cold, dry spell settled over the city.

A good night to stay inside, Gaultieri thought. A good night to stay away from Nick Carvaggio.

But it was too late now. Whether he liked it or not, he had the feeling that Carvaggio was going to be in the driver's seat from here on in.

He kept his thoughts to himself until they were in Midtown Manhattan and Carvaggio directed him to head across 38th Street. He drove past the shops, bars and security-gated department stores and then, just before they came to a stoplight, Carvaggio told him to slow down and pull over.

"Where?"

"In there," Carvaggio said. He took a remote control door opener out of his jacket pocket and pointed it at a metal shuttered garage door on the right side of the street.

The overhead door rumbled open as Gaultieri swung his car off the road, then headed down a ramp that led into an empty hangarlike building. His headlights flashed on bare walls.

There was nothing in the space but concrete columns, and a bunch of desks and worktables stacked up on one side of the room. A harsh yellow security light, which had been triggered by the opening door, cast a circular cocoon of light down onto the oil-streaked floor.

"Park over there and shut off the engine," Carvaggio ordered.

The wheelman did as he was told, then said, "What is this place?"

"Just a place," Carvaggio said. "We got lots of them."

"For what?"

Carvaggio shrugged. "For whatever we need. Staging areas. Storage space. Mausoleums."

"Cheerful."

"Practical." Carvaggio looked over his shoulder as the Explorer drove down the ramp.

The truck swung in a 180-degree turn so that it faced back up the ramp. The man behind the wheel killed the headlights, but stayed inside and kept the engine running.

"Now what?" Gaultieri asked.

"Now we both get out of the car and walk out into the open. That way my partner can see that I'm still alive and you're still a thinking man."

The wheelman looked over at the other vehicle. "He doesn't take any chances, does he?"

"No," the ex-hit man said. "And neither do I. So leave whatever piece you're carrying in the car."

"Can't do it," Gaultieri said, instinctively gripping the wheel as he shook his head. "And you can't ask me to do it, Nick. I can't go face him without a gun. It's like asking to be killed."

"If we do have to kill you, it won't be tonight," Carvaggio said. "And with or without a gun, whenever the time comes, you won't be able to stop him or me." He nodded at the Ford. "But for now, the man over there just wants to talk to you. And he wants to do it without having you try anything crazy. Because then he *would* have to kill you."

Gaultieri looked hard at Carvaggio. "Give me your word, Nick. You've always been straight with me. Swear that nothing will happen to me, and I'll consider myself under your protection and put down my gun."

"I swear, Stefan," Carvaggio said. "You've got my word

on this. And my word holds with my partner. You're safe all the way. Tonight, anyway.''

Gaultieri exhaled slowly. ''All right,'' he said. Then he carefully reached into his underarm holster and removed his Colt automatic. Holding the grip between his thumb and forefinger, he set it down on the floor and followed Carvaggio out into the open.

BOLAN HIT the remote-control button to shut the garage door. As the overhead door clanked shut like a collapsing accordion, he climbed out of the Explorer and swung the door shut behind him. After the thunderclap echo rolled across the empty space, the room was deathly quiet.

And Stefan Gaultieri looked deathly pale as the Executioner walked toward him.

Bolan stopped when he was about ten feet away and crossed his arms in front of him. He was dressed in black, ready for night work, a commando against a civilian.

''Before we start,'' Bolan said, ''I've got one promise to make to you. Same one I made to Nick. Sign on with me, and I'll see you through this in one piece. But if you stay with Sienna, you won't walk away.''

''I've been thinking the same thing lately,'' Gaultieri said.

Bolan nodded. ''Good. But if you do come on board, it's all or nothing. You have a part to play and there's no backing out. Cross me at any time, even think of crossing me, and you're dust.''

The Garrison wheelman looked at Carvaggio, then back at Bolan. ''Nick signed on and he's still alive, so it seems like it might be a fair deal. Besides, Sienna could turn against me any time. All things considered, I'll take my chances with you. One thing, do I get a bonus for signing on?''

''Matter of fact you do,'' Bolan said. Then he outlined the bargain he'd hammered out with Hal Brognola. New name. New life. A chance to walk away from the killing trade.

''This includes protection from Victor Sienna?'' Gaultieri asked.

"There won't be any Victor Sienna to need protecting from," the Executioner said.

"Jail time?"

"Dead time."

"Yeah," Gaultieri said. "With Vic, that's the only way it can go down. He won't ever back off."

"That's what we're counting on. That brings us to your part of the deal."

"What do you need?" the wheelman asked.

"Let's start with Hank Prescott's killer," Bolan said.

"Prescott's the name of the Fed who Nick was supposed to turn himself into, right?"

Bolan nodded.

"Yeah, well, it's a bit late for that," Gaultieri said. "The guy who actually killed the Fed got clipped in the Patricio crash-up. And I do mean clipped. Guy had about thirty rounds drilled right through him."

"Glad to hear it," Bolan said. "So the guy who actually pulled the trigger is dead. What about the guy who set it up?"

Gaultieri hesitated from force of habit, then said, "He's still around. It's Drew McNeil. He worked out all the details. He didn't want to do it, but Vic gave him no choice. And ever since that day, things have gone wrong for the Garrison. Dead wrong."

Bolan shrugged. "The people we're dealing with will want to hear your story when this is all over. Everything about the Prescott assassination, everything about the Garrison. Could require your testimony. You up for that?"

"If it's gotta be that way, yeah," Gaultieri said. "But first I got a question. You don't exactly seem like the kind of government blue suit we've dealt with before. What exactly is your connection to the government?"

"More like a disconnection," Bolan said. "Just consider me the middleman between you and the Protection plan. You make it past me, then you're in with them. And if you don't, well, no one has to know about it."

Gaultieri looked at Carvaggio for confirmation.

"It's true," the ex-hit man said. "Prove yourself to him, then you make it through the door."

"Okay," Gaultieri said. "I give up a dead guy and I give up McNeil. Fine. But for this kind of deal, you gotta be looking for something more. What else do you want from me?"

"Nothing," the Executioner said. "In fact we're going to give you something."

"What?"

"We figure Sienna's got everyone in his crew out hunting for Rupert Sawyer," Bolan said. "He wants him pretty bad."

"Yeah, like he's the Antichrist. That *Case Closed* stuff drives him up a wall. He also figures if he gets the producer, he can get a lead to Nick here. And you. So how's that figure into things?"

"Simple," Bolan said. "We're going to give him to you."

"You're giving up Rupert Sawyer?"

"That's the plan," the Executioner said. "That's about the only thing that'll draw Sienna out of hiding."

The Garrison wheelman looked stunned at first, but then as Bolan spoke, realization dawned on him. Sienna was out for blood where the producer was concerned and had offered a reward for information on him. Bolan would see to it that Stefan Gaultieri discovered the producer's hideaway so he could collect that reward from the Garrison chief.

It would be a legitimate setup. The wheelman would actually make contact with someone on Rupert Sawyer's staff, a researcher Brognola had planted in the production crew. The researcher would supposedly be an old friend from Sawyer's network days who was down on his luck and needed a job, an old friend who knew all about Sawyer's habits and his isolated retreat.

The wheelman would follow the researcher to a bar where the staffers hung out, wait until the man looked drunk, and then make the approach. Money would exchange hands, and so would information. The phony researcher would give up the location of Rupert Sawyer's hideaway in Connecticut, complete with his private phone number.

Chances were that some soldiers from the Garrison crew would be hanging around and watching the staffers. If so, they'd see Stefan Gaultieri make the approach and verify that Gaultieri bought the information from the producer's old assistant. It would appeal to Sienna's world view. After all, who better to sell someone out than an old friend?

When Sienna checked out the address he'd find that Sawyer owned the place for years. A Garrison crew would check out the place and report back to Sienna that it was occupied by two people—a man and a woman. Maybe a couple of guards would be seen around the retreat now and then.

The Garrison would descend on Rupert Sawyer. Only Sawyer wouldn't be there waiting for them—the Executioner and Carvaggio would.

After he listened to Bolan's plan, the wheelman nodded enthusiastically. "Yeah," he said, "it'll work. You sussed this guy out perfectly. But one thing bothers me. If Sienna raids this place, he'll bring everybody with him, including me. I don't want to buy it out there."

"You won't," Bolan said. "Just stay in touch with us until it goes down." The Executioner spoke in his no-nonsense manner, as if the future he'd mapped out had already happened and seeing it through was just a formality. "When it starts, you hang back and we'll make sure you're out of the firing line. Then you get your ticket out of here. You still up for this?"

Gaultieri nodded. "It's my only out."

"Then let's make it happen," the Executioner said.

14

The black Ford Explorer followed Interstate 95 out of New York and traveled along the Connecticut coastline for about twenty-five miles.

Once he hit Bridgeport, the Executioner turned north onto Route 8, leaving the densely packed urban sprawl of the coast behind and heading up into the wild backcountry of Connecticut.

Nick Carvaggio followed several car lengths behind, driving the wide-bed pickup with the polar white snowmobiles in the back.

A fresh afternoon snow was falling on the countryside, but it melted as soon as it hit the road. The driving was clear, and they made good time as they drove north, even when they left the state road for a series of country roads that wound through out-of-the-way hamlets and villages.

The forest-lined roads connected them from one storybook village to another, past antique shops, bed-and-breakfasts and seventeenth-century town halls.

Some of the villages were home to corporate outposts that had fled the big city environments of New York and New Haven for a more peaceful and untroubled rural landscape. Now their glass towers and modern complexes stood almost side by side with church steeples.

But the farther north they drove, the more traditional the villages became.

After about an hour and a half of driving, they reached Lantern Hollow, a village with a population of 1,530 that looked like a colonial oasis surrounded by wild forests and fields.

Bolan swung into the country store next to the town hall, gassed up the Explorer, then bought some supplies to see them through a short-term siege.

He carried the packages out to the back of the Ford, opened the gate and set them next to the other tarp-covered essentials—sniper rifle, automatic shotgun, mines, explosives, ammo and satcom gear. Enough to get them through their mission in one piece.

Carvaggio stopped at the store just as Bolan was leaving and repeated the procedure, stocking up on gas and food, adding them to the winter warfare gear stashed near the snowmobiles.

They drove north along the Housatonic River for a while before turning east again, following a narrow winding road through high snowbanks and deep ravines. After a stretch of hairpin turns carved out of the forest, they finally reached the private road that led to the country retreat of Rupert Sawyer.

All told it was about three hours from Sawyer's digs in New York City. Three hours and three centuries.

The producer had spared no expense in creating a lodge that combined seventeenth-century Swiss and Nordic architecture with a mix of American colonial. No one style won out. The end result was a blend of gables and shutters, field stone chimneys and a cathedral-shaped roof.

Off to the side of the house was a barnlike garage, and behind the house was a large privately stocked pond that almost qualified as a lake. It was frozen solid and covered with snowdrifts, strips of birch bark and skeletal tree limbs that a windstorm had blown in from the forest.

A light was on in the house, a perennial lamp that Sawyer kept on twenty-four hours a day. And the private road had been recently plowed.

It looked lived-in.

Bolan and Carvaggio unloaded their gear into the house,

drove the snowmobiles down the pickup's ramp, then parked them in the garage with their noses facing outward.

They left the Explorer near the gravel driveway that circled in front of the lodge.

Then the two soldiers reconned the area and prepared to greet their visitors from the Garrison. When they finished setting up their preliminary defenses, the two men went back inside Sawyer's country house.

Bolan went into the study and pushed aside dozens of videotapes stacked neatly on a counter near three TV monitors and editing equipment. The videotapes were all carefully labeled with the subject matter and date of broadcast. Most of them were from Sawyer's *Case Closed* show or other documentaries he'd worked on. Bolan pictured the man sitting up here at his electronic altar, splicing together monuments to himself. Rupert Sawyer reporting on Rupert Sawyer.

With the tapes out of the way, the Executioner opened up the satcom suitcase and set up the encrypted communications gear, giving him a secure satellite link to Hal Brognola's Manhattan number.

Even with the secure lines, Bolan made sure the communication stayed brief when Brognola picked up the receiver. All he said was, "This is Striker. We are in position."

"Acknowledged," Brognola replied. "Everything is in motion." Then he broke the connection.

One of the things Bolan's call set in motion was the security arrangements for Rupert Sawyer's retreat. It was strictly for show. Every couple of hours a unit from Hal Brognola's SSU team would travel through the area in a county sheriff's car. When the Garrison got around to scouting out the place, it would look like there was a regular watch on Sawyer's retreat.

Soon Brognola would have teams of marshals flown by helicopter to the nearest state police barracks.

The airborne teams would be on hand in case the operation got out of control. But if things went as planned, they would remain on standby until after the strike went down. Then the marshals would fly into the area by helicopter to extract Bolan, Carvaggio and, if he carried out his end of the bargain, Stefan Gaultieri.

THERE WERE TWO CALLS on the second day of Bolan's stay at the producer's retreat.

The first call came from Hal Brognola. He raised Bolan on the satcom unit early in the morning to update him on the movements of Stefan Gaultieri. The wheelman had made contact with Brognola's operative on the producer's staff and went through all the right motions about buying the information on Sawyer's hiding place.

The big Fed let Bolan know that Gaultieri had also made his call to one of the phone drop numbers the Executioner had supplied him with, a number that was connected to an SSU listening post. According to the message he left at the phone drop, Gaultieri had given the location of the producer's hideaway to Victor Sienna. The wheelman was following his instructions to the letter. It looked like the Garrison was getting ready to make its move.

The second phone call to the Connecticut retreat came in the afternoon. This time it was the phone in Sawyer's study that rang.

It was a private line that Sawyer had kept carefully guarded over the years. But now, according to the digital display on the phone, someone was calling his unlisted number with a Manhattan area code.

Though Brognola's people still had the producer under wraps in New York, his phone was patched into the Connecticut house and hooked up to a speakerphone so Bolan and Carvaggio could listen in on the call.

After the third ring, Sawyer picked up the phone. "Hello?"

Sawyer's voice was as clear and static free as if the producer actually were hiding out at his country home.

"Is Rebecca there?" The caller's voice sounded casual and

eager and just a bit confused, like a suitor calling for someone only to find an unfamiliar voice there.

"You've got the wrong number," Sawyer replied.

"Sorry," the caller said and hung up.

Bolan looked at the former Garrison hit man, who'd been staring down at the digital readout screen, trying to place the number. "You recognize the voice?" the soldier asked.

Carvaggio shook his head. "Could be someone new McNeil brought in. Could be someone I know but just can't place. What do you think?"

"I think when Hal's people trace that number they'll find it's a phone booth or a restaurant in Manhattan," Bolan said. "It's got to be them. They played it smart by staying on the phone instead of hanging up. They didn't want to spook Sawyer, just convince themselves he's here."

"Now they know," Carvaggio said. "And now they'll come down on us with everything they have."

"Looks like."

"Most people wouldn't hang around if they knew what was coming," Carvaggio said.

"Most people aren't fighting the kind of war that I—that we—have to fight," Bolan said. "At least this way, we'll know when the shooting starts. You ready for it?"

"I've been ready since the day Victor Sienna framed me as the Judas goat."

VICTOR SIENNA SAT in the front seat of the copper-colored Jeep Cherokee and watched the snow-covered thickets of forest blur past his window.

He was moving toward the battlefront, and he wanted to be in the passenger seat to watch it all unfold, to execute the plan just as he and McNeil worked it out. That would normally be McNeil's job on an operation like this, but this night Sienna felt the need to be on the front line with his men, directing them, leading them.

He smiled the first real smile in several days.

His enemy was within reach, and Victor Sienna was going to personally take him down.

Sienna glanced back at McNeil who sat in the back seat of the Cherokee. He, too, was looking out the window, but he didn't have the same edge. He seemed calm, as if this were just another night in the New England woods and he was checking out the scenery.

Sienna understood his attitude. McNeil thought they were using too much manpower to go after just one man and one woman who wouldn't have a chance against them. Like using a hammer to swat a mosquito.

Rupert Sawyer's weapon was a camera; Ambrosia Lyons' was her beauty. Neither weapon could be remotely considered a threat to the convoy that was moving through the tree-lined county road. The entire available Garrison force had been called out for this operation.

Several other vehicles traveled closely behind the Jeep, ready to follow Sienna into battle. They'd been driving for most of the night, splitting up in random packs until it was time to rendezvous.

Now the time had come.

It was just past midnight, and the Garrison scouts covering the retreat had reported in that the latest patrol car had come and gone. There was plenty of time for the Garrison to make its strike before the next one came. And if they were still there when the patrol came back, then the patrol would be taken care of.

That was one of the reasons why Sienna wanted all of the Garrison soldiers on this one, to handle anything that came along. If they ran into Carvaggio and the crew helping him, the Garrison would have more than enough numbers to come out on top.

Sienna also wanted to be there to let his men see him in action, see him interview Rupert Sawyer. Instead of a microphone he'd use a gun. If done right, the producer would tell him everything he wanted to know about Carvaggio.

Or maybe the producer no longer had a lead on the man. It didn't matter, Sienna thought. It would still be entertaining.

Either way, this night, the producer of *Case Closed* was going to be canceled.

When they were just under a mile south of the producer's private road, the Garrison chieftain waved his driver off to the side of the road.

One by one the drivers followed suit until the trail of vehicles stretched far down the road. Dark shapes climbed out of the cars and scurried down the snowbanks into the woods. As the soldiers moved through the shadows toward the distant house, Sienna nodded to the driver.

The Jeep pulled back onto the road and headed for Sawyer's private road. The driver killed the lights as the Cherokee turned off the main road and swung into the mouth of the long private drive. Victor Sienna took out an automatic pistol, waiting to greet the man who'd made him a target of ridicule throughout the underworld.

STEFAN GAULTIERI STEPPED softly through the snow-covered field, easing one foot at a time through the crusted surface.

He was part of a three-man team moving stealthily through the woods, or as stealthily as they could. It had been awhile since any of them had been in the field like this. They still knew weapons and war, but their most recent missions had been in the streets.

It took awhile, but gradually they regained part of their rhythm, gliding rather than walking. Gaultieri could see other teams moving forward in the distance. The foot soldiers advanced rapidly, spurred on by the sight of the bright yellow window light and the curling stream of chimney smoke. To them it looked like an unprotected outpost.

A walkover.

Gaultieri was operating on a different kind of knowledge. As the steps of his mates crunched softly into the snow, his steps moved slower and slower. His furtive approach soon turned into a creeping advance as the soldiers paced on without him.

He stopped and leaned against a tree, melding his shadow with the trunk of the thick, sturdy oak.

From somewhere in front of him he heard one the men calling his name in a hushed whisper. He stayed in his hiding spot until the voice called him again. The voice sounded worried now.

Still the wheelman stayed silent. But the soldiers wouldn't give up.

"Stefan! Where are you?" one of them said. "You okay?"

Realizing the team was getting spooked and might raise the alarm to the other soldiers, Gaultieri called out to them. The last thing he wanted was to have them beating the bushes for him. As of now, Stefan Gaultieri was no longer part of the team.

"I'm here," the wheelman whispered. "Just twisted my foot."

"Hurry up."

"I'm coming," Gaultieri said. But he waited until he heard the men continue their advance again. And then waited another half minute before he stepped out from behind the tree and started to walk in the opposite direction from the Garrison war party.

Suddenly a white shape erupted from his feet. Before he could cry out in surprise, a hand clamped over his mouth. And then he saw a face looking out at him from under a white camouflage shroud.

The face was streaked with white and gray paint that blended with the forest. It was the man who called himself Striker. He was painted for war.

The camouflaged warrior held his grip on Gaultieri's mouth until the wheelman's fright subsided.

Gaultieri realized that the man had also taken his submachine gun from him. It all happened in a fleeting second without his being aware of it. But the 9 mm Heckler & Koch machine pistol with the sound suppressor was now in Bolan's hand.

"There's been a change in plans," the man said in a hushed voice. "Too dangerous to have you wandering around back here. They've got a mop-up squad roving around."

"I'll get by them," the wheelman said.

"Not the way you move. You'll run into them or they'll find you. Either way you won't be able to explain why you're going the wrong way."

"Where do I go?"

"Circle around to the west until you come to a stream," Bolan said, gesturing his arm in a motion describing the safest transit. "Follow it to the pond, then go past the pond and stay on the western side. We'll rendezvous later and airlift you out of here."

Gaultieri nodded and reached out for the Heckler & Koch, but the Executioner pulled the submachine gun out of his reach.

"But I need a weapon out here," the wheelman protested.

"We're all safer without you carrying one now. You're hereby discharged. Now move out."

BOLAN WAITED until the wheelman was out of sight and sound, then took his place and fell in behind the Garrison team.

The Executioner moved quickly, not worrying about making too much noise. The men in front of him were expecting a straggler to catch up to them, so if a few sounds reached them it wouldn't be a cause for alarm.

In just a couple of seconds it wouldn't matter what they heard.

Even so, Bolan's years of experience kept any sounds he made to a minimum. The soldiers didn't detect the Executioner until he was about ten yards behind them.

The first man to spot Bolan was a tall man with a Sterling submachine gun, its familiar long barrel silhouetted against the white snow in front of him. The gunman turned back toward Bolan, expecting to see the wheelman but instead saw an amorphous shape. His eyes went wide when he saw the white mass bearing down on him.

He also saw the stout barrel of the Heckler & Koch submachine gun the Executioner instinctively trained on him. It was too late for the man to shout or react. The Sterling subgun was held at his side, and there wasn't enough time to aim it at the white-camouflaged enemy.

There was only enough time to die.

A 3-round burst caught the man high, obliterating his brain with a skull-crushing sound. As the man dropped into the snow, the Sterling fell from his clutching fingertips.

The Executioner took a step to the right, staying in a low crouch as he triggered two more bursts from the H&K. The 9 mm rounds ripped into the second gunner, stitching him from hip to chest, tossing his carcass into a web of interwoven branches.

Originally Bolan had thought of taking them out in total silence, but that would have taken too much time, and the rest of the Garrison was closing in on the house. Better to get the jump while they were all in the ideal position.

Walking through a kill zone.

The Executioner kept moving, uncertain whether the other teams realized their outer position had been breached. The silenced rounds from the Heckler & Koch weren't especially loud under normal circumstances, but in a forest full of gunmen the coughing sounds were enough to draw some attention.

Bolan scanned the forest in front of him and saw several man-sized shadows looking in his general direction. They'd been moving in the darkness but had stopped suddenly, their silhouettes splintered by trees, brush and the uneven banks they'd been crossing.

While they were still trying to sense what had happened, the Executioner strafed them from left to right.

Spear-shaped flashes from the subgun's barrel cut through

the darkness as Bolan squeezed off a series of well-aimed bursts. With so many targets and a variety of cover, the Executioner had to aim by instinct rather than sight.

The sense of timing developed over years of fighting had a telling effect. The fusillade took down two men for good, caught a pair of gunners who'd been stuck in the open spaces and forced a number of other soldiers to dive for cover.

The first man had unleashed a stuttered full-auto burst that suddenly stopped as Bolan's 9 mm rounds cut into him. The second man chopped down by the Heckler & Koch's deadly fire landed flat on his back and triggered a burst into the sky.

That left a small army of gunmen in the woods.

Bolan figured he had about six rounds left in the 30-round magazine so he burnt off the rest of the clip to give himself a couple more seconds of cover. Then he dived to the ground into a small gully and crawled on all fours.

Subsonic bullets cut through the air above Bolan as he moved away from his last position. Shotgun blasts thundered through the trees, blowing off strips of bark and breaking off limbs. Pistol and automatic rifle fire punched holes in the darkness.

It was a deafening counterattack from the Garrison.

Too much for Bolan to handle with the empty Heckler & Koch. The subgun he'd taken from the wheelman was a weapon of opportunity and had only the one magazine. He left it behind as he kept on moving away from the field of fire, head down, feet pushing into the snow.

Bolan's main field weapons were his Beretta 93-R and the Accuracy International rifle he carried. But he also carried a more potent weapon—a small remote-control detonator that weighed about eight ounces.

The gunfire ended just as suddenly as it started. After their first instinctive barrage, the troops were holding their fire. They knew that if anyone had been standing, he would've been cut down by now. And if anyone was still alive, he was dug in and they'd have to come for him.

The gunmen called out to one another as they started to

move out. Two small groups split off from the main body to move in on Bolan's left and right flanks. The main group started moving slowly forward.

Bolan forced himself to stay silent as the men closed in, beating the bushes for their prey.

The closest Garrison hunter was about twenty yards away when Carvaggio opened up from a firing line off to the right.

The 5.56 mm Ameli light machine gun cut down a half dozen Mob soldiers who'd been stalking toward Bolan's right flank. Their arms flew up, their weapons clattered against tree trunks and their bullet-riddled bodies toppled over in awkward harmony, propelled by the heavy 5.56 mm cartridges weighing them down.

Carvaggio kept up a sustained fire, hammering the rest of the troops with the heavy firepower in the light plastic box magazine. There were two hundred rounds of ammo in the magazine, connected by open bottom links. The links and spent cartridges were ejecting from the Ameli at a rate of fifteen rounds a second.

The ex-hit man moved like a ghostly figure through the tree lines, smoke and flame ripping from the barrel of the machine gun. He held the Ameli at his side and used the shoulder sling to maintain its balance as he triggered long bursts of the high-powered NATO cartridges.

He was firing in a staccato rhythm, pulling back on the trigger for several seconds in one position before moving on and resuming fire. The constant movement allowed him to zigzag his fire through the trees and rout the Garrison soldiers from their positions.

Under cover of the Ameli machine-gun fire, Bolan slowly raised himself, aiming at the soldiers nearest him. Two of the gunners had sought cover behind a low barricade of fallen trees on a snowy incline.

They were looking in Carvaggio's direction, ducking back for cover now and then as the ex-Garrison hit man unloaded a wide arc of kill fire at a jackhammer pace.

When the Ameli moved from them, one of the men crept

forward and propped his Colt automatic rifle on top of a splintered tree trunk. He swung the barrel of his rifle toward the Ameli-wielding commando, figuring he had a sure kill—until Bolan drilled him with a triburst from the Beretta 93-R.

The Executioner pitched to his left and shot the other man just as he rose from the ground to fire at Bolan.

But the Executioner's rounds struck first. The man's aim went wild, then went dead as he crumpled in the snow.

Bolan continued picking off gunners who'd sought cover from Carvaggio's devastating fire. Then he covered his approach until the ex-hit man managed to link up with him.

By then the 200-round magazine was empty. Both warriors faded back into the depths of the forest as the scattered Mob soldiers regrouped and headed for their position.

As they loped downhill toward one of the snowmobiles they'd planted in the woods earlier, Carvaggio threw down the disposable magazine. On the run he fished out another, smaller magazine with a clear plastic cover from the pocket of his white-hooded jacket. He locked the 100-round magazine into place and aimed the barrel of the Ameli toward the advancing soldiers. He could hear but not see them.

The backup squad was also closing in, coming from somewhere off to the right. Soon Carvaggio and Bolan would be caught in a pincer movement.

But so would the Garrison.

Bolan jumped behind the handlebars of the white snowmobile that sat in the bottom of the gully. He stood with his feet planted firmly on the floorboards, the Beretta nestled in a wide pocket of the winter shroud, sniper rifle slung over his shoulder.

A moment later Carvaggio jumped on the back of the machine, ready to ride shotgun with the freshly loaded Ameli pointing upward.

Sienna's troops were still out of sight, but the heavy footfalls of the advancing war party were loud enough to let them know that in the next few moments the gunmen would appear.

Carvaggio preempted their attack with a full-auto burst when the Mob soldiers appeared on the ridge. The Ameli machine gun fire whipped uphill like a guillotine, kicking the first rank of gunmen off their feet and forcing the others to drop out of sight.

Bolan started the engine and gunned the machine uphill and out of the left side of the gully. Carvaggio kept up the covering fire as the snowmobile erupted from the hill. It went airborne for several yards, then came down hard, bouncing on the shock absorbers.

Bolan thumbed back the throttle when he was on level ground, then darted his right hand inside his jacket to pull out the remote-control detonator. With a quick tap on the keyboard he triggered the first series of blasts.

The woods turned into a minefield, setting off the charges that Bolan and Carvaggio had planted throughout the forest.

Shrapnel and exploding sheets of white-hot flame ripped into the feet and faces of the Garrison troops. The high explosives were pointing inward, shredding the area the Mob soldiers had been led into. It was a classic box formation that hit them from all sides.

As the underworld hardmen milled about in shock and horror, Bolan triggered the second sequence, expanding the kill zone to catch the soldiers who'd made it out of the first perimeter.

Then he gunned the snowmobile and rocketed across the moonlit landscape, following the trail he'd reconned earlier. With Carvaggio still riding shotgun and spraying the forest with fifteen rounds at a time, they were able to head for the pond without catching much return fire.

As soon as the skis touched the solid surface of the ice, Bolan yanked hard on the handlebars and brought the snowmobile to the western edge of the pond. He and Carvaggio dismounted as it skidded for the brush.

With a quick motion of his hand toward the lodge, Bolan keyed the last blast sequence.

The walls flew out with concussive force, echoing through the forest. The mushrooming blast ripped holes in the ceiling, collapsed the deck that surrounded the lodge and sent splintering windowpanes flying into the night.

The explosions marched up Rupert Sawyer's private road, digging huge mortar-size gaps in the gravel drive. One after another the fiery blasts sprouted from the ground, punching flame, stone and high explosives into the bottoms of the cars that had followed Victor Sienna's Jeep down the road to the house.

As the dark clouds and chaos surrounded the remnants of Sienna's force, Bolan and Carvaggio merged with the shadows of the woods.

VICTOR SIENNA STOOD in shock, holding his mute 9 mm Sturm, Ruger automatic in his hand. His army was being cut down all around him, and there was nothing to shoot at.

First there'd been a firefight on the far side of the woods. McNeil had sent most of the men gathered around them into the forest as reinforcements. They'd reached the zone just when the first set of explosions went off.

No one had come back to report on the casualties they had taken.

Perhaps no one was left.

Sienna stepped through the twisted husks of metal that sat on the ground like inflamed metal skeletons. Tires and wheels lay flat upon the gravel, beneath blown out windshields with blood and bone specked on the glass.

It was like the aftermath of an aerial bombardment.

Sienna had brought the entire Garrison here, thinking that it was going to be overkill. And it was overkill—but for the other side.

He looked around the flame-seared woods. In the distance he saw some of his men standing or crawling. They were straggling their way to eternity, severely wounded but still trying to hold on to life.

Drew McNeil stood beside him. His right-hand man was untouched by the barrage but unable to move, stricken by the sight in front of him.

They'd both left the Jeep at the same time and had been heading for the house when the heavy fighting started. Now the Jeep was demolished by the explosive charges and so was the driver. Parts of him had merged with the broken bits of metal and chrome that were now scattered upon the snow.

Sienna's dream of empire was dying just as quickly as his men. It was too much to bear. One minute they were on the attack, the next they were completely broken. "You led us into a trap," he said to McNeil. "Get us out."

McNeil's weary eyes studied him with scorn. "No, Vic," he said. "You led us into this trap. You wouldn't listen, you had to make it happen your way. Well, it happened. Here it is, Vic, everything you wanted."

"You planned it—"

McNeil shook his head. "Just following orders."

"So follow some more and get us out of here."

"You want out?" McNeil said. He glanced toward the forest, where there was sporadic gunfire followed by periods of silence before it erupted again. "Only way out is through them, or him, or whoever the hell is out there."

"It's Carvaggio," Sienna said, speaking the name of his one-time friend and ally as if it were a curse.

"And company," McNeil said. "They're coming this way."

Sienna waved the Ruger in front of him like it was a good-luck charm. "Good," he said. "It's past time I used this." There was still a chance to salvage something. The hate that was bottled inside him now merged with hope. Hope that the man who ruined his empire would finally get what was coming to him. At least that way Sienna could still triumph.

"Nick!" Sienna shouted. "Over here!" He yelled out the name several more times until he was certain his voice had reached the intended target. Then his voice fell softer as he whispered to himself, "Come on, you bastard."

NICK CARVAGGIO STEPPED carefully toward the edge of the thick forest, moving closer to the driveway from where Sienna had called him.

The Ameli was empty, discarded somewhere back in the woods. In his hand was his 9 mm Steyr Tactical Machine Pistol. The TMP had a fresh 15-round clip, and it was aimed at the smoldering wreckage in the driveway.

Carvaggio had circled around through the woods so he could angle back toward the driveway. Now he was facing a gauntlet of wrecked cars and beyond them the smoldering ruins of the lodge.

Making sure that he was protected by a thick line of trees, Carvaggio called out to Sienna and waited for the answering call to pinpoint his location.

For a moment the forest was silent, except for the distant sound of burning branches falling into the snow, hissing as they were extinguished.

Then Sienna shouted back to him. "I'm here, Nick."

The ex-Garrison soldier placed his voice on the other side of a wall of wreckage. "Come on out then," Carvaggio said. "Let's settle it."

"Wait. It doesn't have to end like this. We can both walk away. It's over."

Carvaggio laughed. "I know you too well. You started this thing and you can't stop it. From now on you'll think I'm the one who beat you. You won't be able to live with that. Neither will I. I'm not spending the rest of my life waiting for you to get up the guts to come after me."

"It's your call," Sienna said. His voice was nearer now. "We'll do it the way you want, just you and me. You come out, I'll come out, and we'll see who walks away."

Carvaggio stepped into the last pocket of shadows from the forest, not presenting a clear target.

Sienna did the same thing, hovering near the edge of the wreckage.

DREW MCNEIL CROUCHED about ten feet behind Sienna and peered around the charred edge of what used to be a pickup. He kept his head down and his Ithaca shotgun at the ready. From his vantage point he could just barely see Carvaggio's shape in the woods.

He breathed out his tension. He knew he could get Carvaggio in a couple more seconds. But right now there was still too much cover protecting him. A few more yards and Carvaggio was dust.

For that crucial moment when he had to bring the shotgun out in the open, Carvaggio would be able to see him. But the ex-hit man would be concentrating on Sienna, giving McNeil just enough time to let loose.

"He's coming," Sienna said in a soft voice. "I'll bring him out, you kill the bastard."

Sienna made himself more of a target. "Come on out, Nick. Just you and me. Let's do it." He started to raise his Ruger in front of him, taking aim at the shape that was stepping from the cover. Without turning back to face McNeil, he said, "Now. Do it!"

McNeil leaned forward and started to whip the shotgun into position, knowing that he had Carvaggio at last. There was nothing that could stop him...

Except that his right shoulder was disintegrating. Blood, bone and muscle exploded in the air, painting the shotgun that fell from his hands with gore.

McNeil spent his last second alive deciphering the sound of the sniper rifle that had felled him. And just as he recognized what had happened to him, another heavy round crashed into his skull.

The second shot slapped him off his feet like a nail gun bolting him to the ground.

THE EXECUTIONER lowered the Accuracy International sniper rifle when he saw the second shot take McNeil to another place. The 7.62 mm round had scattered his skull and his thoughts onto the winter white ground.

Bolan had come up from the opposite side of the house while Carvaggio closed in from the other direction. From that angle the Executioner couldn't get a clear shot at Sienna, but at least he'd leveled the playing field.

Sienna had called for an equal fight and now he had it.

VICTOR SIENNA HEARD the shots and watched his man fall, then he saw Nick Carvaggio running toward him.

Sienna squeezed the Ruger's trigger. Once, twice, three times. It bucked in his hands as Carvaggio fell.

But he was falling the wrong way. Carvaggio tumbled forward, and as he lay almost prone on the snow he squeezed off two bursts from the Steyr TMP, two bursts that zeroed in on Victor Sienna.

The first got Sienna in the legs and toppled him sideways. The second hit him as he fell, spinning his upper body, arms pinwheeling wildly until he thumped into the snow.

Carvaggio lunged forward, triggering another burst into the body of his fallen friend, making sure he was dead.

Making sure the Garrison wouldn't rise again.

FIVE MINUTES LATER Bolan and Carvaggio rousted Stefan Gaultieri from the woods behind the pond. The wheelman stared at them like they were ghosts. He hadn't expected to walk out of this one.

But Gaultieri stood by quietly as the Executioner called in the SSU helicopter squadron from the nearby base. Then they waited by the edge of the woods near the pond.

It took awhile before the choppers arrived, and Gaultieri managed to keep his silence until he heard the first mechanical drone cut through the sky above them. Then he started waving like a hitchhiker in a hurry to go home, or leave home behind forever.

The three of them headed for the first chopper, eager to get out of the battlefield before any of the media zoned in on it.

Bolan's work was almost done. The Garrison was finished. All they had to do now was come up with a body count and a cover story.

EPILOGUE

The day after the Garrison fell, Rupert Sawyer appeared on a special edition of *Case Closed* to announce that in weeks to come he would present an inside look at the underworld war between Mob chieftain Victor Sienna and his Judas soldier, Nicholas Carvaggio.

Sawyer mentioned several times that he was personally involved in the investigation and in fact had helped bring about the end of the war, a war that had literally hit home for the producer.

And that was the subject of the first episode of his series on the rise and fall of the Garrison—Rupert Sawyer, producer, investigative reporter, undercover asset to the law-enforcement community.

Standing in front of the ruins of his Connecticut retreat, the producer looked soulfully out at the camera as he laid out his involvement from the beginning with one of the men who was killed at the lodge, a man named Nicholas Carvaggio who turned to Rupert Sawyer in his hour of need. Nicholas Carvaggio was dead now, Sawyer informed his viewers, but his story would live on in future episodes of *Case Closed*.

"HOW'S DEATH TREATING YOU?" Bolan asked when Nick Carvaggio walked through the shuttered metal doors of the 38th Street garage where a late-model Dodge Caravan was waiting for him.

"Never felt better," Carvaggio said, shaking Bolan's hand.

Carvaggio had a different look about him. It matched the ID he now carried, one that had been provided to him by Hal Brognola.

The ex-hit man looked older. His dark hair had been dyed gray and cut in a conservative style.

There was little about his outward appearance that connected him to the assassin who used to be known as Nicholas Carvaggio.

Only his eyes gave a hint of his past and his future. Whatever the name, he was a serious man. A capable man. And for now he was a man with a clean slate.

He climbed into the Caravan, switched on the engine, then started to roll toward the open door.

The Executioner walked alongside him for a few feet, then rapped his hand on the side of the van. "Do us all a favor, Nick," he said through the open window, meeting the ex-hit man's eyes. "Make sure you stay dead."

Take
2 explosive books
plus a
mystery bonus
FREE

James Axler

OUTLANDERS™

NIGHT ETERNAL

Kane and his fellow warrior survivalists find themselves launched into an alternate reality where the nukecaust was averted—and the Archons have emerged as mankind's great benefactors.

The group sets out to help a small secret organization conduct a clandestine war against the forces of evil....

Book #2 in the new Lost Earth Saga, a trilogy that chronicles our heroes' paths through three very different alternate realities... where the struggle against the evil Archons goes on...

Shadow THE EXECUTIONER®
as he battles evil for 352 pages of heart-stopping action!

SuperBolan®

#61452	DAY OF THE VULTURE	$5.50 U.S.	☐
		$6.50 CAN.	☐
#61453	FLAMES OF WRATH	$5.50 U.S.	☐
		$6.50 CAN.	☐
#61454	HIGH AGGRESSION	$5.50 U.S.	☐
		$6.50 CAN.	☐
#61455	CODE OF BUSHIDO	$5.50 U.S.	☐
		$6.50 CAN.	☐
#61456	TERROR SPIN	$5.50 U.S.	☐
		$6.50 CAN.	☐

(limited quantities available on certain titles)

TOTAL AMOUNT	$
POSTAGE & HANDLING	$
($1.00 for one book, 50¢ for each additional)	
APPLICABLE TAXES*	$ _____
TOTAL PAYABLE	$ _____
(check or money order—please do not send cash)	

To order, complete this form and send it, along with a check or money order for the total above, payable to Gold Eagle Books, to: **In the U.S.:** 3010 Walden Avenue, P.O. Box 9077, Buffalo, NY 14269-9077; **In Canada:** P.O. Box 636, Fort Erie, Ontario, L2A 5X3.

Name: _____

Address: _____ City: _____

State/Prov.: _____ Zip/Postal Code: _____

*New York residents remit applicable sales taxes.
 Canadian residents remit applicable GST and provincial taxes.

GOLD
EAGLE®

GSBBACK1